THE POWER OF TIME

The Power of Time

JOSEPHINE SAXTON

CHATTO & WINDUS

THE HOGARTH PRESS
LONDON

Published in 1985 by
Chatto & Windus · The Hogarth Press
40 William IV Street, London WC2N 4DF

British Library Cataloguing in Publication Data

Saxton, Josephine
The power of time.
I. Title
823'.914[F]   PR6069.A96

ISBN 0–7011–2955–7
ISBN 0–7011–2956–5 Pbk

The following stories have been published previously:
'The Power of Time' *New Dimensions 1* Robert Silverberg, Editor (Doubleday,
New York, 1970; paperback, Avon, New York, 1970)
'Food and Love' *Cosmopolitan* 1975
'The Triumphant Head' *Alchemy and Academe* Anne McCaffrey, Editor
(Doubleday, New York, 1970; paperback, Del Rey, New York, 1970)
'To Market, to Market' *Woman Space* (New Victoria Publishers Inc, Lebanon,
New Hampshire, 1981
'The Wall' *Science Fantasy* 1966
'Dormant Soul' *Fantasy and Science Fiction* 1969
'Elouise and the Doctors of the Planet Pergamon' *Again, Dangerous Visions*
Harlan Ellison, Editor (Doubleday, New York, 1972; paperback, Berkley Books,
New York, 1983)
'The Snake who had Read Chomsky' *Universe 11* Terry Carr, Editor (Doubleday,
New York, 1981)
'No Coward Soul' *Interzone* 1982
'Black Sabbatical' *Fantasy and Science Fiction* 1971
'Living Wild' *Fantasy and Science Fiction* 1971

Photoset and printed in Great Britain by Redwood Burn Limited
Trowbridge, Wiltshire

Contents

For Mr Rochester and Emma

The Power of Time

'It shouldn't present much difficulty if you approach it in a positive way,' I said to the Chief of the Mohawks, Flying Spider. 'Your tribe is expert in this kind of thing. All you have to do is number the parts, get it translated in terms of a computer jigsaw multi-dimensional complex, get the land measured out and prepared in advance – new sewage systems and so on, flood the Trent and the Soar to form an island – aw, c'mon Spider, you can do it...'

My power complex that I never thought about, working on his power complex that he nurtured and lived by. He was very powerful and his tribe had worked for five hundred years to make it so, and other tribes too; time was when Flying Spider's ancestors had been a very small minority, working high above the streets of New York, building on higher bits, repairing, cleaning. Work other people would not do, nor could do; the Mohawks took naturally to heights.

Yes, Flying Spider was powerful all right: he owned the whole of Manhattan Island. His ancestors had sold out for twenty-four dollars worth of trinkets, and he had bought it back for an unimaginable sum. He didn't only own the land, either, but every bit of every building, and all the companies too except for DuPont on the eleventh floor of the Empire State Building who had a special concession for making all the tribal costumes free of charge and before any other order. Like Spider for instance always wore full regalia, masses of gorgeous feathers but rain-and-stain proofed; you could have poured printing ink all over him and it would have brushed off when dry. Not that anyone would do such a thing, not to Flying Spider.

[9]

So Spider was powerful and rich and so was I. There were only about a hundred of us as rich as that, all descended from former depressed peoples and groups, like about five generations back my great multi-great grandmother was secretary to the Stir-Crazy Housewives League Ltd, England. That's what I call progress, I mean, out of the sixteen million or so people left on this planet after the Great Emigrations, I should end up being one of the Elite. Everybody else lived well too, but we hundred or so Top People decided how well. I not only wanted to get one up on Spider though (that's just a kind of hobby we had, buying things from each other and then proving it more valuable than the price paid), I wanted Manhattan Island for myself. You see, my family have always had a kind of thing about Manhattan, it's been a kind of Mecca for them, although I can't say quite why. It has been a tradition to sit at mother's knee and listen to tales of Manhattan. But I had never been there. Yes I know it sounds a bit odd what with travel so easy, anti-grav sledge would have got me there in half an hour but not only had I always been rich and powerful, I had always been – well, English Eccentric, which is a type you have probably never heard of but in my case it took the form of never leaving the village where I was born. Travel never appealed to me; three-D teevee was as much of the outside world as I wanted to experience. I had everything I wanted right there in East Leake which was Reservation Country for the Ancient Britons, a small village that made two leaps in its development. First in the thirteenth century when it got itself built around the church, and second around the twentieth when they added a few thousand horrible houses, a supermarket, a library for those that could read and a health centre for those going crazy from loneliness and boredom. Only the privileged and eccentric could survive such a place, I then thought.

So in that situation it was not surprising that I became the victim of a whim. It was a kind of nostalgia for something I had not seen, something almost genetic, passed on from that female ancestor – for it was said that she had actually been there for a visit. I have a pair of her false eyelashes set in lucite and they look like underwater caterpillars ... they had some very bizarre fashions at times in the past.

I had better explain it quite straight now just in case you haven't got it. What I wanted to do was buy the whole of Manhattan Island and have it re-erected on the site of East Leake, a village between Nottingham and Loughborough, in England. It was only a matter of marking every piece correctly and sticking piece A on to piece B.

'Okay okay, it's a challenge. I'll transact. Let's say the entire thing including inhabitants within six weeks, in working order?'

'That's what I had in mind, Spider. Is that your earliest delivery date?'

She finished typing the last letter of the day as Secretary of the Stir-Crazy League and went to look out of the window for a while, through the cotton mandalas of Nottingham lace. Mailman should be due, more mail, please let there be more mail. There was.

Congratulations on being winner of one week in New York City. Your guess number of Sugar Tweeties in one ton accurate absolutely not counting plastic turkeys which was the catch. Our rep will call to arrange tickets reservations escorts to suit you.

After the initial shock and fuss there were envious goodbyes, passionate kisses that were at once expressions of perfect trust in fidelity and betrayals of trust – after all she's a good-looking woman, all those escorts laid on, standing in line to take her out. Manhattan at her feet for a week. Brand new clothes, lovely shoes which were really seconds, a lot of care and attention to health and looks. Lucky woman zooming up to thirty thousand feet, far above the cat-spit of the rest of the Stir-Crazies. She was full of silly worries and frightened of flying, but the man in the next seat, who was really a boastful bore, kept her amused by telling what it was like to spend a month on a Greek island. Oh, she thought, it must be marvellous to be a rich American and travel a lot. He was stopping over in New York to take in some culture in the form of off-Broadway plays, one must not allow the mind to stagnate. Secretly she thought it was too late for him, but said out loud 'Nossir'. In American.

The JFK Airport, two valises at her feet, hand clutching purse, raincoat, passport, tickets, just standing there wondering what to do. More people in one place than she had ever seen before. The temperature was in the nineties and humid, she prickled. With fear as well as heat, for she sensed something horrible. What was it that was evil? It vibrated everywhere in the very breath of the place. The organisers of the competition arrived to whisk her off in a yellow taxi driven by a huge handsome black man, somewhat oblivious of the fact that there were other cars on the street. The noise was incredible, car horns going all the time, tyres screeching – a thing one never heard in England, but in America they always seemed to corner on two wheels and brakes, people calling, traffic rumble, subway roar, police sirens. Police sirens, did that mean a murder? Could be. And then it seemed to her that she could smell and hear the vibrations of Hell, she could see how it had all come to be, suddenly one day the lid of the Pit had crumbled up because of the pressure, and all this had come oozing out, out of the earth, materialised as City. She wanted to go home, she wished she had never come . . .

But she never said so aloud, kept smiling and looking and asking, kept the false eyelashes fluttering. The hotel room they gave her was clean and comfortable and very much too hot, and she expected to be fetched in the morning to go on a tour of Fifth Avenue dress shops followed by lunch in the Russian Tea Rooms near Carnegie Hall. No sleep to speak of because of being confused and feeling strange. She didn't know, but it was jet lag. Her home and family seemed like faded photographs already. The next day after some rest, everything improved.

For lunch there was a pancake stuffed with goatsmilk cream-cheese, caviar and sour cream, and vodka. She began to feel better, the centre of a great deal of unaccustomed attention, and it was all very pleasant. The escort for that day was charming and intelligent with a golden silky beard and impeccable manners. They discussed Russian literature and she blessed the time she had spent long ago reading *Crime and Punishment* for she could recall some things about that he could not and thereby avoided looking stupid. He told her that the witch-balls on the chandelier were Christmas trimmings from six years previous. So, they were fallible and human in America, even if this was a Russian place. It certainly was not all noise and rush and bustle and food in cans.

A conducted tour of the East Fifty-Seventh Street art galleries in the afternoon, an introduction to kinetic art. Glass globe on black cube, inside the globe a long symmetrical loop of neon moving back and forth and changing from red to blue regularly. She found it particularly hypnotic and compelling and found that it was trying to say something to her in between hooting bleeps. Buy me and take me home. But it cost an immense sum of money and the cash she had with her prize was meant to be spent in dress and cosmetic shops. A woman didn't want a piece of sculpture – she *was* a piece of sculpture. Not quite understanding how insulting this tortured compliment was, she went along with the escort on the schedule.

The city was wonderful and everything seemed exciting. Nowhere else exactly like it ever on Earth. And that in itself was exciting.

'Yes, sure, Spider. It's the perfect site for it. A disused gypsum mine right under the hill, stretches over an area approximately three hundred square miles, you can use what you like of it to suspend the new sewers and subways and all of that in, it'll be a cinch, I mean, East Leake is built over a vast cavern, you won't have any blasting to do at all and it's like the Rock of Ages for strength, they don't even get a split in the wallpaper from subsidence, and you won't need to flood much of Nottingham to get it all in, I was talking to the surveyors only this morning, you see, there's no problem at all, don't make any. Down to the eleventh floor and DuPont giving trouble? Build them a solid concrete base with elevator, and when the whole building is transported put DuPont's floor back on to that, they'll have everything they're legally entitled to but who else will care? Anybody else grumble at coming to England, offer them the same treatment, tell 'em they can stay behind. They'll come to their senses, what business are they going to do on Manhattan Desert Island?'

I was really flying with the idea, it was taking shape already, only a couple of days after I had signed the deal with Spider. I had had to sell out thousands of square miles of Finland to do it but as I had no intention of going there I did not care. I had never been to Manhattan, it was coming to me! I sorted it out with the town councils and started on the evacuation of all the inhabitants in the area, and when we actually got the measurements it included West Leake, Sutton Bonington, Hoton and Costock, Stanford and part of Bunny. But as I pointed out to them – what was their problem? They would benefit. I was having it seen to that everyone got a better house than the one they were leaving, that new factories and shops would be built, that their whole standard of living would improve not to mention the retirement pensions for *everybody*, not just heads of households. They might have been Ancient Britons on Reservation Country, but they were open to reason if it smelled of comfort. By the time I had finished talking to them they couldn't wait for the subsonic rasers to move in.

Everybody stand back! The alarm hooters making all of Sherwood Forest tremble, all of Charnwood shake. And then, the strange drone that was almost a silence, quite quickly, the whole area I needed became dust which was of course siphoned off to my breeze-block factory in Yorkshire. 'I may seem to create chaos but I don't like waste,' I said to a Flying Spider who was stunned with admiration.

'I do believe you have genius,' he said to me. That's what I call progress, I thought, it had only been a matter of weeks since our first head-on meetings and he had thought me unadventurous and neurotic with my dislike of travel, and hopeless at buying and selling. That compliment from him gave me a boost – he was a powerful fella.

The escort for the day was a delight to be with: he was a large young man with unconventional clothes and hair and a wild grin which frightened some people, but not her. He bought her lots of vodkas and Camparis on the expense account, and when she looked around at the city she felt that she was falling in love with it all. Something in the air was like those evenings out with her husband before they were married. What had happened to that? Once, they had had such splendid times, and felt so good.

'Well if DuPont won't come across and it means that there will be only one hundred and nineteen floors to the Empire State, then I have to have it built right on top of the hill, on the site of Adastral House you know? Appropriate name, no? Yes, I do insist, I want it to be as tall as it was, higher above sea-level than its original site. Think of the view! On a clear day I'll be able to see as far as Northampton or Derby, depending on which way I look. No, I'm not interested in the fact that there are other taller buildings. The Empire State is historic, which is why I suppose it had been so carefully preserved – and must be so again. By the way, the flooding of the new rivers went perfectly, there's not a ripple difference in the shape of the water around New Manhattan, the currents run exactly right, you can move the ferry tomorrow, check that the toll-gates on the tunnels and bridges are sorted out properly, like the Pennsylvania lane will now be the lane for North Wales. We'll make a tuppence or so too, people will drive down from

Edinburgh to ride on the ferry at night, it's quite spectacular, I hear.'

Spider was delighted with me, I could tell from the way he laughed. He liked women with imagination. He told me that already the city was in pieces and stored on the Palisades and the Poconos in the order of re-erection and that whole blocks were on their way across the Atlantic by anti-grav sledge. They had been obliged to use subsonic rasers on whole tracts of forest which I would not have allowed, but Spider said that the method of storage and shuttle was essential if I wanted fast delivery, and there was nowhere else near enough. I ordered replanting at the earliest time possible.

I took a two-seat sledge to watch the foundations of the Empire State being relaid right on the site I had specified. I hovered around for hours and could hardly explain why I felt so scared. I put it down to excitement. After all, it was no mean thing I had set in motion. It was a First all right. I couldn't sleep that night even though the luxury houseboat I had fixed up on the East River, formerly known as the Trent, was as comfortable a place as any I had ever known. I was not to sleep properly for many nights. It was soundproofed against the twenty-four-hour activity of anti-grav sledges homing in with the next bit of the jig-saw, armies of fibreglass and old-time concrete mixers, the clang of scaffolding, blowtorches, cranes, lorries, drills and other machinery. No it wasn't the noise that kept me awake. Every day I went floating out over the growing city to watch, checking the avenues with a map just for fun. It looked like scum and lichen at first with square mushrooms sprouting but as time passed it rapidly took on a coherent shape. Glossy yellow sunrises would reflect off flight after flight of glass, some of the smaller buildings even had flags flying and people began to move in. Every hour a new sledge arrived and furniture and boxes and people began to settle in, back into their homes and shops and offices. Faces appeared at the windows to see what the view was like from the new location. Most looked disappointed for they looked out on exactly the same bricks as they ever had. One old fellow in an apartment on West Eighty-Eighth complained that we had been the cause of the death of his cat. He accused us of planting his acacia tree out of place, because his cat had been used to jumping from the fifth-floor window on to a certain branch, and the first time it tried it in the new location, it fell to its death. We showed him the plans to prove that every stone was in place – the cat must have lost its touch. I was sorry about that, but everything above ground was exactly as before. Below ground there was the new sewage system with a built-in rat-gassing system. My idea of course but I had paid to have it invented. Offer enough money and people can invent anything. So, no rats and no spillage. The people of Manhattan would like me, I thought, and even as it was they did not seem too perturbed. Life for them would go on much as usual, and if they wanted vacations in the States, I paid. I had all that kind of detail covered.

What I particularly liked to watch were the spidermen high up. They were better than cats, height just did not scare them. They were both sexes all doing similar jobs. Spider's tribe didn't have to work of course, but it was a tradition and they liked the work.

There was a thrilling time when the Big One was finally up and I floated past and there was a blazing sunset behind me and the reflection flung back at me was like scarlet fluorescent blood, and then blue sky, and I flashed back and forth to get the sight again and again until the greenish clouds of early night came and I descended away from my tower of glass, out of my mind with exultation that I owned the most beautiful city ever built. I lay in bed that night feeling that someone was trying to get a message to me, but I knew I was overtired and ignored it. I got up before dawn and looked out on to the river. Somewhere near the island there should have been a thing called the Statue of Liberty, but I had forgotten to include it in the deal. Anyway, I thought, who wants sculpture that size, I had the whole of the Guggenheim and all that stuff if I wanted Art.

I was just a little depressed about the whole project around that time I must admit, but I put it down to extended impatience which made me feel ill. Six weeks seemed a long time to realise a dream, but as Spider said: 'You don't want the Chase Manhattan in Battery Park or the Penn Station under the elephants in the Natural History, do you?' He put me down properly by saying, 'It's *organised*.' It was the way he said that word. He outpowered me, but I was still the one with the imagination.

'What shall we do next when this is over?'

'Suggest something,' I said nonchalantly.

'How about a merger?' I shrugged but not rudely. Secretly I was shattered with pleasure. A merger with Flying Spider was a great project. It was as if I had been dreaming a dream for centuries and it had suddenly come true.

There were two days of the Competition Trip left, and she was feeling wonderful. She wondered how she could ever have thought the city frightful, it did not now seem possible. She was with an escort in a superb restaurant, slightly drunk and very happy. He was a pleasant companion and very attractive. He poured vintage claret which she was not used to ('actually at home we usually have plonk') and they drank it with squabs in a delicious sauce full of olives. The salad was perfect. By the time they got around to fruit salad in Kirsch and then the excellent coffee she was truly flying with well-being, happiness, joy. Her companion was beautiful and had a fabulous tan. She asked him where he had got it and he smiled without annoyance. Not a tan, he was a full-blooded Mohawk Indian. By day he worked as a spiderman high up on girders, and he only did the escort job to make extra money. His wife was very ill and medical bills were exorbitant. But, he said, they were not to talk of that. He had something wonderful to show her. The sixty-fifth floor, the Rainbow Room.

Huge windows through which he indicated a fabulous view. Somehow at that moment they had clasped hands, and she could hardly breathe for the shock of what she saw, it was so beautiful. The mist was below them in the canyons, moving towards them menacing and amorphous was the Empire State Building like an insect presence from Outer Space, a glittering treasure in the sky. Just coming in to land, perpetually coming nearer. She spread out her hands to it, stunned by the mystery of architecture that is unearthly and unreal, compelled to love this strangely Gothic place which masqueraded as Modern. She wished a deep wish to come and live here forever. She loved the place, and felt loved back. At home.

Chief Flying Spider apologised for being one day late with the goods. It was DuPont's fault: they had decided at the last minute that they wanted to come in on the move, and so the problem of how to insert their offices back into the Big One had to be solved. I came up with the unique idea of floating it all the way across the Atlantic on several layers of anti-grav sledges all inter-computerised so that there would be no hangups like the entire thing sliding down into the fathoms. DuPont resented losing working time and I wanted them in fast, so it seemed obvious to me to float the entire thing over at one blast, typewriters and computers clicking away, temporary short-wave telephones installed, elevator doors double-locked. About fifteen thousand sledges were fastened all the way up to the top of the Big One from the twelfth floor up and lasers sliced through the entire floor just above the ceilings of the tenth, and up it went at a preset moment like a plumbline sweet and true, and in slid DuPont still yakking on the phone and hardly a drop of coffee spilled. Services were reconnected and everything was checked for perfect fit. I had them pin certain places with steel rods and an electromagnetic charge, making the join stronger than it had originally been. All the windows were tested for warp – we didn't want glass exploding, but there was no strain anywhere. Spider thought I was bright to have thought of doing it that way and I thought him clever to have accomplished the dream. After the merger, we felt that we would do things which would shake the world.

There were then only details, like making sure that all the new commuters' homes were satisfactory – the overwhelming opinion seemed to be in favour of the English countryside.

Already the subways were roaring, and I was very pleased with those.

The escort for that last night was a very nice man who was to take her out to dinner and then the theatre. They were to see three one-act plays in an off-Broadway theatre and she looked forward to the evening very much. (Take in some culture on the way home, as the man on the plane had said.) She took especial care with her appearance, thinking that she often did so at home, and that her husband took it for granted. She missed him less and less each day and thought with horror of going back home to that flat village and the Stir-Crazies secretarial work and the housework and the loneliness of life as a wife. But she told herself not to be selfish and silly, for this was just a trip, and she was lucky, people who were selfish and greedy risked losing everything.

All during dinner she told her escort about the previous even-ing when she had stood on the sixty-fifth floor in an ecstatic con-dition, she rattled on all during the excellent clams on ice and softshell crabs in butter, and tactlessly rattled on about the incredible beauty of New York City, Manhattan Island, America, right until the curtain rose on the first play. During the interval she told her escort all about the escort of the previous evening until she perceived a small knowing smile on his face, interpreted it and blushed. He was paid to be attentive and kind, she felt that she had been boring. And indiscreet.

When she got home in a cab, there waiting at her door was the

Mohawk, dressed in his working clothes. She did not hesitate for a moment but invited him into her room.

They kissed a few times and lay back reeling. Yes, they agreed, they were in love. No, they agreed, they were going to do nothing about it. There was nothing they could do. His wife was sick and needed him, her husband was waiting for her at home. It was the most powerful and awful hour of her life, to find the one true person and lose them. Her feelings she could contain but she felt that they burned her from inside and that she would never be healed.

He left silently and she neither wept nor could she sleep. At dawn in a drugstore drinking coffee she came to a formula for transmuting pain and love: she gave all her love to the city, for-ever, and ever. Her pain turned into a kind of elation, and every sound of the city waking up gave her pleasure. Nothing would succeed in hurting her now, she felt sure.

Spider called me: 'It's all yours, complete with trash in the gutter and roaches. Wanna conducted tour?' I picked up the lucite block with the false eyelashes set in it and I swear the damn things moved. Like crawled, or winked. I had to laugh. I was very over-tired but full of energy; it is amazing what a sense of accomplish-ment can do for the nervous system. I put down my paperweight and told Spider no, first there was something I wanted to do. I had a crazy longing to go and see Manhattan Island all bleak and bare. He was horrified.

'The first trip you take outside your own backyard and what do you go and see – it's all happening *here*! You made it happen, you got what you want. The trouble I went to...'

'I know, I know, it's just a feeling I have. I want to do it.' I hung up. I was nervous about the merger. Our combined powers might be too much, together we could possibly accomplish awful things. On the TV they were interviewing the former residents of New Jersey and places around and there was a noticeable lack of sentimentality about their former homeland. The weather was the only problem. I was getting that fixed. I wanted the seasons extreme like real New York, not the English softness where you were not always sure what season it was.

It was all set, it was mine. There would be the official company meeting to sign the merger. Before I set off on my trip I called Spider.

'By the way, what were you thinking of doing with the site of NYC?'

'I thought I might do an Ancient Indian Reservation...'

'See you later,' I said, smiling.

She stayed awake every moment until she got back home. The plane journey had been fabulous, intense blue runway lights, the lights of the city from the air, an electric storm and black silk clouds ripping on the wings, the whole sky illuminated like her sudden discovery of a new love, plunging into cloud like its loss. But then straight up to a sight of the stars, and ahead into pale liquid glass containing one last bright star, permitting herself one last exploding thought of him and of how it might have been and then consigning it all to outer darkness, because if she did not, something utterly dreadful might happen.

I hovered over the desolate site of Manhattan and wondered why I had come, it had been silly. It was utterly dreary and kind of haunted, the earth flat dust. I headed for home and made it in less than an hour. I did not land immediately but decided to have a good look around the new place first. When I first saw it I thought I was suffering from sleep-loss hallucinations. The sky-line was trembling. Moving around idiotically. And then I began shouting warnings to people who could not hear. Buildings were toppling over sideways and I narrowly escaped being crushed by the steel cupola of the Woolworth building, gliding past me like a rocket and exploding into scales somewhere below in the abyss.

I sent my sledge straight up and began to cruise, circling, switched the controls over to automatic-avoid. It was the gypsum mine caving in, of course; it had been roofed in firm for thousands of years but this was after all just too much. All the engineers and consultants had said that it would take it, that it would be fine – but they had been wrong. Maybe the subsonic lasers had done unseen damage, maybe it was my wanting the Big One right on the top of the hill at the thinnest point of the cave roof. I could not hear anything much in my sledge, but I could imagine. All the screaming and shouting and crying out, yells of disbelief and horror, echoes of explosions as power lines hit subway cars, fires everywhere, gas leaks, buildings falling and bursting like fruit, yellow cabs like beetles under bricks, horns howling, then the sucking downwards, a thousand feet of sparkling white gypsum grinding against itself and spreading back miles of surrounding yellow clay, the pressure so great that Beacon Hill ten miles away became three feet higher above sea level – the oldest rocks in Britain would take another million or so years to flatten out.

I homed in, aware of vast winds and flashes of light, scarlet and blue, explosions, sunset, dust and fire and electricity both manufactured and natural, and then I saw what I was seeking: Spider on a parapet of the Empire State, waving to me for help. The building moved back and forth and I strapped myself in and opened the dome. I could hardly breathe for rising gas and dust. I could not hear him. I reached out to him, I tried again and again, I screamed to him to jump across but I had forgotten the automatic-avoid. He leapt into empty space and I zoomed out of the way of his falling body. Down it went hurtling over and over, I stayed to watch the island sink, like the lid of a great pit was lifted, the void claiming its own again, it was a triumphal roar, a greedy sucking, closing over, the abyss eating up what was its rightful property.

It was a long time ago and on Earth. I emigrated. I had no money left and no friends, no home, no choice. I don't have anything much now, no power. I didn't have any then. I have never had any, or I would have made everything go very differently.

Lover from Beyond
the Dawn of Time

Homage to H. K. Giger, and with respect to H. P. Lovecraft

My recording begins now. This batch of material is to be put into the *camera* section of the Mental Health Bureau for attention in the near future. Tegrindesfor, archivist recording, eleventh section of year 6666.

It is with much difficulty that I have managed to decipher the papers found in the room of Malleena, the eccentric new inhabitant of the Land Complex number 223, who has recently disappeared. I myself will decline comment, the reasons for which reticence the researchers will readily appreciate, except I must state that the material in itself is more or less useless as information as it is obviously the product of a very sick brain. There are various matters to be cleared up in connection with this material, and it could possibly provide a clue to the origin of a squatter reported in that same complex, but I do not think it will help in locating the corpse or person of its author. The material was written by hand but we have managed to translate it into speech. I read this slowly which will give an odd cadence but I have rehearsed and colleagues find it intelligible if incomprehensible. Material begins now:

I had been assigned a unit well above the water-level, high in the area which was once called Switzerland. It was a huge block of several thousand together, so I did not anticipate loneliness. Now that we all speak one language, I thought, I shall enjoy promenading the long corridors, meeting new people. Once in my childhood I was moved, and could communicate with nobody at first. My rhythms dictated that I should have free time in the minority group, but there would still be sufficient people awake to ensure a happy social life. It was a new block and all the units were not yet filled, but I knew how lucky I was for so many people are assigned units below the water, and I felt certain that I should suffer from the discomforts of this, adaptation not yet being perfect. I was therefore very lucky. I have the unusual hobby of reading books, which as we know is considered very eccentric, but something in me is very atavistic and prefers to decipher and write lettering rather than watch a screen with images or listen to sound alone. An antique book could last me many sections, and I had two. One was a very great curiosity about food in pre-flood times in which various powders were mixed with food to make it hot or mild, an idea which does fascinate me, and another Book of Records by Guinness, a strange fabulation about imaginary people who spent their lives doing the most extraordinary things. The imagination of the author is beyond anything else I have read, but he manages to make it sound authentic.

My unit was on the lowest floor, right in the centre of the building, and this made me feel safe. Old units or outer units afford me no comfort, I do not care to look out on eternal greyness; weather upsets me, it is primeval.

I was the first to occupy this unit so there were no personal marks on it at all, everything was immaculately clean and neat, so I closed my door behind me with delight. I had a new home. Immediately the viewing screen came to light with a message for me. I was invited to a mixed-sex party for newcomers in nineteen parts time. I replied to the invitation with pleasurable anticipation. Celibacy was not going to be a problem.

I began to unpack my boxes, putting away my clothes in the closet, relishing the hygienic feel of the place. I had occasionally come across old clothing or the remains of eating in rooms and found it quite disgusting. I was therefore very puzzled to enounter a faint odour emanating from the bottom of the closet. It was horrible.

I have problems describing this odour for we have so little to compare it to, but I would guess that sulphur dioxide and bacteria in rotting meat or stagnant dirt would approximate to it, with some strange overtones of very sweet scents, musk and patchouli, the kind of thing some people sometimes wear at social occasions. I recoiled from the closet and activated the air purifier. I searched for the source of the nastiness but there was nothing. There was no fault in the structure through which the smell of a wild animal, a mouse for example, could possibly seep. It is not unheard of for buildings to have colonies of small animals in their basements amongst the works, but there was no way for a smell to enter my unit if it came from such habitation. The smell disappeared, I finished my packing, and when I noticed on my checker that it was past my sleeping section I decided that I was overtired and overexcited and had imagined the smell. I took a dreamkiller and laid myself down on my bedstream, adjusting the temperature of the airflow. My last impressions before closing my eyes and turning off the lights was of a safe and pleasant living-space, immaculate, and anticipation of the party.

That party was a great success. There were about a dozen newcomers, all pleasant outgoing types, and the men among them were quite suitable for me and I made an alliance immediately. I recall that occasion with nostalgia because it was the last social occasion I attended at which I felt normal and at ease. We took food together, and there were the usual drinks and drugs. We danced and mimed and I went with the new lover to his unit to spend a pleasant section and congratulated myself that I would have everything I needed in 223. He agreed with me that we would be suitable partners. His name was Ilexin and he was quite young, a mere seventy-two without any visible changes in his muscletone as yet. My physical form is still perfect as it was when I was young, but I am eleven years younger than Ilexin. I have not yet given birth to children, but had been considering applying for permission. That idea is now irrelevant of course, I no longer desire a human child. Now I do not know my future, I live from one sublime experience to the next and I am not the person I then was, for experience changes and enriches. My friends had noticed. I soon found a woman friend, a good person who took an intelligent interest in my hobby and who had the even more unusual hobby of writing poems. Her name was Hegellin and she can conjure up images in the mind and turn them to words as the ancients did. We got on well, but as events progressed, I began to neglect her. Ilexin also noticed.

'Malleena, perhaps you need a visit to a clinic? You do not seem happy and you daydream a great deal. Did you know that you are unsociable? Perhaps you feel that we are not suitable partners after all?' he suggested mournfully. I reassured him. I told him that I had been a bit lax on keeping to my correct rhythms, that I got interested in reading some of my favourite things and forgot to sleep, and that it was affecting my health, but not seriously. I knew that such an excuse was thin, for if I seemed much worse to them, my friends would insist I go to a clinic. I could never tell them the truth. If I had told them even a part of my new experiences, they would have taken me for full treatment at a clinic immediately, and then I would no longer be Malleena. I dreaded that, such an occurrence has always been a phobia of mine. I can not understand how so many people give themselves up at the slightest aberration, without fear.

One sleep section soon after the party I went to sleep as usual but did not take a dreamkiller as I was very tired and full of drugs and alcohol. What happened later I put down to this condition, for it does occasionally happen as we know, that people halluci-nate quite strongly. The idea that I was hallucinating saved my sanity at the time, for I could not have borne the reality.

I woke in the dark, hearing a faint music in the air. It was like strings and drones with deep distant drums behind, and it felt not interesting but threatening. But my senses were chiefly assaulted by smell – the same smell I had inhaled on my first entry to the unit, but this time it was much stronger. I cast around for the controls for the light and air-purifier and could not find them at first, and when I did a most extraordinary thing occurred: they would not work. I had never had that experience before, it was unheard of and it shook me into sweating terrors. I decided that I must be ill but I could not think what to do if the services did not work. I was confused.

Then the light began to appear, as if it shone gently on to the opposite wall, moving gently with a glow like that I once observed on a rotting dogfish in a biology laboratory. But there were shadows on the wall, cohering gradually into a dim vision. This had something of the effect of a hologram, it had that kind of reality about it, but I felt certain that it was not a hologram. I knew it must be an hallucination, yet some other part of me already knew that it was real.

It seemed to me so horrible that I was ill with fear. But I felt compelled to watch.

The light became stronger, clarifying the image. There with me were creatures not of this world. I had never visualised such horrors even in my worst nightmares, although they seemed to relate to some of my dream disturbances. The whole vision was dominated by the most frightful figure, an enormous creature with a head like a goat with frightful horns, and inward-looking eyes which expressed a terrible evil. It had a dual sexuality, with an enormous erect phallus, and huge breasts which were formed like the heads of the most ghastly babies, suppurating with unspeakable sores. The entity sat on a row of skulls. I had seen things slightly resembling this in our museums of ancient history, and thought that I must be in the presence of a religion which nobody has believed in for several thousand years: Black Magic. I now know that it is not really that, but something I can not properly record for I do not fully understand it, and I am also on an oath of secrecy about certain things. But I was correct in a sense, for Black Magic was the term once used to name the outer mysteries, a term belonging to human beings.

As we know, this is a pragmatic-existential universe, so I was therefore labouring under considerable intellectual strain taking in the situation at all. There came then a whispering voice with the music, hoarsely singing to me, for I could hear my name.

'Malleena, Malleena, we need you,' sang the voice, thrilling me entirely with both fear and pleasure. The ego loves to be named aloud in song. Perhaps I was foolish to so respond but I some-times think that our lives in these times are empty, and our energies will therefore cling to anything of interest even if it is potentially harmful or even obviously – how shall I say – evil? I know that human ideas are not the only ones, and not the most important.

'Malleena, approach.' The figure beckoned slightly with one clawed hand and the eyes seemed to move slightly. Slowed with terror I rose from my bedstream, my pulse racing, confused because curiously exalted, and then fell into a dead faint. Hours later I awoke feeling cold. Everything was gone. I checked, and it was the hour I should have been out, eating with other people. The light and the air-purifier were activated.

I was exhausted and had no appetite, so I crept back to the warm bedstream and lay musing about what had happened. Of course it was an hallucination, was not the mark of such ex-periences their very feeling of total reality? I would desist from alcohol and drugs for a few days and would take dreamkillers for several nights. Then there would be no danger of being taken to a clinic. I knew it was my duty to keep healthy, but my phobia was less trouble to me than my guilt so I told myself that all would be well and that it was just a matter of self-control. How was I to know that I might as well try to re-freeze the polar ice-caps with willpower!

I slept dreamlessly for many sections, further upsetting my biorhythms which might never now be righted, for I have for so long been awake when I should sleep and have stolen sleep when I should be awake.

Oh lover in darkness, come for me again tonight. Bring with you your allies, your minions, your slaves, and take me at your will.

And then I was woken again by the music and the awful stench, which in some curious way I seemed almost to like although this was strange for I knew it to be terrible. I inhaled it as if it was fresh and delightful, like some addiction to something poisonous. The scent fired synapses in my brain that I had never been aware of; it was like a traveller in ancient times getting his first scent of his native shores. And the music, a familiar feel about it lifted my spirits to great happiness, although not a kind of happiness I had known before. It was a new emotion to me, more akin to fear and yet I could not call it anything but joy. My feelings were inverted in a way I could not have guessed possible. Once more the figure beckoned, and I saw other figures around it. Frightful presences, half machine, half fabulous beast. They were the dealers of death, and of ecstasy in death. They tempted, reached out sensually with clawed hands and licking tongues, unearthly in their total lasciviousness. I stood naked and shaking with apprehension and felt the brush of soft leathery wings on my flesh. I felt the lick of hot tongues on my thighs, the exploring scratch of hairy paws. I was powerless against this violation, for it afforded me the most intense pleasure I had ever experienced. I could not call out or even moan. I was lost.

I awoke much later, again very cold but in a state of euphoria, and then my mood changed totally. I felt defiled and ashamed and utterly filthy and I rushed to shower myself, scrubbing and rinsing, trying to rid myself of the memory of the things of the night. I determined to make an appointment at the clinic, but later changed my mind, for I was convinced that what I had experienced was not an hallucination, and could not be cut out of my mind, for it would return again and again from outside of myself. And yet, did not lunatics think it just that way, swear that their experiences were 'real'? I was afraid of not knowing the difference but I was convinced that everything was real. I was correct. It is certainly real.

To keep up appearances I occasionally saw my friends, inventing what excuses I could. Ilexin did not mention my mood or responses when we made love but I am sure he noticed even then that my mind was elsewhere. He had been perfectly satisfactory, but now I knew of other pleasures, and could not help comparing him unfavourably.

My visitors did not come to me every time I slept but they sometimes appeared during my waking hours and it was this which was spoiling my normal life for I found that I stayed in my unit, living in hopes of a trysting, and neglecting my ordinary recreation. And I began to communicate with them verbally. I found my tongue.

I asked them who they were. They told me that they were the ancient ones, and that they had existed since long before human history. They still had access to this planet, but only through a very few places. That part of the earth over which my unit rested was one of those places, for they had been summoned there thousands of years ago. How long ago? In the twentieth century as it was then called, a human had invoked them by depicting them on the walls of his room, and later on paper.

'His parents kept what was called an apothecary shop, a place of drugs, but he was a super-intelligent being, and he knew what we looked like by seeing into his own mind,' said a female with long legs terminating in clawed feet.

'I used to use this young man through his mind, and he could give us shape with his immense skills in draughtsmanship.' I marvelled at such a story. People no longer draw or paint, it is archaic. To think that an artist could recreate images on the walls of a room, so that the subjects of his skill would always be able to manifest there.

'I loved that man,' she told me. 'I gradually took his soul. Now he is part of me. We are immortals of course,' she said, taking my hands in hers as a preliminary to one of the shattering physical encounters that she could perpetrate upon me. 'I loved him, and now I love you. Malleena, we all love you.'

'But why me? Just because I came to this unit?'

'You are lucky. You came here, and as it happens, you were suitable. Not everyone has it in them to become one of us.'

I did not want to become one of them. I felt myself a dilettante at experience then, I did not wish to lose my very existence as payment for the bizarre pleasures I had found. I felt caught between two kinds of extinction. I applied for a change of living accommodation. I was refused. And of course, I could not appeal, there was no reason I could invent that the authorities would have believed. I determined to socialise more and take dreamkillers when I slept. There was no question of leaving the building without authority of course because there is nothing out there but damp earth and fog right to the edge of the ocean. I must take stern measures with myself, I thought, I could rid myself of the visitations if I made myself morally strong. How could I have been so naive and self-deceiving?

No person who has not had these intense experiences and been in the grip of the most hidden and dark forces can know how compelling they are. I would rather have fought alone a severe drug addiction than stop meeting my creatures. Everything else in life became pale and without interest or importance compared to what they had to offer. How can I explain it to anyone? Who can believe that to be whirled through freezing fires and possessed by demonic forces, ravished by chthonic entities and taken to the very brink of extinction by the sheer excess of sensual pleasure can be preferable to a normal healthy existence? These days there is nothing except a normal healthy existence, how could anyone possibly understand, least of all a doctor in a clinic? It is preferable. Every time I have been with them in their dark rituals and allowed myself to become part of their unimaginable conclaves, I return disgusted, ashamed, resolute, but soon begin longing as one does for a lover, unable to think of anything else until that glorious moment when I inhale their scent, and see their glowing lights appear, and dance to their music which is not like any other sound. I have become a woman between two worlds.

But there are more hazards to my adventures than I have yet hinted at. As I have said, it is not always during my sleeping time that the world changes for me, although of course it is always in my unit, that bridge between two universes built so long ago by that brilliant artist. One day I had made an effort and been to socialise with Hegellin, my dear friend whom I had been neglecting. She had sensed much amiss of course but I had put her off as best I could. She suggested that perhaps I pay more attention to my sex-life, that I was possibly suffering from a deprivation syndrome. I do not know how I prevented myself from bursting out laughing at this kind suggestion. But I felt better from the encounter, and we spent pleasant time together chatting, and I assured her that my sex-life was fine. My spirits were high and I was comfortable within myself when we parted. I entered my unit and closed the door behind me, and almost died of terror.

I was standing, not in my unit, but on the very brink of a bottomless abyss. I have never liked heights, I am not used to them and cannot cope with the sensation of vertigo. I froze there, poised with my boot toes just over the edge of a shiny shelf, and when I attempted to step back I found there was no door, only a solid wall behind me without purchase for a panic-stricken hand. I was collected enough not to stare down, so I looked up. It was a shaft, dimly lit, with no perceptible roof. Perspective took the end of it from my sight. There were narrow wooden steps fixed to the side here and there, but many were broken and they all looked undependable and some of them ended nowhere, over that eerie vastness, encased within the sheer walls. I took courage and looked down. From the very depths came the sound of wailing and throbbing, a draught of cold wind smelling like the meat freezers when they are being defrosted, and like a broken urinal if ever there could be such a thing, stale and miserable. The murky light had a faintest hint of colour in it, a strange kind of pink, a suggestion of green. I knew that the end of my life had come, there was no way out, no place to go, no turning point. In such straits it is said that strength comes to people, there have been acts of heroism beneath the sea during accidents. With all my remaining strength I found no heroism, only the will to scream for salvation. At first my voice would not work, but then I called for the lover of my soul, the central figure of all the creatures, who I knew had more strength than I and who had said that I was needed. I stared ahead at the blank wall which seemed to drip with some foul slime, and gradually there appeared before me a machine creature, a tentacled engine of torture with a gripping device worked by nuts and bolts of ancient design, held at either side by some vile entities with skulls out of which grew terrible guns.

Looming over this creation which I had at first thought to be floating in space but which I then saw was erected on a kind of platform of appalling snakes and other strange creatures with wings, which had emerged from the wall, was the beginning of another image. It was the chief creature of them all, come to my cry, the alien countenance I now knew so well.

'You have been chosen,' it informed me, and I could only wonder for what I had been chosen. Just then, I wanted only to return to normality.

'You are to be the mother of our Earth-child,' it told me, whispering seductively over the emptiness of nothing. 'If you will come close, you shall be privileged to be my only Earth-bride, and together we shall make a creature invincible to all forces of destruction, a being which will have the power to do miracles, which will be totally beautiful and have eternal life, and who will change your world.' I began to feel less frightened at the sound of his voice for it always inspired me with courage and good feeling, there is no voice like that one.

'We have waited for millennia for such a one as yourself.' I could not speak, but the question of 'why' ran through my mind.

'This new being will give birth to others of its kind in your world, and they will change it. Your world is full of woe and destruction and blindness about the real nature of things. We have the secret of changing what you call horror into what is truly beautiful and ecstatic. This is the only way.' I already knew that what I was being told was true, for since I had been with them I knew that things which I would once have called pain were not pain, and things which were ugly and evil were truly marvellous.

'What shall I do?' I asked.

'You will be given the utmost privilege we can bestow, if you come to us and lend yourself to this birth machine. We shall impregnate you, and the new being will begin its life in your body. You will be remembered for all time as the one human being with the courage to offer themselves for the greatest cause there has ever been.' I began to glow with warmth then, I began to come alive again, and to breathe normally. The idea was taking a hold in my mind and the desire to comply was already very strong.

'Come to me now,' it said. I then felt to be in a different state from any normal state; I was invincible. I could float across space, I could be burned in fire without death as the result. I opened my arms and stepped forward, drawn by a powerful feeling which I can only describe as love, the desire to become one with the other, and to take into myself the seed of a glorious new race.

I was lifted by claws and tentacles and stripped of all my garments and I was turned upside-down. I experienced everything as the most perfect ecstasy. I fitted into the birth machine, knowing that it had been made just for me. It was measured for every curve and bone in my body. I was fastened in by living straps, sensitive to every one of my breaths so that they held me but caressed me at once. My head was slowly clamped into the metal jaws of the vice so that it could not move. My legs were held by winged creatures, and then slowly, and knowing the exact moment of the meeting of two worlds in my glowing flesh, I was impregnated by the god himself and herself, the perfect one. Their view of things was more powerful than pragmatism, than existentialism, than reason. It was the most powerful force this world has ever known, and that is why in ancient times it was treated with fear and revulsion, and named 'evil'.

I dissolved into glorious flames and felt my blood surge up beyond the heat of fire and I seemed to be gone forever, taken on an ocean of total bliss.

And then I was cold and greyly asleep on the floor of my unit, euphoric, shuddering, with my own blood upon me. A strange slime covered everything in the room, dripping slowly, glowing with its own light. I stayed there in that state a long time, needing nothing, until eventually a message came on to the screen enquiring after my health. I replied that I had been feeling tired but that I would be in circulation again soon. There were no more questions asked. I cleaned my room, and myself, with difficulty.

That was almost nine sections ago. I am not visibly pregnant, as I would have been if I had successfully applied to be a mother. But I know that I am pregnant, I can feel growing within me the creature that is to be the first of a new race. It circles in me, swimming and jumping in my humours, I nurture it in my flesh. I have not been visited by my lover since that time when I was chosen, but I know that when I am ready to give birth, soon, they will come to me and take me to their birth machine for my ultimate destiny of usefulness, which is to thrust into the world, this world, a new and perfect being. I am impatient, I hope it will be very soon.

I have no lovers now. Hegellin does not bother to call me, for she knows that I have become unsociable and without anything to offer in the way of discourse or games. To them I am dull, and they believe that I should hand myself over to the clinic for rehabilitation, and how can they ever believe that they are wrong? They see only with human eyes.

Last night a messenger came to me. It was a winged worm with eyes which opened inwards on to unimaginable worlds. It said to me through a mouth with many jaws: 'Be ready!' So I wait. It can only be a matter of a very few sections until I am ready to give birth. Or rather, that my child will be ready to use me. I am utterly committed to the role that has been chosen for me.

When the abyss opens at my feet, and the birth machine waits, I shall be ready. This world needs my new creature. This child will save the world.

Report from the Bureau of Archaeology and Sociology, Accommodation Section 334, eighth section year 7179. Personal progress report.

All the preceding material was salvaged from a bureau block in the area now under excavation. It would seem that the text refers to the site on which it was found, as it was indeed an accommodation block, Land Complex 223 as the text indicates. I have as yet no further material to continue the history of the mad woman who originally wrote the text but everything indicates that the building was destroyed by a means we have not yet detected, soon after the final dating. It is interesting to note that the 'story' is not all fantasy. There was for example an artist who made pictures exactly fitting the description the woman gave of her fantasies. These are ancient works, microfilmed and stored in the Himalayan Records, Art and Literature section, sub-section Religion. A friend of mine is studying religious art of that period and during a conversation he suggested to me that I look up H. K. Giger. He once lived in what was then known as Switzerland, and published a book in an island long since sunk called Britain, a part of Old Europe. It would however have been quite impossible for anyone without special permission to have access to any of these records; as far as is known the Himalayan Records have always been extremely closely guarded except to bona fide scholars. Her interest in books may be the clue, but the text states that she had only two, one of which, the Guinness book, is still in Records, the other could be any of several Indian cooking books, hardly an academic record! We must at present put the resemblance down to coincidence.

The character of the 'story' suggests that the woman was suffering from a psychosis which is still not unknown in these times. A recent case concerns a woman who claims that she has a lover with wings and claws who claims to be the son of an all-powerful god. She is of course in a clinic awaiting treatment, so it is always difficult to get interviews before the psychosis is eradicated. A typical feature of this syndrome seems to be that in some way the world will be changed because of the union of two life-forms. It would be interesting to do a study of people with the ability to read and write to discover if the denial of use of these talents alters brain chemistry in any way.

I shall be going on location in the near future to save time in travelling and transport costs, and intend to set up camp near where the material was found. I shall be alone on the trip, so shall need to apply for extended food supplies, water purifiers, and the use of various machines, and transport. I trust that the directors of this institute will see fit to aid me in this project, which will I think bring much light to bear on the effects of the sociological structure of the people living in the area I am studying. End of track.

Food and Love

She is preparing for a dinner party the next evening. Her lover will not be there but at another dinner party. There are pigeons on her menu. She likes to do things well, when she can afford it. It will be unstinted.

A curse on the cat, who has evil teeth in a pigeon; out it goes into the damp afternoon. And: your poem, it is marvellous. I can not write poetry. But I can cook.

Pigeon liver is not delectable, so out it goes, along with the little necks, traces of gut-slime, and the clung feather. The tail feathers are something else – some of those, the ones with the nicest markings, shall be kept for decorating the final dish. The kitchen light illuminates red hair falling forward: a bowl intended for marinade now contains two tears. The secret ingredient.

Washed. Washed through and out, to be clean. The flavour must not be too high, for there are several tastes to suit. Clean, drained, neat, with their pathetic little claws curled. Neatly tied with exquisitely fine string, a collector's item of string, for a child who collected twine of every kind. A passionate collection, each one with its own knot. The pigeons are captive, eviscerated.

Dear love, if it were not for the poem, for the future, I would throw the whole lot to the cat, and observe their more natural fate with bitter amusement. I am a bored woman, and cooking, for me, is not what it was.

And yet, an entirely new flavour and smell, I have sensed this possibility strongly, and will follow that where it leads. If one forbids negativity, great things may occur. But how to put my heart into a task, when it is leagues distant, beating to death against deprivation?

So thinking, washing down the chopping-board, beginning to concoct a marinade, and turning over the pigeons in the strange bed of the future, she allowed herself to be a plant, for a moment, for safety. An anticipatory lick and flare into life, meristem and sepal do not suffer the same pangs as racked and bound flesh.

Red wine and yoghurt, garlic and bay, basil and tarragon, and peppercorns crushed like skulls, the flying creature shot down with a scream over a wood. With arrows, these birds would burst apart, they are so small. She reminded herself to mention the shot, to the guests. She did not want anyone to jump up, screaming, spitting out bits of lead, or gold. Bruised juniper, too, a few.

What will he eat, at that other dinner party? Duck and oranges. And tiny sponge fingers soaked in rum. I would like him to eat my food. The food I am preparing. I would like to watch him taste. I would like to see him eat anything, for he has a wasting disease, and will starve to death soon.

She had made a pâté for the first course. Mushrooms, ox liver, several herbs, fat bacon, eggs and a little oatmeal. A coarse peasant pâté, cooking slowly, *bain marie*. There would be toasted rye bread, without the crusts, and rococo mounds of unsalted Normandy butter, emerging from an inland sea of ice-water.

My love is starving but he may take a morsel of duck, a little orange. It will have been deep frozen, not natural and good, but the skin is perfect. A choice of desserts, conversation.

Perhaps they will discuss the recent science programme about weather. Everyone discusses that.

'Did you see how there is to be another ice-age any moment now? Apparently, yes. Eighteen inches of snow, but it doesn't melt in summer, the winds change, more snow, iced over immediately. Nothing to eat, nothing can grow. Everything deep frozen.'

'God!'

He will hardly hear the chatter, but will suggest playing Mozart after dinner. He will be asked which pudding he prefers. He will decline both. One of the guests will naively suggest a solution to the oncoming ice-age.

'The world ought to have a heating system installed now, a sort of soil-warming scheme. That would prevent an ice-age.' Someone will speak across.

'Even if we ate less, it wouldn't mean that the starving would be fed. Would it?'

'No indeed,' the hostess will say, smiling. 'Have some more. Eat. Do.'

She took a bath, and rested on the bed, one dry vermouth to hand, with ice. There was only an hour, and several culinary details to pay attention to before the guests' arrival, and she had to dress. She does not want to have the party. The aroma of braising pigeons fills the house; the meat is perhaps high after all, for she senses corruption.

She has never had a failed dinner party. Perhaps this time will be a new experience – the disaster? Clean in the mouth, chill aperitif, exhale that odour. Correct the sauce with dried apricots, astringent and fragrant, all will be well.

Eventually, all the guests are together, and she serves drinks. Music plays not too loudly, the lights are dim and the room is warm. Complaints about the weather merit an offer of a seat nearer the fire, and another drink. Eyes brighten and people like each other. She excuses herself and goes to the kitchen, looking at the dining-table as she passes, pleased with its appearance. No ostentation of flowers in limp imitation of Dutch painting; no blinding colour in the linen, no candles. Utterly white damask, perfectly clean cheap glass and shining steel. Two bottles of Mâcon stand breathing, the pâté undecorated on a white china dish. She has eaten poor food in magnificent surroundings and knows that the way she presents things is superior.

The scent of nutmeg in the Duchesse potatoes, each one of which is like a perfect sculpture (they could be set in resin and sold for high prices in art galleries), makes her smile. An ocean liner and the Spice Islands, a line from a poem she could not write, from a poem he did write, offering her those things. Not the earth, the moon, but more precisely, an ocean liner and the Spice Islands.

The experienced hostess protects her face as she opens the oven door. Eyes sealed with hot mascara a once-only comic horror. Not to be able to open the eyes, curled warm at dawn, affirming the lustful watcher! Dark flesh, reflecting light, licked all over like kittens. Naked on white linen, held close so that juices run. If the flesh offered is inferior, burned up with wanting, scarred, split, glazed with sweat, will there still be a feast? Will the food be rejected if it is not perfect? Put to the side of the plate unwanted. Like a girl-child on a bare mountain, exposed to the ice which will creep up around bones, a glassy exhibition of the horrors of excess.

The sauce is perfect. It is not tainted, it is rich and mature. A smoke of garlic, and pearls of fat from bacon, each slice curled round like sleeping cats, relaxed and striped. The mushroom gills are separate and erect: swimming and breathing creatures, she arrests their progress from one biological form to another, pushing them back into the shallows. She gently explores the breasts, and they are deep and tender.

With closed eyes over a moment of bliss, she almost drops the tray on the floor. She reprimands herself, clicks back into the present. Great concentration needed to bring these acts to perfection, daydreaming can be disastrous. Dinner is served!

Gasps of delight upon tasting the pâté, and compliments on the wine which has both strength and softness. On her knee, under the table, a very strong hand. The man on her left has been overcome with amorousness.

'Have another slice of pâté.' The hand grips her upper thigh, and she convulses, half amused, half in pain, and knocks over his glass. This seems to be amusing rather than embarrassing, and the company embark on funny stories, funny voices and accents.

'I'm terribly sorry – I'm very clumsy,' and she covers the spreading bloodstain with white linen.

'My fault entirely, I should have drunk it!' The man on her right is really enjoying himself. He is large and rosy and dearly loves his food. He is also a nice man.

'Marvellous pâté, absolutely marvellous. The last time I ate pâté even half as good as this, I was on my way to Woburn Abbey. We missed the way, stopped at an hostelry. We eventually turned up at the wrong abbey, can't think how.'

'Don't you love Normandy butter? Can't you just taste the creaminess, unspoiled with salt, its texture glides over the tongue like pure silk on a bottom.'

'So I said: Woburn, Schmoburn, what does it matter so long as you're abbey?'

The table is cleared ready for the main course, and she presents the massive bottle of Ruffino. She anticipates it, her blood is excited at the thought of that nourishing crimson liquid. Ancient gods were adored with wine like this, it is a link with other worlds.

When she walks in with the dish of pigeons, the fans of tail-feathers at either end play, there were sounds of delight, screams. There is a still-glamorous ex-actress present who can not take drink without becoming excessive in everything. Now, she is almost hysterical, barely suppressing screams of mirth. It will later be revealed in a heart-to-heart chat, again over too much wine, that she was so strongly reminded of their dead budgie with its pathetic claws, lying on its back in its cage. Death can be so funny. But, some other one began a round of applause, an unlikely but sincere event. She rushes back into the kitchen blushing, grips the worktop refusing to weep. Graciousness and equanimity! So she returns to serve the food and eat her share.

'It is necessary to be savage to eat pigeons, the best bits can not be got at with knife and fork,' she explains; she is being patronising but is unable to bear the sight of waste. Some present would be too delicate to rend the food apart with bare hands, and suck the bones.

People delve into the salad for slices of avocado and black olives, which have slid to the bottom, absorbing a delicate dressing. The texture and taste of avocado causes deep shudders of pleasure. It is more than an acquired taste, it is an addiction, a raging need, a key to transcendental planes. Oils of avocado are used in beauty creams; light and life, I shall be beautiful all through if I suck this. It slips, caresses the tongue, melting in the head, awaking possibilities of sensation quite outside the ordinary. Balm and elixir, transforming substance. Changes take place on a cellular level, alchemical meetings in another world.

Dark flesh pulled from bones left like mother-of-pearl on a shore of fragments, beachcombers find jewels, transmuted life-forms in warm caves. Flirtatious propositions seen through rubies, laser beams of inspiration.

And again, the white damask, background for the dish of pears, freshened with frills of cream.

'I detect a hint of clove, absolutely delicious!' Teeth slide through this translucent succulence, and without shame smears of cream and syrup are licked publicly, no drop shall be lost.

Later, moving around with coffee and drinks, she is convinced of their sincerity, when they express appreciation. Her ego glows a little, and why not?

'You must have put a lot of hard work and love into that.'

'Yes, it was a pleasure.'

In the night eighteen inches of snow freeze beneath eighteen inches more, and twice more this happens, a damask winding-sheet for the bones of a lost civilisation on a naked mountain.

'What is there that is real which lasts forever?'

Deep-frozen planet without biological forms, no creature to eat another down a chain of life. The last people ate thin broth, then roots, had no appetite even for each other. It was not like a restaurant, and in the other half of the world they did not play Mozart over the coffee. The belly echoes, temblors of lost hope. There is more than one way to starve to death, and he sits at a loaded table, throat closed. Her eyes fly open and she turns over on the snow.

'I overate. Too much to drink.' A resolution to fast, a purification with spring water, denial and sacrifice.

She dreamed then of new recipes, new flavours, more perfect combinations than ever before, nourishment for the flesh and the spirit. The picture was of fluttering wings ascending into a bloody firmament: her invention, the food which changed all who ate it into gods. For only immortals survive the ice.

Silence in Having Words:
Purple

To Philip the drummer who gave me some words

Never before had a tennis ball come between a man and a woman, playing its part in a chain of events so disastrously, but in 7081 AC–DC, Caatreuse, great dictator, self-styled, and very unpleasant person, issued a statement offering severe reprimand to anyone bouncing objects of eroticism on Sunshine Boulevarde. Until the advent of Caatreuse, the Boulevarde, a small township originally formed of free-thinking, happy, loving people, had been somewhat chaotic but surprisingly successful. Its inhabitants were fugitives from a far-distant Terra corrupted with division, inequality and aggression and had been in existence for some twenty Terran years, which are not the same as Sunshine Boulevarde years, time on the nameless planet of which the Boulevarde was a tolerated colony, being subjective, at least to human perceptions. It is probably something incomprehensible to mere humans, but as almost no contact had ever been made this was not to be known to the nameless indigenes. There was no doubt of the indigenes' peaceful nature and lack of interest in Sunshine Boulevarde; they, unlike Caatreuse, saw no harm in the colony.

Caatreuse had somehow arisen and gathered round him grim troops, people who, unlike all other colonists, wished to destroy happiness; his methods were perversion of knowledge, the poisoning of love by insidious ideas and the punishing of artistic endeavours. He had not at first been thought to be anything but a person deserving of compassionate help; lovers and artists had laughed gently at him without fear. It had seemed impossible that in the blessed climate of their new world anyone could seriously have reasons for destructive behaviour, but insidiously he had gained recruits and was now a threat; politics were afoot where before a gentle anarchy had rendered them a distant bad memory from Terra.

The light of the days on Sunshine Boulevarde is often purple due to beneficial chemical reactions in the atmosphere, and during such phases quite ordinary objects can become objects of eroticism, for example a tennis ball in the case of Bjorn Nord, whose African father had named him for a Terran sportsman in ancient Terran history, much as a Mexican might name a child Socrates in the hopes of a philosophical turn of mind being encouraged. Bjorn had not become a tennis player, he played the Yoranga, a particularly sonorous and melodic drum, and part of the training for a Yoranga player is the rhythmic squeezing and bouncing of tennis balls. That he playfully squeezed and bounced one on the way to visit his pupil and Lover, Aariarla Dancer, during a phase of violet light automatically made him a target for Caatreuse's thugs.

As is well known, purple light turns on female vibrations to such a degree that few males can take it; they wilt, shrink, flip, flop, retreat, mumble, stutter, flitter and, as it was once termed on Terra, come too soon. But real men, the happy and relaxed Sunshine Boulevarde men, love that purple light, that violet, sort of heliotrope gone mad, and do not blow it just like that but go on to better things. Chi'thuna rituals were not reserved for an initiated few under a religious umbrella on this colony, but were a usual source of ecstasy. It was evident that Caatreuse had somehow managed not to benefit from Chi'thuna, and he and his thugs envied this ecstasy; a state of envy automatically undermines male capacity as will any negative emotion. Failing big guns of which there were none on the planet, a few shotguns being the only armoury, the banning of bouncing of tennis balls could have its effect. To inflict pain is the sad delight of some, and alas there are thousands of ways to inflict pain and all its attendant ills.

A society which has allowed a traitor to gain power is a society in trouble, but it had been against the gentle anarchism to prevent this happening. Now, Sunshine Boulevarde was not all bliss; it had in place of some of its drug experimenters, wine appreciators and sexual ecstatics, quite a few drug addicts, drunks and people in fear of sexual love, and others at the ashes of hope. Neither Bjorn nor Aariarla were among these but they had suffered from a certain loneliness. They had of course had partners for the Chi'thuna, sometimes called Suprasex, but even so something had been missing; they had been drinking rather too much wine and smoking rather too much blissweed in order to smooth the rough edges of the saw which rakes at unloved necks, destroying energy flow and wrecking constructive mentation. As is well known, lack of good loving prevents the beneficial effects of Blue Heaven Energy, that most powerful force which unfortunately wrecked the life of the scientist who first noticed it, he being imprisoned and driven insane because at the time it would not have been advantageous to those in power to have Blue Heaven Energy in the hands of the general populace. And that scientist had not messed around with it to half the extent that Sunshine Boulevarde colonists did, which may be seen as an improvement over a great span of time, Caatreuse notwithstanding.

Bjorn had messed around with Blue Heaven quite a lot at one time and his frizzy black hair had grown waist-length in a week and his dark skin taken on a rosy glow of health. Aariarla had messed around with it quite a lot and her entire muscle-tone had improved, her dark blue eyes become luminous with health and her straight hair had sprung into curls overnight. Also, certain aches and pains which may or may not have been symptomatic of serious disease were disappearing because she took acupuncture sessions Sunshine style, and this tunes perfectly that Blue Heaven Energy, or, as it was once known on Terra, Chi, pronounced anyway you like as only Chinese can get it right.

Together, these two people, as might be imagined, were as near to perfect as possible. Also, they had much in common.

Which is why Aariarla wept one night after she had told Bjorn she loved him and his rough reply had been: No you don't. She had been longing to say that, it was one of her ways of expressing herself but her timing was out and Bjorn preferred unspoken things. They had been dancing and Aariarla had danced too often with other men and Bjorn had become ruffled. Why oh why, Aariarla was later to ask herself, had she not seen then that Caatreusian philosophy was eating at the growth of the rose? After her words had been rejected she became more subtle, speaking in the way of Sunshine Boulevarde: 'Abreaction, sachay, another ten Heptaparas I give at judgement,' but this of course meant that she would never hear in words the meaning of his little twisted smile. Even before their more obvious troubles then, at the very back of her mind, Aariarla had a dread that all was not as perfect as it seemed. There being no perfection without imperfection is a useful attitude for not paying attention to imperfections. She preferred to trust implicitly, for without trust, no love.

'Come on along Thalassawise,' said Bjorn holding out a tennis ball. 'Here be power,' and put it in the hollow of her flexible neck and her thin shoulder with its smooth, untroubled skin. She held it, flexed it, moved it around, learning fast and becoming more supple in many parts for the improved playing of the Yoranga. Her flexings resulted in a fit of coughing and some strange internal pains which should not have happened if her Blue Heaven Energy had been flowing correctly: later she reflected upon the question of whether loving had made her feel better than she truly was? Such questions border on the Caatreusian and allow doubt to enter; at the time of the wracking coughs and strange pains she took herbs. Other little pests were nibbling at the fruits of love for even given that time on Sunshine Boulevarde is subjective, would she ever have spent it in harming the petals of an unfortunate daisy muttering 'loves me loves me not' and as the petals fluttered even poor thing, cheating as she saw the last petal open its mouth to duet 'not' so missing a heartbeat to make it come out right.

That subjective time; on every planet time is experienced differently of course but in the colony and as in old songs, the minutes can seem like hours or a thousand years pass between an indrawn breath before an orgasm and the choking caused by having forgotten a thousand-year-old cough pastille.

The longest moments ever were those when Aariarla waited for Bjorn to call, tension slowly mounting in those only partially trained neck muscles, juices running to waste, mirror-beaded braids on end with desire, thoughts running over and over like looped tape.

And then he would simply turn up, changing the pace, a tennis ball in one hand, the Yoranga gripped by its dorsal fin in the other, and a huge spliff of blissweed stuck in his sensuous mouth which developed that slow smile once they had got things sorted out and the curtains drawn. Aariarla told herself to stop her silent mantra 'I live I love I love you' because she knew he would mislike it, but offered instead to sew the hems of his garment; only to touch will heal. Who needs sacred oil, a few drops of Three-in-One will fix the machine and there she is, in service again, Love-twenty-three (Boulevarde scoring system) and fuck-all, no advantage to anyone.

Aariarla had always devoutly worshipped the Yoranga which had led her to Bjorn for lessons. Her main art form was dancing, and the rhythm of the Yoranga dovetailed splendidly with her inborn talent. Worship is not the same thing as love and neither entity is applicable strictly to playing either tennis or the Yoranga, depending of course upon the degree of semantic extravagance found desirable. Tennis is the sport of snobs and has not been rhythmical since 1923 when for a full seventeen minutes two ladies and two gentlemen played pock-lock-pock-lock with such precise timing and no dropped shots, forming an invisible pattern of traces across the court like a Cat's Cradle that the audience were hypnotised into a mass religious experience, but the less said about that the better.

Aariarla's mother back on Terra had thought tennis the sport of snobs and many thinking people including Aariarla would agree with her, and it is not rhythmical; Yoranga music is the music of the spirit of love and is rhythmical: Aariarla and Bjorn both had rhythm and were of different sex. And yet, Bjorn said to her: 'You can't Yoranga like Yang, young you Yoranga like Yin, half and half is the whole of the law.' Stunned. A shocking statement in a society of gentle anarchy, she didn't want to quarrel so let her mouth hang open as if in awe, thinking, maybe he's joking. She'd never noticed music having sexual division, maybe she was unobservant, maybe it was an esoteric part of the training to have to listen to crap and not express dismay?

It was after that when Bjorn got done for bouncing, just as they were meaning to play their own game in the Boulevarde purple evening. Two thugs came and took him off to what Caatreuse had renamed the Tower of Punishment. It had once been a dance-hall and pool-hall with all-nite Hopi-Indian fast-food bar but he had occupied it, and gentle anarchists do not react very fast to such actions so it was *fait accompli*, *coup d'état*, game set and match in two hours, subjective time. Nobody really minded, Vietnamese food was becoming fashionable and there were dozens of dance-floors and pool-tables. No violence, just elbows, sneers and uncomfortable vibrations, powerful and insidious weapons.

Aariarla howled a song of despair; off-the-cuff rhythms, bluesy words and double-tracked with antique Brazilian woodblocks once owned by her great-aunt – it wasn't bad for a first try but it had no effect. If only they had paid more attention the night when Bjorn had idly told the cards whilst smoking blissweed during their teabreak: he had picked an astonishing run of good cards to follow the nine of cups which had been found on the floor of his magic-carpet mending shop where he exercised another of his talents daily. The cards had only one dodgy picture, the Knave of Swords. Did it now signify Caatreuse's spy, or something more sinister? Good luck, love, prosperity and creative force – and this Knave.

So Bjorn was imprisoned and his waist-length locks were not long enough to Yang-Yin a Rapunzel and Aariarla's mirror beaded braids though somewhat longer than during a naughty Demented Nun-for-fun phase, insufficient to construct a rope. Nobody to ask for help, it would have been interference. Naturally there were no police either wonderful or piggish. Ingenuity was called for. Mirror beads reflect sunlight, flashed, perhaps, a message?

It was a calm warm day of quiet, even the fluten flora had mutes, the sniffing lepidus pissed against hushed trees hung with silent harps, the moments were all magical light and soundless. By a river the Tower. But what was that heavy breathing? Evenly controlled, count seven in and hold for seven. Seven out and hold for seven, on and on but yes, rather heavy. No phones, not that, someone preparing for a Chi'thuna ritual with an attack of poli'oli'ama-ga'lite virus cough: a ghost of herself from a lively day like this when she and Bjorn had been by the river in love and sickness. The scent of garlic, mint, thyme, licorice and smouldering mullein all obtained at expense on supply ships from Terra which sometimes brought another fugitive to the colony. That wheezing day she had hi-jacked Bjorn from his carpet mending and led him gently but not by the hand which he had withdrawn stating that holding hands in public is childish (she had deemed that another esoteric test) and they had found a quiet place to blow smoke gently on the water, the Deep Purple light an enchantment and enhancement of all life. They had observed a punt containing an archetypal couple. She with long hair, a bunch of tuesliam, sesam and verealiam ready-to-wear for drowning in some pool, momentum lentum.

Bjorn had asked, rhetorically: 'Is the river better than the sea?'

She had replied, 'It is different.' Even though they spoke in code they both knew what they meant and if that afternoon was not love then there was no such thing, which is what she dreaded most of all as she now flashed a message to Bjorn in the Tower: 'Superiority incarcerant desire reclamation.' He leaned out of the window and shouted back down with a heavy brown voice which fell hard on her: 'What reclaim, do I like this with a pool table?' Her beads went dull, she could not think what to say. The ghost in the magic moment had a fit of coughing on an indrawn breath the like of which transforms lovely women into hags. Bjorn went on to explain: 'Woman divides and falls his beer and man. Companions of like minding, nothing serious at this stage but with a straight face at a thousand miles an hour buddies replenish, and I need my sleep.' He was brainwashed already? Drunk? Poisoned? What Caatreusian divisive junk was that to emerge from the mouth of a full-blooded Yoranga player who understood Chi?

'Sleep?' she screeched to the tune of a saxophone and an atonal clay flute.

'Rounded with, a little one,' and that was the prison guard butting in with a quotation he'd learned at the Wide Open University Summer Orgy, back on Terra.

'Yeah, sleep, even the spirit must sleep for sustenance,' said Bjorn, gazing not at Aariarla but at a passing swallow helping to make the summer and in more danger of a long sleep than it could yet know.

'But I love you!' she screeched silently and he silently pretended not to hear. What he heard was a lot of twittering messing up his thoughts which revolved around an axis of it being better to stay with the lads playing pool than get mixed up with all that two-sex-two-step business. Aariarla wept and he sneered, tearing a bit off the curtains, letting it flutter down for her to blow her nose upon, hearing her blubbering, thoughts said: 'Migod women are all water and blood and snot and sweat and twittering.' But the twittering was that of swallows, not really swallows but minia-ture eagles called swallows on Sunshine Boulevarde, nesting, building nests in his locks, just arrived from other lands, singing: kendo-nimmo-kendi, meanwhile shitting in profusion building a slope to the window in guano-like glistening steps, tiki-taki-tiki-taki-tow, bird language.

When Aariarla had gone home to think and gather herself, without thinking anything of it, Bjorn stepped out of the high window and simply walked out full of beer and piss. The guard didn't give chase, the prisoner would return, if not voluntarily then on some other, harsher charge.

But next day was not his return day, for in confused euphoria of what appeared to be yet another delightful aspect of gentle anarchy, he visited Aariarla uninvited, not even thinking she might have a life of her own to lead. Which impression she gave with glad singing and a big showoff to him of her latest Yoranga accomplishments. He asked her, 'What did you place on my plate?' but she was too happy to spoil it all with words and smiled. They played the drum all night giving no thought to Caatreuse and his henchmen (it is hardly necessary to explain that the Caatreusian movement was exclusively male but it must be mentioned for those who unthinkingly wonder at no mention of female thugs) and Bjorn demonstrated ten new rhythms, none of which she straight away repeated. In fact, one of them which should have been simple she fluffed over and over until she felt humiliation and despair, aware that her attention was more on her desire for Chi'thuna ritual than learning a Yoranga rhythm.

'But Aariarla you have many musical branching from dancing, you need repeat to greatness.' How kind. Her heart leapt causing a coughing fit which reminded him of his unfortunate mother whom he sent letters to annually, back on Terra. His mother had experienced many illnesses and much hardship, he was proud of her. Bjorn began to lecture Aariarla about hardship, knowing nothing of her past. She listened for a good lesson but heard only envy and guilt. His mother had consoled herself only with tea and toast, not wine and fine food in purple light.

'But I never wealth, I acupuncture to be clean jump and dancer, why I bring myself to light, some pilgrimage you wot not Bjorn, and still with insidious. Reason.' But he compared her with Zsaz-satomore, self-seeking lush, no pain, whereas his Mere and Grandmere, crippled, doing crochet with a smile, knitting cheer-fully in a bed of pain, how admirable even though abandoned by her husband who had needed active woman to grasp his achieved arm. Aariarla thought, reconciliation, smooth him over this bad patch, his incarceration has deranged him. She made a cup of Quickbrew Emmotion which was a mistake. He kept asking her, how was it, how was it, his mother, through all, not a word of complaint, so submissive in misery, lovely woman?

'I don't know, I don't know, I don't know your mother,' said Aariarla bewildered, feeling needles all over, prick prick. He told her, suffer in silence is correct, and she told him, I never com-plained. He said, right, you have no complaints. He shook her in emphasis to get an answer and got one.

'Maybe your mother was dumb!' A woman without a tongue would never nag, complain, it had to be that. Or else perhaps ter-rified of beating if she whined. It was too late, Bjorn was angry for she had insulted his mother. Righteous, unforgivable, too far.

'My Sainted Aunt!' moaned Aariarla, tired out. This was not Bjorn at all, his words were mothballs and shelvings, avoidances, rotting lace in stale lavender, ghosting from light years and other times. Warped. She was not breathing evenly, felt aches and pains, held open the door through which he stalked, the slam at his back and a crunch under his feet, the glittering gravel she had laid with her own fair wheelbarrow and bloody shovel. Ace of spades, all cards having double meanings.

The little dawn eagles sang that the worst which might befall them, the latest Caatreusian edict: all birds to be shotgunned.

Had he rapped her knuckles like a mad father? Was there an

antidote to this poison? Think back to Terran tropes, what had she done with this? Not since landing on Sunshine Boulevarde had she apologised to someone who had hurt her, the kissing of smelly feet, I didn't mean it; such idiocy was purely Terran, here, the situation had remained unrisen, disguised as non-existent.

Ten years later by subjective time, five minutes, she put on her tennis shoes all ragged below a velvet robe and ran, panting, cold before the sunrise, sweating, pure misery shouting: 'forgive me forgive me', and caught up with his closed door which he opened, glaring. He was not pleasant and made her grateful for a very small mercy, enjoying himself very much. With his arm round her shoulder, stiffly, she could breathe again. But he was a wounded soldier and would sue for damages.

'I shall not tournament for three days, we have a life and I must lead it, men are men.'

Could anyone behave like this on Sunshine Boulevarde? She was aghast. There were dark, ragged clouds patching up the sun which was yellow today, warm but diametric in the spectrum. Could all this be blamed on the chemistry of the planetary winds? She ran home then to visit a woman friend, muttering 'the son of a bitch'. And for an hour she poured her despair into her friend's kitchen, drinking the last drink in the house at breakfast, and the woman said: 'He is not good enough for you.' Her Bjorn, not good enough. Oh, but she had thought him very good indeed. And still, projecting back to Terra, a slum not far from the birth-place of Bjorn, so much in common, where they would have said: Yoranga hobbyist, women do not play drums, Chi'thuna ritual so much trappings, blissweed is a nasty drug and then she heard it, what he had said that night. She had not wanted to hear it but he had said it, said it, said it.

'Women should have their mouths sewn up.'

Pure Caatreusian rhetoric. Not literal. Horrible. Issuing from between his sensuous lips. She retired to her own room and screamed at a pitch to make the pictures fall off the walls, tennis balls bounced, her heart missed two beats and with a terrible groaning noise like ice floes the world disintegrated. She staggered over to the shattered window to look at the footprints in the gravel, standing where she had often stood waiting for him to arrive, hours later than a promise. But worse and worse, she was not at home, in her distress she had madly and inadvertently run herself right up the steps of the Tower of Punishment. Blinded to reality. Walking by the Different River, a silent woman walked, worth more than rubies. In which case Bjorn could not afford one, the situation was priceless from some angles.

Imagine: unable to moan in ecstasy, sing in tune, speak up for herself. Glubber gobber glucking, eyes rolling, coughing ghastly behind a bloody slit. So much for love.

Now on the river glided one black swan and seven little ugly ducklings and many tight lotus buds.

On the river bank sat a large black lepidus disguised as cute and cuddly, curly and lolling but it had already eaten thirteen ducklings, one each morning before the crust-hurlers came. It grinned in satisfaction at recalled crunch.

Aariarla was frightened and tried blaming herself for everything. 'With my clavering I overkilled something beautiful,' she said aloud but it did not quite fit, it was from a Terran video in the backyard of her birthrights. The black lepidus heard and looked upwards greedily, surrounded by unmuted fluten flora shrilling; it sucked hope from her with eyes as big as saucers.

'Good boy, nice boy. Seated!' But they did not speak the same language, it leered and lolled, sucking with eyes as big as dance-floors. She wished that Bjorn would relent and rescue, but he was a mender of magic carpets, a Yoranga player, and not a god-damned animal trainer.

Unknown to Aariarla, Bjorn had other problems. After pick-picking on a very old tune on Aariarla's mandoline the fatigued metal strings had snapped back trapping his fingers, the tune having no fade out but ending in cacophony twangling.

Aariarla wondered if all that Chi'thuna ritual had been merely futility rites. A crackling and screeching could be heard by those listening. The decimation of all twittering birdlife was being carried out by Caatreuse's men with the few available shotguns, used for the first time on that planet. What would the indigenes make of that? Might a reaction be provoked? Peace and love had been the conditions of colonisation. She looked in vain for the guanaco steps but they had been shovelled by those only fit. The only birds remaining, the ducklings and the one black swan. There was no conscience over the killing, and even as she watched the lepidus crunched one more fledgling, cheekily brazenly encouraged by the shooting, permission to kill. The crunching sound was like a welcome footstep on gravel and her bloody tropism leapt in hope, triggered but she knew it was an hallucination: like the telephone ringing way back when but it was only a bird in a tree doing a Percy Edwards on electronic devices, and now the bird was dead and all wires crossed.

Pulling herself together she turned and ran for the door but crashed into the Chief Torturer who had been standing behind her for some time. He was trying to thread a needle with a broken G-string from an old mandoline. He had a mean, closed face and several badges pinned to his leather apron proclaiming him First Class Citizen, Protector of the Fatherland, Official Bird Decimator, Love Strangler and Ripper of Precious Carpets. A frightful figure, no gentle anarchist he.

'Oops!' twittered Aariarla, but he did not flicker. She ran round him to the door but it was locked, she ran to face him again, at a loss for words. He had around his beer-belly a chain from which dangled terrible instruments of torture.

Various sizes of sewing needle both round-eyed and crewel; a silent whistle which would ruin the impending explosion of Blue Heaven Energy in a pre-orgasmic woman; a tiny rack for overstringing nerves; a pair of pliers for snapping tempers; a flat tool for flipping lids; a sharp lever with super and subsonic action for digging abysses between world-views; a beautifully wrought gold and silver box containing a grease which when applied to any instrument would render it out of tune; a spray-can full of ghastly fog to obscure the radiance of a loving smile and a particularly horrible little rubber thing designed to push all the wrong buttons. His leer was dreadful. He put a knot in the end of the shining threaded string and gazed intently at her lips.

'I have been mandated to labial stitching in time.' His accent was harsh. He was now trained to drop women like hot bricks, to shout peevishly at people who dance for joy. He had undergone surgery to create a blind spot so he could see only what he wanted to see and his ears had ugly little flaps grafted and he heard only what he wanted to hear. That such people had power on Sunshine Boulevarde! How had that happened? It was so. Molecules in the breeze?

Aariarla tried to think quickly and efficiently. Long ago she had talked herself out of awkward Terran situations, but if she did not remember how very soon this would be impossible, not a word in edgewise, first or last.

'Sewing is floral for muscle, tuesliam blossom men are sewing these days not aprons like bloody tough guise.' She spoke in an unconvinced tremulo being a seamstress and knowing the skill and stamina required.

'Nonsense, worldbeating tailors are not eunuchs,' he snapped with an impatient gesture which gave her the edge on him because he held the needle in one hand and the knot in the other, pulled unthreaded, damn. He grunted in annoyance narrowing his narrow eyes to narrow slits focusing on the eye. It was the needle through which camels had passed on the way to wealthy paradises full of virgins, greasy and blocked with the fine foods of miserable women. She would have played for time but she had no Yoranga. Had she been wealthy she could have bribed the lout.

'Do you recycle your mother very?' she asked him. He glared.

'Implication softening, as a lad of twenty-three I did a right thing, I am fixated you dare?'

'Not leaping I gently enquire thinking of her pride to see you sewing, maingoolies in Caatreuse so big a boy.' He blushed with something, perhaps frustration at disease in needle threading. He leaned against the pool-table to steady himself which gave Aariarla an idea.

'For drinks,' she challenged, picking up a cue and blue. He was tempted but stalled. Play against a woman?

'My mother suffered under the Tretchkov more than you dream, she never played pool but knitted suffering jumpers.' Goodness gracious! More pitiful women with large sons.

'I suppose a saint not aunt,' said Aariarla sweetly, learning fast and hating duplicity. Aariarla's own mother had stood up for her rights, spoken out against oppression, boredom, suffering, deprivation; been cut off from her birthright for it, had 'bitch' tattooed upon her forehead in Gothick lettering, drugged out of existence finally, and never been near a tennis court in her life. The torturer gave in, resolved to wipe the floor with this female, sew up her mouth and for good measure her only yoni, and curse her with bad menopause, arthritis, cancer, nerves – make a real woman of her, Sunshine purple or golden notwithstanding. He loathed that purple effect, it made the bitches stand up on their hind legs, demanding satisfaction.

They set up the table, ordered drinks, and by some fluke she potted the first two and by the law of averages fluffed the third completely. After her first glass – it was the time of the female circadian rhythm for maximum effect from grape alcohol, not to mention the two moons both being in the Quarter of Charon, one full and one new – she began to think: this is a human being after all.

'You think this,' she slightly slurred at him, 'I should not pool lightly now when Blue Heaven waits the needle, my appointment today returns.'

'Only rich bitches get tuned upwards so, what rotting for you, observed dancing Dervishing prancing, we know.' She didn't want to discuss her Fallopians with him, it would cause scorn as always in male males.

'I pain much, all seems not what and I need.' Bah, she had carpets on her floors, hot water, good food. The imagination of the female made him sick. And yet, he had a problem and had thought of Blue Heaven tuning which here as on no other planet was said to be effective. Turned on by the idea of her secret pain he took his shot, short-sighted but too proud for eyeglasses. He could not tell her about the problem but was curious.

'Where piercing for Heaven tuned there?'

'Different implosion never like, nine impulses decided methodical, elements known.'

'Wherewithal?' Shooting, scoring.

'Sensory,' she said, taking his wrist lightly and listening in, knowing a little of the subject. He watched her listen so did not notice a great bird swoop in at the window, place a tennis ball on the table and swoop off with the white. It was the black swan from the Different River who had formed a plan to save birds and undermine Caatreuse. It dropped the white ball near the lepidus croaking 'fetch boy' and the animal galloped and grabbed, damaging its meat teeth and in its nasty surprise swallowing the ball, glup. It ran off howling, the torturer heard it and collected himself.

'Well sensing then energy pin woman?'

'I help the needle for your loss is hearts key.'

'Blathering twilights, in this bunch that turnkey.' He fiddled about beneath his leather apron and brought out a clanking bunch of keys, it was there somewhere, he felt certain – and also the key to the door of that Tower room. Aariarla guessed which key for it was encrusted with blood.

She took her shot, noticing the tennis ball, quickly pretending to fluff and offering to puncture for healing if he gave her the needle.

Meanwhile Bjorn was carving a piece of wood with yet another talent, sitting by a dream with his Yoranga and a blissweed spliff, congratulating himself on having had two lucky escapes: one from the Tower and one from woman. He was still under the influence of his imprisonment which had most certainly excited some throwback genetic imprint. She would, he told himself, have used his body, taken his money and taken off; didn't all women do that? Except of course his mother who, as luck would have it, was a woman. Elsewhere in another arcade of his continuum he grieved for spoiled love, lost friendship, excellent pupil, but he turned away from those thoughts as unmasculine. He hacked at the wooden carving, an African totem, and almost cut off its nose to spite its face.

Outside in the yellow light an ice cream van played an old Terran tune which went:

It's now or never, da da da da,
It's now or never, dum, dum, dum, dum,
Tomorrow, will be too late,
It's now or never, my love can't wait.

For a brief moment his affections melted but he picked up his Yoranga and played it like a guy, which is to say, mucho Yang bang. The Yoranga at full throttle can be heard for seven miles and the Tower of Punishment was a mile away. Aariarla heard the drum but the Torturer did not, he never heard love-songs, even played like that.

'Oh Bjorn, my dear friend,' silently sang Aariarla, 'you do care for me after all.' Which was rather sad because even though he might have liked to, the song was not for her and he was choking his love to death before it strangled him.

The Yoranga was not speaking to her, but it gave her new hope, and even false hope is better than despair. The Torturer was ready for his treatment; even more important than the game.

'Rightings. You prick me then this prick you for claverings, eternal shutup. Preferring satin stitch, hemstitch, feather stitch, chain stitch or blind stitch, ha ha ha ha.' A bubbling sinister smirk of mirth.

'Whichever the Yin top feminine style, but first your shot at the ball,' and misliking her own sly flirtatious smirk but of necessity sticking on to it, she took the threaded needle from his fingers.

Being short-sighted and agitated at the thought of jabs, and being preoccupied in working out a clever-dick double cannon, he did not notice the swapped ball, so he achieved a violently fluffed stun-shot, a ripped cloth and a very puzzled facial expression. He cursed in humiliation, leaning over the table peering, and she stuck the needle very hard into his bum. As he grabbed with both hands ow ow ouch oooh she clutched his chained keys and dragged him squealing to the door and quickly put together male and female with a metal click of much satisfaction; open door, grab one of his hands and smack it to the doorframe and as she left slammed the door with all her frail feminine worth.

Dirty fighting quickly learned, no gentle anarchist she now either, things were improving and getting worse. Was it molecules in the air, particles reacting, something less obvious than purple love rays, golden happiness rays, what? Or just the natural cycle of events such as, whatever it is, it changes, as say Sufi teachers but do not change that saying, it is thousands of years old.

His howls could be heard for seven miles.

'Relish that self with its medicine,' she could not resist shouting a last word, rejoicing in a normal mouth.

Outside was beautiful. The black swan bowed as it took the remaining ducklings under its wing, sitting upon its collection of strange eggs. Aariarla ran like hell, hoping to find Bjorn at work mending carpets but his shop was locked, and at his house no answer. Where now? Home – the way led through a pleasant park with trouble-absorbing trees. Even a colony of happy people has a few sad hours, and this place had been planted to ameliorate those times. A troubled soul sat alone now, a very old woman who asked the time of day.

'But it's subjective, you are new to colonise?' The lady looked and thought, not certain of the accent.

'I came newly yes, retiring widow and alone. So far the scene is not mine.' Not bad for a beginner, Aariarla could get the sense of that.

'The sesam and tuesliam are glory for,' she showed, pointing and smiling, a new consoling role upon her.

'Yes. I speak to him dead, they laugh but forgetting is not easy so I forget.'

'The present moment is the best.'

'Yes, but madness pointed from my sister, unkind envy sent me packing.'

'The fountains play rainbows.'

'Seeking love and freedom but too late.'

'No friendships sailing?'

'Relatives sheerline and annual, I had children and now get letters, three or four.' The air turned violet and rainbows then are more unearthly than even another planet can explain, so they watched together in enchantment and Aariarla thought: my future, white hair, arthritis, aches, loneliness, persecution, a park bench. No Yoranga, no Chi'thuna. Is it? No reply. She touched the twisted hand of the woman, pale and swollen, glanced into eyes showing traces of suffering and fled to find Bjorn back at work.

'Aariarla.' He seemed a bit nicer. He had been smoking blissweed with the boys. Together they looked at a magic carpet. It had been ripped, played tennis upon, had wine and bitter tears spilled on it, been sewed by a hamfisted female seamstress, bled upon by a woman caught out by the two moons of a tricky planet, pissed upon by a lepidus and shat on by swallows, but still its colours glowed.

'Yesterday two rejuvenations briskly.'

'To be a worn-like carpet wearied.'

'Restored but never new.' There was a slight threat in his voice, you can't get round me so easily. Aariarla trod with care.

'If while carpet better?' She wanted to kiss him.

'Maybe. Maybe not. When a woman says yes she means no. When she says no she means yes.'

'And when maybe?' He did not speak, very loudly.

'Yoranga evening?'

'Maybe.' She dare not speak, all codes could be misinterpreted. They could hear marching and noise. Troops with a megaphone. Their names on a wanted list of happy people. Happy? This was happy? Bjorn began packing up his work.

'Go from my quiet hour,' he said with assumed authority. Now, he would not smile, perhaps the fading of blissweed, but he mouthed a sullen kiss which she hungrily sucked from the air, returning it with many, skipping away warily aware of being hunted. Perhaps she should disguise herself for a while? Not believable that such a thing could ever be necessary here, their haven, their state of peace, their safe colony far from oppression: infected.

The sun was setting slowly like home-made grape jelly. She thought: How can goodness and beauty be defended without aggression? Demonstrations of love, by example. But already that had failed. Why? Get into politics, that scourge of Terra? How boring.

In her room there was a sprig of tuesliam but she did not disturb its petals to test the love of Bjorn. She must trust him. And when he visited her in the evening, which he surely would, they must think of some constructive plan to undermine this harassment of Caatreuse. Who was Caatreuse anyway? Nobody seemed to know much about him except that he could somehow attract followers. She tended her plants, made the room clean and tidy, rolled a spliff ready, opened a bottle of fresh green wine, drank some of it herself to steady her waiting nerves, polished her mirror beads, practised on her drum for a while, wishing she

[66]

knew the difference between playing Yin and playing Yang. Surely all music was made up of both elements?

She played a heartbeat, a two-step, a rhythm for those tuned into the Chi'thuna way of love and a melodic rhythm which ought to have made all barriers between people tremble and fall to dust. She was lonesome and fought with a queer feeling in her stomach that something was wrong somewhere, but played on with determination, saying, it is only the disturbing adventures upsetting me, nothing basic.

'This is a test, a part of my training, my trial by fire,' she told herself, remembering that not long ago Bjorn had told her: 'Trial by fire, second Yoranga test.' But she was now in pain and it was not easy to tell if the pain was in her emotions or in her bones or in her deepest flesh. Perhaps a little smoke of blissweed would help, although this was a risk as blissweed could as well enhance pain as pleasure.

She struck a match, forgetting that the recording machine was switched on and later she would replay distant gunfire. She played strong rhythms and later she would replay sound formed into ricocheting cubes, dropping like hot bricks. She sang:

'Beautiful blacklocks, why don't we dream?

Don't rest on your laurels and cause me to scream;

Drum up some energy, snakelight and wings,

Come to your lover and hear how she sings.'

She waited. And waited and waited. She thought she heard the telephone but it was another old mandoline string snapping. She thought she heard his steps crunching but it was the cat's rough tongue on the bone of a dead bird. Only one word, she prayed, knowing she wanted much more.

Tablaquadabla. Nothing. Nothing.

Next day she decided to be pragmatic so disguised herself. First she unthreaded the mirror beads from her little braids, then she wore a pair of shades, turned her embroidered skirt inside-out, wore her sweater tied around her waist like a tennis player, but

[67]

affected a painful stoop and grimace of pain, which was easy to do for it matched her aches on all levels. She tore holes in her stockings.

She must go and trade for some new mandoline strings; someday she meant to learn to play that instrument. Also, some more tapes for the recording, they were full of strange sounds which she did not wish to eradicate.

And then, in the music shop, people were gossiping. She heard that Bjorn had been imprisoned again because he was a secret agent of Caatreuse and was considered a traitor for having a lover and repairing magic carpets.

Had he only ever been her lover as a spy then? But that did not make sense for she knew nothing which all the happy people on Sunshine Boulevarde knew. But worse, Caatreuse was going too far, everyone was disturbed and frightened. Bjorn had suffered a terrible punishment, physical injury had been perpetrated. His eyelids had been sewn shut. He would be turned out that day to wander helplessly. She must go and help him, and yet, she did not now know if he was a traitor, and to whom. First he had turned her on, and then he had turned on her.

Sunshine Boulevarde was beginning to resemble Terra. What could she trust? She must go somewhere quiet to think.

The gardens. To think. Love alone was not enough, it did not conquer all after all, on the contrary, it seemed to attract its opposite.

The old woman sat watching rainbows. They were not in a violet phase but the effect was very beautiful. Aariarla sat down and without meaning to, wept.

'You again all changed, I know your voice girl. Tell.'

'Causes are lost men, my fears small sympathetic. Not Bjorn and music only, disastrous on the Boulevarde.'

'Subjective time my theory. Newly here I perceive two worlds of packed perceptions years go by, warping deep elaborates, and in no time it is the end.'

'Twenty Terran years were golden here in purple.'

'Envy glows slowly to fuse.'

'No blame.'

'No time backwards or my husband fountains also, living real in golden not ghostly habit and a bookworm.'

'I love Bjorn.'

'Yeck! As well love water in this Different River, one colour in this fountain, love, yeck yeck, what drop of water is the same twice before your eyes?'

'We were perfect together. He was my Lissner-Chrysler, my deep offer, my usher, my sha'lafearma.'

'Yeck! Fast carseats and blue tassels. My husband was a Joker Smith, a wokanard and a kute 'aluke. But you grow out of it.'

'But we had potted palms and olives, late crash at Tiffany's, klone-Pluto for menu and rouge ostentatious.'

'It always seems.'

'Retrieving returning regaining?'

'Can a good woman make a good man better?' Was Bjorn good, was she? Nothing held fast.

'Fetch him to me for a treasure rare such I needed on Terra many times, forbidden though that sewing brutal and chthonic practise, unique oracle thing for telling.'

'Mutilated oracle?'

'A touch of sorcery.' Aariarla didn't know what to make of that, but yet she went to find Bjorn, and there she waited by the tower, looking like an old sick woman.

The black swan glided by followed by ducklings and other little creatures.

'Kill him kill him,' it hissed. Kill? Her beloved? Murder on Sunshine Boulevarde? The end of the world. The swan and its strange brood drifted back.

'Not killing really, the protest burns my anger at the bird-deaths.'

'Ecological misinterpret everywhere.'

'Madness madness,' it hissed, gliding away.

The iron doors of the Tower opened, and within those Caatreusian doors opened the restaurant doors swinging, and through them Bjorn was pushed, not seeing.

Aariarla hobbled as fast as she could towards him, full of love, pity, fear. He groped about, and she, horrified at his wretchedness, took his outstretched hand. He snarled and withdrew, all touch dread. But she took his sleeve and pulled, remembering that holding hands was childish, led him gently, childlike. What a pair they made now; she in disguise as an unloved and sick woman and he mutilated.

Soon they were with the old woman again, and that old woman stared and stared at Bjorn and said nothing. At last she said: 'Each moment is a surprise.' Her accent became more Terran, some ancient twang of mixed tongues. Some lost continent called Lancashire, full of witches; Africa, the home of half Bjorn's ancestors, full of witchcraft; Mexico, full of dictators, enchiladas, anthropologists and sorcery, all lost but not vanished: undercurrents of hidden oracles seeded across centuries of subjective time and vast oceans of sinking space. Aariarla looked at Bjorn while the old woman looked into the fountains and Bjorn looked only inward, seeing something somewhere. Poor Bjorn. How could he mend magic carpets without eyes to see the stitches and colours? Aariarla and Bjorn both had distant genes in some foreign land called Wales, her greatest grandfather the herbalist in some mountain village: a recipe, take one blue lizard with its eyelids sewn, and ask it questions. Yes, the old woman might have something, she recalled as a little child what she had thought to be fairy stories. There had been giants in those days as well.

Grandmother in Black Swansea beneath the mountain, at twelve years old picking up the pins in a sewing shop, and passing on to generations her stitchcraft, learned in Terran poverty; she too with small complaint aloud, a lifeship of hard sailing.

This old woman here now told Aariarla to roll up some bliss-weed and offer it to Bjorn, and the disguised young woman, impressed, did so, holding out the smouldering spliff to his sensuous lips, his unmarked orifice. But, a man as an oracle, that was weird; and yet, had he not told the cards albeit overlooking one dark picture? Bjorn inhaled and then again, relaxing over his suffering.

'Yes, in a chords with his inward music, she never lies down the Pythoness, holy snakes climb life trees higher than Yin and Yang, it can be done in a flash.'

Aariarla listened to the old woman with respect, and looked at the dried crusts of blood on his lashes, feeling lust and pity, the pity of it that this could happen here. The stitches shone, some string attached, she murmured endearments to deafness: 'Cherokee! Brave Warrior!'

Everything was quiet except for the recycled rainbows, the pock-lock and angst of a game of tennis being played the other side of a yew hedge and the coarse laughter of the black swan as it broke the arm of a child who had tried to strangle a little chick. The swan had a huge collection of many kinds of egg and was hatching. The oracle suddenly spoke in tongues.

'Ugga-ugga-ugga, me speak long time no see.' The sound of tennis was interfered with by a contingent of booted feet. Aariarla shuddered, these were strange times.

'Now, girl, the tripod of your questions.' So she considered and then asked.

'Traitor when me true Caatreuse?'

'Not now, sometime I did.' Oh shame.

'Your mother love intacta virgin green the boy?'

'Yes love but such neglect, the mind keeps green.'

'And Aariarla, was and is that loving?'

'Some.'

'What is love?'

'I do not know the meaning of the word. Feelings known are

not feelings sworn, nor sworn were, the blissweed talks and ecstasy persuades, one of the boys is one of the boys.'

'What of Chi'thuna in my time?'

'Man and woman can not live without one another.'

'Should all women have their mouths sewn up?' There was a
long pause and she gave him a drag of drug.

'Never never mutilations of the temple.'

'Caatreusian philosophical rise or falling?'

'Much luck both sides.' How true.

'Yoranga yin and yang, your Aariarla playing, you and I proceeded fiery trials?'

'Another world.'

'Game playing?'

'Pool and football with the lads.'

'Richness of pools for far journeys?'

'Do not importune the oracle.' The old woman interrupted
with a gesture and herself gazed into nowhere for a while.
Aariarla dared to touch the hand of the oracle, noticing its scars
from sewing carpets, its stains of bright colour from the dyes:
over the dark skin were heliotrope, saffron, indigo and madder.
He neither flinched nor responded.

'Hear me now.' The old woman too spoke in tongues of a kind
and asked the oracle.

'I wish to know, is one more right than two or two objective
truth and eternal, all people of hierarchy?'

'Nobody has any rights.'

'True on Terra true on Sunshine Boulevarde?'

'True and true, we are not human for ourselves.'

'Now: your own mother suffering without a narrow squeak,
no women's rights and yet, the women's wrongs but knitting
pickles and detergents ever ask?'

'I admit her sealed lips waxing my denials waning.'

'Well then, in plain Lancastrian lad, she were bright enough to
know that complaining got her nowhere but scorned, and, while

we're on about it, if you are such a good son, you could have been a lot kinder when you were back at home, you moody little sod.'

A gaping silence.

Eventually two tears squeezed themselves from between his eyelids, slow, burning, acid, bitter tears. They were so hot they dissolved the stitches and a twitching began.

Aariarla thought, Sunshine Boulevarde is full of miracles and purple light but it also has red herrings, yellow bellies, the blues, shrinking violets and mood indigo. And as for orange, wearing it will block bad vibrations, sealing in as well as repelling. Is there oh is there true love between man and woman she breathed to the waning oracle waking to a new life, light invading him painfully, healing his wounds and bending his conditions.

'Love is temporal in subjective Time, Time is eternal and love is a breath indrawn only to be caught again by the breezes full of something.' The old woman made a gesture of impatience at Aariarla. 'Get that disguise off, they won't want you now but you don't want to go around looking like a sick, unloved old woman. Do you never learn anything?'

'The Yoranga.'

'Teach yourself, you've got hands.' And learn other things too, the hard way. Such as, the several uses for tennis balls, what a dangerous thing happiness was, how difficult it was to find a lover who was not a traitor or insane, that perhaps none of it mattered except ultimately.

Sighing in the heliotrope evening, Aariarla went off leaving Bjorn and his mother together. The fountains ceased. The tennis courts closed. The swan hatched out a strange brood. The torturer emitted a little squeak as he pricked his finger and fell asleep, acupunctured like a hundred-year-old egg. Immediately spiders wove webs and briars were stimulated into growth, a long wait for a kiss began.

A renovated Persian carpet took off vertically without its cargo and flapped into deepest space, mistook for a black swan in flight against the drowsy sun.

One lotus bud on the Different River opened very slightly, projecting a strange luminous beam into the lonely Boulevarde night.

New Aesthetics

Parabolic extrapolations are what will save the world in time of need. Science fiction writers believe this, and so do some scientists. For example, a zoologist, professor at an English university, was heard to say in public that if we were to survive (the problem was not lead pollution or the bomb, but food supply) we must change our entire aesthetic structure. As well say that in order to bring down the crime rate, ideas of good and evil must change, but this fellow really meant what he said. He considered it decadent to want good natural food; technology was here and must be employed. There was no essential difference between steak fed on good grass and steak fed upon chicken shit and processed newspaper. In America he had eaten deep frozen spinach which had a packet along with it marked 'taste' – this did not attract me, being one who thinks that canning beans is going too far. Spinach must be washed seven times, drained, and simmered in cream. But while feeling angry I was saying nothing – cutting out cattle and becoming totally earth-food oriented is not a good total answer either, I thought. But if you are going to have new aesthetics, you may as well go the whole hog, including the postage. I don't know what sort of a cook his wife was, but she looked pragmatic in a mean sort of way. I thought, it only needs an enzyme pill to aid the human digestive system; the zoologist flatly stated that it was impossible. I don't like that word, no great scientist likes it much, either. But I can't structure enzyme pills, I'm only an ideas person. That's what fiction is for.

'You are just an old-fashioned sensualist,' said Thomas's wife, with self-righteous disgust. 'Fancy complaining about the quality of your evening meal, when everyone knows that the world is in a state of semi-starvation. Do you realise that there are children in China who pick up chewing-gum wrappers out of the gutter and eat those in order to stay alive?' Thomas realised it, of course; how could he not, having been told it daily for years, having read it daily in his newspaper for years, having fully ingested the information? Should he also feel guilt and shame?

'Picking the best bits out of your food and eating that first is also retrograde behaviour,' she carped on. 'When you show discrimination about what you eat, then you need to see a psychiatrist, in my firm opinion.'

'But we haven't had a copy of the *Guardian* for many a long week, Sadie. Every night the same, what do I get? The *Grayshire Sentinel*, what kind of nourishment is that for a hardworking man, I ask you?' She snorted disgust at this, and virtuously tore off a column of *Spare Rib*. It crackled as she chomped it and he turned away with refined feelings twinging on stalks. People who ate noisily! Yeeuch!

'Maybe you forgot to take your enzyme pill, Thomas?' she chided, knowing very well that she had watched him swallow it not an hour ago. Without the enzyme pill, one's palate became insensitive to the charms of paper besides which of course, digestion of it was impossible. Everyone knew that, but sometimes people forgot, and then they got bellyache and boils.

'I am digesting it perfectly, thank you. Every word is as protein with a high vitamin content, dear one. I took my pill and you know it, therefore I shall not be ill from undigested paper. No, I shall keep going on this stuff, having first read how the Lady Mayoress presented a shield to a centenarian, how a gang of teenage youths have been imprisoned for browsing in the public library, and how the price of water will be doubled within the year, even the unfiltered ... I eat and benefit. The *Grayshire Sentinel*, the most delectable paper money can buy! Ha! That may be true for some, but I want something more substantial. In fact, I demand a copy of the *Sunday Times* together with its colour supplement!'

There was a shocked silence, and he was pleased. She would tell the neighbours, maybe, that he was moving towards the Right. She would presently accuse him of being a social climber, a Conservative, or even a Fascist. She could say what she liked, he required a change in his diet from time to time. The thought of consuming the 'after' part of a skin-disease cure had made his mouth water. Why should all the rich and educated have all the privileges? Anyway, he was educated, and his very soul was starving – to Hell with New Aesthetics! Variety in diet raised one's level of being!

'You are an enemy of society, talking like that. The Harrisons down the road even wash out detergent packets and eat them. Mrs Harrison says she has noticed no ill effects, and the money they save they are dividing up two ways. Half goes for paper clothing for the children, which they eat when it begins to wear out, and the other half is for charity, for starving foreigners.'

'How virtuous of her. Well, I have an even better idea. Spend money on good papers for me once a week, I'll eat them if your conscience hurts you. And if you want to humiliate yourself and get one up on the Harrisons, try eating toilet tissue, used of course.'

Sadie walked out weeping. He had gone too far. But it was difficult to resist saying something which would *really* offend her, and point out her secret misgivings about belonging to the New Aesthetics Party.

He finished his meal with the crossword puzzle, having first solved it, and then he went into their other room to read a book. Sadie was still out, probably grumbling about him. Halfway through the story he realised that he was still hungry, so began extravagantly to gnaw the pages as he read them. It may well be considered madness of a kind to prefer the flavour of Kafka to Ian Fleming, but Thomas did so.

So, he was a regressive and a snob!

He must be careful, though, for there was a political movement afoot to persecute people like himself. Only the other day he had read about a party of students of English Literature, who had incarcerated their Professor in a university library, without any enzyme pills.

'He will starve because of his atavistic tendencies!' they had written on the library door. They should be careful, or they would martyr somebody, and reactionaries would rise against them. He might himself become a martyr, he could almost see it happening.

Goat's milk yoghourt for breakfast, the very best, thick as custard, with a sharp orange and a little Tasmanian leatherwood honey. Tender Californian prunes and bran, that despised substance once thought fit only for rabbits or pincushions, finally proven essential for health, to the delight of that group of people or paranoids known as Health Food Fanatics. Oh bliss, oh breakfast. In a more Edwardian mood of course we might occasionally indulge in such delights as kedgeree made with oak-smoked haddocks, a pale tinge of saffron blending with the rich yellow of the yolks of free-range eggs. Bright yellow haddock is of course dyed and deadly. Or kidneys sautéed in the drippings of milk-fed Normandy bacon, touched with needles of rosemary...

Thomas's happy martyrdom was curtailed, for in came Sadie, contrite. She admitted that she too preferred a better brand of paper, and she showed him the gift she had purchased for him on the black market. It was a very mature copy of *Vogue* with a painted face on the cover, and inside, photographs of exquisite clothing and jewellery that was no longer seen in real life. They drooled over the pages together, and the culmination of the evening came when Sadie chewed up a picture of a perfect pair of breasts and then kissed her husband, ejecting the pellet into his mouth in a downright Dyonisian fashion. He had a wild fantasy of making love to her on a bed covered with newspapers, recognised it as anal-oral, dismissed it with difficulty and enjoyed their union in more conventional style.

'I'll try not to nag you, Thomas, but I get frightened sometimes. All the wives make such a lot of the moral aspects of New Aesthetics, you know. It's a competition as to who can eat worst!'

'Well, just you remember who you married, when you talk with these women, my Sadie. This way we can survive and stay happy. In my opinion, you mix morals with food, you've got trouble.'

The ultimate extrapolation of bagels and lox is to present the whole delicious pile of fresh curds and smoked salmon on fresh and very rough wholemeal bread. Toasted cardboard we don't need. And if we were alone, and rich, we might have just that for lunch, that or nothing. Food in the middle of the day makes a person sleepy but when there are guests this is not a problem for the talk will keep the blood circulating. Someone is sent out with a jug for some real ale, and the baby anticipates its sieved liver and whatever by urgent gurgling. Plates are put to heat, food is chosen from what is available. There will be thin slices of smoked short-back bacon, thick slices of rich black pudding, little triangles of fried bread, and a large dish of perfect scrambled eggs. Perfect we mean when we have just got the barely mixed yolk and white to set, well seasoned with sea-salt and black pepper, in melted, not hot, butter or good margarine. The curds will be large and shining and will remind the poetic or the greedy of silver and gold. There will be cream and parsley in the dish as well, just enough to make the texture smooth and to flavour gently... The food is served on blue and white plates, with a willow pattern, and the coffee is very good ground coffee, filtered into a hot Denby jug. We are all content with life, we recognise ourselves, silently, as amongst the fortunate.

What Thomas and Sadie did not know was that her brother Henry was a great deal more immoral and decadent than either of them. They had heard, with a thrill of scandal, of a drug that the wicked were taking, which not only had the enzyme properties of rendering paper digestible, but of making it taste like avocado shrimp salad, Colorado Beefsteak Diane (flambé Courvoisier), Apricot and Almond Gateau with fresh cream Chantilly, Brie and farm-baked rye crispbread, and Kenya Coffee Dublin. Two or three times a week, Henry indulged in the drug, known as Gourmet's Gumdrop, and he and a selection of girlfriends (one at a time), tripped out to imaginary restaurants and indulged their Eclectic-Sybaritic-Epicurean-Hedonistic passions together.

Henry had always been attracted to anything evil, and if evil could be combined with pleasure, then he was the more strongly attracted. He would actually set a table with fine linen (he had once used paper cloth and napkins but they had been eaten), candles in silver holders, plastic roses arranged in an antique aluminium cooking-pot, and actual knives and forks. All these things should have been recycled years ago, but collectors were still secretly selling this permanent type of decadent object to fanciers.

Henry would make a ritual ceremony out of it, tearing the paper into decorative shapes. He was something of a master of origami, and twisted ancient pages of *Scientific American* into shapes closely resembling T-bone steaks, the scarlet jowls of a photo of a tropical bat, when cleverly folded, very well simulating underdone beef, and the edges of a chart showing rainfall in Iceland cunningly masquerading as a trimming of rich grilled fat. No woman had been able to resist his table, and a great part of his pleasure was derived not merely from eating his delectable drugged feasts, his theatrical presentations, his serving ritual and illegal tableware, but from watching the eyes and lips of his loves, when eating what they would be firmly convinced was real food.

'Have a peach,' he would say to some pale starveling, too

young to have tasted anything but paper, but with taste buds only in need of opening. The hallucinogenic properties of the drug would work on her consciousness, and as she took the scrap of paper from his trembling fingers, her mouth would water, and upon sinking her teeth into the illusory fruit she would drool, her eyes would bulge slightly, her tongue would protrude, erect and avid to lick up an escaping rivulet of invisible juice.

'Can you smell the perfume of this fruit?' he would ask, knowing that peaches had a chemical constitution capable of deceiving a blind man that his nose was within inches of a clean female pudenda. The girl would blush scarlet, and he might then offer her a ripe banana, having first explained about those from the Canary Isles, that they were only perfect when almost rotten, and that they were much smaller than normal! Oh, the naughtiness.

Someday he hoped to get together a dinner party, at least eight people around a table with a heap of periodicals, and a dish of Gourmet's Gumdrops. He would get really creative over his accompanying sauces, his allusions to symbolic qualities, his flavour combinations and his psychological analyses. One could discover so much about people just by observing closely what they ate, and how. He might be considered decadent, but he got a great deal more pleasure out of life than The Masses – that amorphous bunch of New Aesthetes, who when they swallowed the nourishment available to them, discovered only that they had a stomach which had been empty.

For instance, that stupid brother-in-law of his, and sanctimonious Sadie! He no longer thought of her as a sister. Since marrying that dummy, she had become mean, moral, miserable. She was beyond saving.

Even in the provinces, there was a tremendous variety of food from which to choose. Freshly killed chickens, geese, ducks and turkeys on one stall, and pheasant, pigeons, partridges, grouse and guinea fowl on another. There were three kinds of local cheese; the soft cream, the hard and tasty, and the one green with crushed herbs, mostly sage. There were sausages prepared in a farmhouse on the hills – great fat pork sausages which did not skulk and lurk on the dish, but which proudly *knew* they were good, and would all be bought and eaten, probably in excess. On the same stall there were tubs of double cream from Jersey cows, and neatly capped pots of home preserves, all singing out to be spread on hot oatcakes or muffins.

The greengrocer's shop was the most immediately alluring. The lettuces, three kinds, were all locally grown, the Webb's especially reminiscent of Art Nouveau renderings of woodland torsions. The tomatoes were all different shapes and sizes, not too ripe but promising flavour and texture worthy of true Love-apples. There was a lurid temptation to make a ratatouille in the display of courgettes, beans, tomatoes, garlic and purplish onions. There were avocadoes in every stage of ripeness, and lemons nearby. There were damsons and bilberries, and winter cooking apples. There were exotica such as Chinese leaves, custard apples, mangoes and fresh beansprouts. There was celery with actual leaves, and leeks which likewise had not been raped with a trimming-knife. Beautiful soups could be made from what profligate greengrocers often threw away. There were five kinds of potato, three kinds of orange, two kinds of cress, four kinds of apple including the unprepossessing but exquisitely flavoured Russet. Spinach, broccoli, curly kale so rococo as to make the dia-phragm dance with mirth, and the first chestnuts of the year. Pimiento green and red, sweet corn sadly suitable only for decor-ation, and green grapes like talismans of jade.

At another shop there was stoneground whole flour, yeast, sesame seeds, a choice of honeys, dozens of kinds of beans and lentils, salt containing perfect crystals for catching the light on the tops of pies.

And a fat mackerel glowering like a sky, a quart of mussels lewdly sprouting beards wrapped in a sheet of newspaper.

And then on to the market came a new food, and it had the advantage of not requiring the prior swallowing of enzyme pills. The new food was called Somatic Healthgiving Ingestion Tabsules, or SHIT. It came in handy packs, together with an aerosol called Nasal Inhalation Choice Engenderer, or NICE. It had the disadvantage of not being readable, but newspaper was scarce: there was very little suitable material left in the world, and the demand for it as either food or reading material was decreasing – SHIT was cheaper. Word was that the invention was another wonderful triumph for the New Aesthetic Rationalists, and that the world was happy.

There were some, however, among which were Thomas and Sadie, who were not happy. Such people, in order to obtain a good bit of paper and an enzyme pill, were selling up their personal possessions, to those few who still craved such decadent things as personal possessions. Life, to Sadie and Thomas, was losing good qualities. Being weakened by privation, therefore, when Thomas went to visit his brother-in-law Henry in order to offer a suit of clothes in exchange for a bundle of newspapers, he confided his feelings of distress. Pride would never have allowed it, but trouble can bring closeness between people.

'I just don't like these new tabsules. Sprayed they may liberally be with NICE but they just don't have the quality of the *Guardian*.' He sat with his knees apart, his elbows resting on his knees, and his head hanging down: abject despair. Henry saw the opportunity for which he had waited. He knew that Thomas and Sadie possessed something which he wanted, and he was convinced that in their present distress he could not only obtain it, but corrupt the pair in the process.

'I could provide you with a full set of Mrs Beeton you know, if the price was right.' Thomas behaved as if nipped sharply: everything about him was attentive.

'What price? And what are you doing with such books? I

thought they were legend only.' Henry assured him otherwise. He had been saving the books, hidden away wrapped in tinfoil for the event of starvation. But the new invention had made such an event unlikely, so the books could be traded. For the set of genuine bone-china coffee cups that his sister had inherited from their grandmother. Sadie had denied having the cups. Henry knew otherwise. They were illegal objects – had Thomas and Sadie committed the self-righteous act of smashing them? He profoundly hoped not. He was not disappointed. Two days later they both arrived, with a package.

'Why do you want these cups Henry? You know that Granny gave them to me to keep in sacred memory of the time when there was still coffee on the planet. I have always felt it to be my duty...'

Henry feared that she might knock one of them off the table as she was unpacking them, maundering on about sacred vessels. He felt sorry for her. He recalled their childhood together. In those days she had been a promising human being, and they had even been friends.

On a rare impulse, Henry made a decision. He made them both swear utterly that they would never reveal what he was about to tell them, and then he confided to them his habit. Gourmet's Gumdrops!

At first, of course, they hardly wished to believe or know it, and there were some sanctimonious sentences about Decadence Destroying the New Aesthetic State. It was surprising to Henry that he did in fact manage to sell them the idea quite quickly.

He explained how his rituals worked; they were tense with anticipation, and looked to Henry as Chef of the Game.

Dinner the night before had been something of an occasion. Not that the food was anything out of the ordinary: chicken, baked potatoes, a kind of ratatouille, and a meringue pudding. Not even a well-balanced meal, but for once the salad was left out, because of the crowded table and number of plates needed. The chicken was only special because of its marinade. For a start it tasted of chicken – natural, free-range, happy and well-fed chicken. It was marinated overnight and was therefore tender, and had absorbed flavours that were so deep within the meat that it had blended with its natural flavour. Basically the marinade was yoghourt with cider vinegar, garlic, honey, crushed peppercorns and cummin, sea salt, basil, tarragon, Moroccan paprika and a bay leaf. The birds had been dissected with a sharp knife, and a knowledge of anatomy bordering upon the macabre, but which Leonardo would not have despised; smashing bones with meat cleavers leaves nasty fragments which get into the mouth. It was later wet down with chicken stock, closely covered, and slowly simmered in the oven. The sauce was eventually finished with an addition of wine and cream and bound gently with cornstarch, and bacon bits scattered over the top which were then frazzled under the grill so that the fat flavoured the dish. The Lincolnshire Red Potatoes were baked in a glimmer of oil and a frosting of salt. The ratatouille was slightly overcooked but the flavours although too well-married were still distinguishable, and even those who found themselves obliged delicately to remove small pieces of cellulose in the form of the black skins of aubergines, did not despise the conglomerate, they ate it with pleasure. There was a reasonable burgundy with this, at exactly the right temperature, opened long before the dinner and resisted firmly by the cook in favour of work-top Martinis. Up to the fifth Martini, or Noilly, creativity increases, and thereafter may take an upwards soaring curve into the sublime, or some accident may occur. On this occasion, only five were drunk, and then dinner was served.

With the pudding a white wine a little less dry but fruity and clean. This pudding. This delectable mountain.

A very light meringue had been baked to a pale gold, in rectangular sheets stuck profusely with Jordan almonds. A pan of apricot purée had been prepared, from small, dark, strongly flavoured Polish dried apricots, simmered to a sharp fruity perfection. A bowl of whipped double cream was waiting, spiked with a dash of yoghourt, an acknowledgement that the taste of cream is long gone from the earth already with sterilisation, and a hint of vanilla, but no sugar. There is a school of thought which maintains strongly that anyone putting sugar into whipped cream is contributing to the downfall of civilisation. Bitter chocolate had been melted and spread into thin sheets, and then carefully cut into small squares. These ingredients were layered together, taking care not to allow the apricot to contact the meringue, but to seal it in thick cream, until the mind and the eye were dazzled and anticipation became something on the borders of masochism.

One guest, a writer known for his eloquence, who had until then contributed to our lively talk, and who was on a strict diet, was rendered speechless and helpless.

'Do you really think you should eat the rice paper off the bottom of the meringues, darling?'
'I don't know, but I like the way it disappears on my tongue.'

Henry gave Thomas and Sadie a Gumdrop each, and some evocative descriptions. It is a monument to the powers of the human imagination, and an interesting question of concern to geneticists, that in spite of never having tasted the food of historical reports, and notwithstanding the drab and minimal quality of their surroundings, they were able to participate in the proceedings with perfect thoroughness.

They 'ate' their way through consommé with sherry; crayfish in Balkan dressing; duckling with bitter Spanish oranges and wild Irish watercress; chocolate mousse made with the very best French chocolate, fresh eggs and double Jersey cream; a delicately mellifluous Camembert followed by a perfect Granny Smith apple; Henry's favourite Dublin coffee and some exquisite hand-made petits fours, each one different, but all containing either fruits crystallised in Greek honey, nuts, or meringue of a disappearing quality approaching magic.

Sadie looked adoringly at her brother across the remains of the feast (metal staples and Scotch tape), and he knew that at the lightest suggestion from him, incest could be an added spice to life. She closed her eyes, and began to drift off to sleep. Henry decided that an after-dinner talk with his brother-in-law would be more in keeping, and he helped his sister over to the bed. She lay spreadeagled in a posture somewhere between inviting sensuality and sheer abandoned ugliness. Thomas's face was pale green, not unlike the inside of an avocado; it had the same oily quality and the same blank expression. Henry was slightly alarmed, he had never seen these symptoms in any of his guests. Suddenly Thomas stood up, clutched his stomach, and retched. A stream of newspaper pulp poured forth, moulding itself into a potential papier mâché cup. He collapsed on to the floor, amongst crashing.

Henry was terrified but equal to the occasion. He hauled Thomas to the bathroom, and spent the next hour cleaning up the room, removing every trace of the debauch.

'Pearls before swine,' he repeatedly muttered as he worked. 'I could do with some help with this. Could it possibly be that the New Aesthetes have a point? Is it after all a crime to be self-indulgent? Pearls before swine, though who could have foreseen this?' It was the repetition of this litany, and his confused ruminations as the night wore on, after he had found it possible to send his relatives home, that led him to a new idea of startling attractiveness. Henry was to become a very rich man, and famous in his lifetime. Or should it be said, notorious?

In times of inflation, many people return to the soil literally, and begin to grow their own vegetables. Patches of land are dug over and manured. Chicken shit is not the best substance for this, being 'cold', although other cold manures such as wool shoddy

and newspaper are excellent for rhubarb. Horse shit and compos-
ted green waste are best, producing the finest flavour and most
reasonable size in garden vegetables. The work is hard, but
rewarding out of any expected proportion: there are not only
edible and nourishing vegetables, there is a satisfaction quite outside the scope of mere economy and practicality. It is better to
share an unpoisoned cabbage with caterpillars, than to eat the
whole of a supermarket cabbage, poison included. Five hundred
thousand tons of potatoes will be grown in the wastelands of
London, so says yesterday's newspaper.

Fresh food will not be treble-wrapped and mummified; freezers will contain only ice, relieving the slaves who were once sent
running to the mountains. When the world contains only one
third of its present population, not only shall we all eat well, but
we shall have time and inclination to investigate literature, philosophy in its many forms including aesthetics.

Henry owned a chain of Underground restaurants, and became
the leader of his own political party, the Creative Atavists. Sadie
and Thomas were in both projects with him, but Thomas was
most horribly martyred in his sixtieth year by a group of exrem-
ist demonstrators fanatically dedicated to New Aesthetics
(which was by then not so New nor so Aesthetic) with a self-
denying rationalism amounting to religiosity. He was starved to
death in the kitchen section of the British Museum, having been
given a solution of water and Gourmet's Gumdrops to sustain
him, while his torturers shouted descriptions of delicious foods
through quadrophonic loudspeakers. This frightful event attracted a deal of attention, favourable, for the Creative Atavists.
Thomas had not died in vain.

With the price of paper being what it is, making any kind of a
living out of writing is extremely hard. Menus are simple, lux-
uries few. It has been suggested that it might be possible to make

a very good living by opening a restaurant, or investigating some other form of high-class catering. And yet, does not food prepared in any large quantity inevitably lose its perfection? How could it be possible to prepare threescore apricot gateau in a day, and still maintain the inclusion of the vital ingredients of care, enthusiasm, and love?

Meanwhile of course, there are some very real problems. In some gutters of the world, there lies paper, which will be picked up by children, and eaten...

The Triumphant Head

My eyes are open and I am awake. There can be no doubt that I am physically awake. He was awake before I stirred in the sun-scarred sheets, I can hear him in the dressing-room next door, splashing about, walking about, singing about, full of it all, and if shaving lotion had a sound, then that too reaches me ... but I must not allow that to distract me in this way.

Having washed all the important crevices and the bits that show of me (good bath last night, reeking of pine essence), I sit here on my comfortable chair, re-upholstered by myself in dark green cut velvet, and as I sit naked on it a pattern of acanthus leaves will grow on my backside, but hold hard, who sits here, looking into the mirror, and why, and *what* is this I see?

So, awake. I question, how awake is that?

Each day at this time I can reveal images.

I utter the challenge.

Beginning with the body, one leg, then the other, one arm, the other, and then the back, on those acanthus leaves, up through the body the stream should flow, should it not, confirming the fact of being awake, so that I experience that ... there was some of that cut velvet left over, I wonder if it would make a hat, sort of Garbo-ish?

That noise? His chest expander. Christ, get on with it, the image, it has to come, what will it be today?

I face the mirror. A Georgian mirror, black and gilt, the corners elegantly encrusted, mended with evil-smelling glue, the cracks masked with cheap gold paint, a good job if I may say so, only the marks of celluloid butterflies placed on its heavy glass by some thin hand now dead, meant to reflect the miraculous patterns seen in nature at the height of summer, a celluloid wonder, and here on my mirror the horrid blur of its pseudopod, marring my beauty unless I lean to the right which I now do, the better to see you with me dear . . .

Begin again – Bruce knew nothing, he was just a student of Arachnida.

To be more than awake for however short a time.

Look in the mirror.

Come to me, two-legged being who will live the day as some dim zombie with the ticket 'Anonymous member Dramatis Personae Planet Earth' stuck on me unless I can pull this off, this fantastic act, to see myself, not as others see me, but as I am. Preferably before that other thumping being, next door, push-ups now perhaps, strains a pectoral fibre, and for what, may I ask? No, I may not ask, he never questions me as to what I do in here each morning. He will be in here, though, asking about breakfast before I've half begun. He will know it is me sitting here by the fact that I shall answer 'yes dear, orange juice in the fridge, kidneys to follow.' Nobody else could say that to him at eight in the morning, in this room. It is outside his experience.

Be still then, choose a small spot on which to rest the eyes, fix it, not with a vibrant glare, but with a steady gaze, seeing and not seeing, and make of that gaze an anchor, so that reality may pervade; one cannot force this process – but you are way off beam again. Thoughts think, body live. If I could say: 'Somebody, help me.'

I am sitting here, a normal-enough practice for a human being, and what are little girls made of? Bones and blood and skin and hormones, and a reliable heart to keep things going until I get them into perspective.

Who is here today, hiding in my living corpse? There must be somebody there, always it is so, but which one?

Supposing *he* came in at this moment, just as my image appeared, would he notice, see it for himself? An interesting supposition, and, at the back of my mind, Robbie Burns, making love wholesale on the beds of heather, and the seas have not yet run dry, and a bloody good thing too, leave that...

I suddenly find I have released an amount indefinable of the source of my energy and do not quite know what to do with it: at this point I must achieve the miracle of stopping thinking at the same time as allowing my thoughts to think themselves, and then, given grace, things might begin to shape up; I may turn this mass of meat into a person, and within that person will be recognisable another, like Chinese boxes, known only to that person next door who is doubtless dressing himself in his chalk-stripe and two-tones, he being a male cognisant of what goes on in the world as 'wife', or, in his cups, as 'the wife', the words implying a certain uniqueness apart from all other wives but understood nevertheless to mean 'her', the wife, we all have them like heads.

Heads. Through the relaxed channels of my flesh flow, life, and run, but never to waste, bring me into focus; who is there today, nok nok nok, who is it, welcome friend, plenty of room in my body, have your say for twenty-four hours, but do not deter me from my aim, that is our bargain. You live, I live.

Things are jumping now, the acanthus leaves are doing fine, and the mirror is still as still, waiting, only a clothes moth hovers expectantly over my cashmere sweater which I will presently wear for the role I shall play today; my body lives, it glows, molten it glows, and my arms, they glow, and my feet, they draw something up through them and resist and glow like the element on the heater that is now singeing that unfortunate moth. My chest passes on the message into my clavicle, otherwise known as right collarbone, left collarbone, up through my neck and chin, to my lips which sing as if a fraction from a kiss, and my nose, tingling, working against me and into an orgasmic sneeze – later, the sneeze, it will keep. Now for my eyes, the right and the left and through the unknown quantities that lurk behind the bones of the triumphant head.

So it is you, today, is it, I half suspected it. Surly, insentient, woman of dusty antimony, mineral lady, butter would not melt, and gaze unseeing into the black depths of space (we all have our off days), and for a moment I saw, before the going and going away of it, in the wordless moment, the image in the mirror.

'Hullo dear, not dressed yet, what about breakfast?'

For a split second the powers of speech refuse the carefully held orbicularis, clinging to the delicate pleasure of a moment ago, but that is nonsense, of course you can speak, you are in command now, you know your lines.

'I'm almost ready, just got to throw on a few clothes. Juice is in the fridge, kidneys to follow.'

'Pity about the clothes, you look nice like that.'

I stand up and lean over closer to the mirror, staring at my face. He sniggers. It is the acanthus leaves. I snigger back at his reflection in the mirror, thinking, 'Does he deduce from this elegant imprint that I have been sitting on this chair for at least ten minutes?'

He goes away, clumping athletically downstairs to forage for the orange juice. Clothes on, and a little foundation lotion will do wonders for these pores and deceive the eye over the matter of an incipient wrinkle. And face powder.

God, what a marvellous sneeze that was, most satisfactory. Powder, there's powder over everything, every crevice of this mirror frame holds a delicate veil of triple-milled silk. Lovely dark eye-liner, green shadow all soft and blurry, mascara, and with a brush and with care bits of pink colour where needed. I brush with vigour the hair, pin it up, cover it with a wig, an expensive and fantastic transformation. I, the gold beauty, my own mother and would not recognise me, nor I either were it not for the fact that I saw the act of putting on the wig, and not only that, beneath that, and beneath that...

Stay with me during this day, mineral lady, you are ugly, but at least I know you, a bit.

If you were the outer image, we would both be locked away in some psychiatrist's cupboard along with other freaks, those with birthmarks over the entire epidermis, deep like rose-coloured leather; I have seen them, spoken with them, and without fail have smelt ineradicable pain in the soul, and suspected great beauty locked within.

But there is no cause for depression or despair; I have my face to hide in, and my mask of make-up, and others' ideas of what I am to screen me, until perhaps I become indeed something else, that need not fear showing itself only for a brief moment, coaxed and cajoled to appear, and then retire behind the veil.

Dust off a bit of this powder with a tissue, put the lid on the jar of cream, set the chair straight, switch off the heater, and go to make breakfast. Looking at the mirror as I leave, I murmur: 'See you tomorrow.'

To Market, to Market

She had so little money left, and time to go before she would have more, that was several days. Everything that could be sold had gone, she had bargained. Her children had to be fed. She wheeled her trolley around rattling light, thinking that the only possibility were bargain packs. It would be a matter of luck what was inside. They were not even frozen and were not always fresh. First, a small bag of weevilly flour to make bread. She had grown caraway to disguise the stale flavour, with success. She hoisted a bargain pack out of the heap. Her money was gone. Two things.

At home the children greeted her, unbarring the door and asking after apples. No apples today. Unable to appease their stomachs, they would fill their eyes: she did not want them to unpack her sack, for unprepared food could be so unpleasant. She kept her children as well as anyone, and did not like their appetites to be spoiled. In devious ways she presented delicacies which were not rejected. She made soup from bones, and ground the boiled bones into meal which went into the bread. There was no waste, she made an art of economy. Her domestic system had a kind of beauty. She found a use for the skins of onions, and forced sorrel under empty cans.

The contents of the bargain pack were not fresh. It was flabby, thud into the sink, greyish where it might have been pink. It had no eyeballs, and when she lifted it for closer inspection the lids flopped shut over shiny caves. Foetid. She could make it into edible brawn with sufficient garlic, but she anticipated the stench of the boiling. The children jostled her, curious.

'It is not good, don't look.'

'Let me see, let me see!' Children were interested in everything. She turned her back to them, explaining: 'I think it is decomposing. I shall try to get it changed.' But she had small hope. A child chinned the sink, rocking and kicking. There was a shriek of discovery. Pointing out: 'Look, look at that. Read it.' It was the identity tag, with the licence number, in the ear. Yes, she knew his number.

She let go but gelid hairs had stuck to her palm. She touched the metal tag, his hunter's licence. They had lived better than this, until he disappeared. Sick memory, the hair on her hand, hair in her hand. Not panicking, but something else inside, turning. Darling. Some relief that after all he had not simply tired. From the wrapper flipped, slipped into the sink, two hands. One flat and one gripped. Cut off at different times.

'Children, we are moving on. Get our things, I mean immediately.' Everyone knew that they might have to move on, for safer places. It was always a matter of time. Of reading the signs. Now, she wanted to go. She could not stay here.

She turned from it all in disgust, with stony determination. But her timing was bad, for there were shadows across the door, with laughter, and knives.

The Wall

It was as if the landscape was divided into two halves, split across by some change in the light, in the atmosphere, in the colours of the air and the earth. It was a great flat valley that rose so shallowly to the summits of the surrounding escarpments that the change in height was scarcely noticeable, but indeed the difference in height between the floor and the horizon was some five hundred feet. A great curving saucer. But the saucer was cracked across from east to west by a difference. The horizon on the north and the horizon on the south when looked at from west or east looked little different from one another when seen in turn, but to bring the eyes forward would have shown how great indeed the difference between these two halves was, and the eyes looking thus would discern a definite line across this area of the world, coming closer, winding upward, until it was close enough to be seen as a wall.

It was a very high wall, thirty feet in height, and it was very ancient in its stone, dark blue, hard, impenetrable, but rough and worn. Crystalline almost, its surfaces sprang this way and that, revealing whole lumps of glittering faceted hardness, with smooth places where mosses and orange lichens had got hold especially on one side, and at its foot many creeping plants, tough twisted vines bearing clusters of ungathered raisins, convolvulus white and pink, and ivy in many colours, thick, glossy, spidery. Here and there stones had fallen from its old structure, two and three feet thick, and in one place, almost halfway across the floor of the valley, there was a hole through the wall, only six inches across its greatest measurement, and three feet from the floor, which was moist red clay on the north side, and dry white sand on the south. The top of the wall was sealed to all climbers by rows of dreadful spikes which curved in every direction, cruel, needle-sharp, glassy metal rapiers set into green bronze. They were impassable in every way, these swords, and stood endless guard between north and south.

The valley was the home of rats and snakes of many kinds, and thousands of spiders ran in the dust at the foot of the leafy creepers, and rabbits burrowed in the clay at the north side and lizards scuttled on the south. There were two sources of water: one a spring which flooded a puddle in the clay – the water here was cold and green and clear – and the other a limpid pool in the sand under a rock, the water therein being warm and slimy and grey except for a slim trickle where it filled. There were no trees to be seen anywhere, only the earth with the sparse grasses, no habitation save the rabbit warrens.

At either side of the hole in the wall lived a man and a woman. The man lived on the north side where it was usually cold and damp, and the woman lived on the south side where it was usually warm and dry. These two were tall and thin and beauti-ful, strong and lean, but something was to be seen in their way of moving that spoke of inner suffering, some twisted thing which showed on the outside, almost imperceptible, something from the heart. He was fair in colour, with yellow-grey hair to his shoulders and a beard of great length which tangled in curls with blackberry thorns and stains of purple juice in his beard from the raisins he had eaten over the years. His feet and hands were horny with callouses from running and scrabbling for wild rabbits, but his fingernails were specklessly white for in his idle hours, of which there were many, he sat and cleaned them with a little stick of thornwood and rubbed them down to a neat shape on a stone in the wall. He wore a threadbare suit of lovat green thorn-proof worsted, a dark-green silk shirt which had been very fine when new, with gilt cufflinks which had only just enough cuff to stay hanging in the threads, and a tie which was not properly tied but which could not be seen for the beard.

The woman was dark and brown like a nut that has been polished. Her hair was very dark and her lashes and brows were dark and full, and her hair fell straight and heavy to her thighs in thick locks with not a wave. Her hands were immaculately clean too, and she had callouses on her knees from kneeling at the side of the pool, washing her hair until it shone. Her breasts were still young and bore the marks of suckling an infant, but that was in another life. She was dressed in a dark blue dress of Courtelle jersey with brass buttons long turned mouldy green. The dress fitted her figure and had a pleat in the back of the skirt, and she showed a little bit of nylon lace from under the dress sometimes, a very dusty white. She always carried a handbag with her. It was a large white plastic beach-bag with bamboo handles, and in it were all manner of bottles containing sun oil, hand lotion, face cream and skin food, handkerchieves, hairpins, dried-up cigarettes, old bills, papers and letters and a paper bag with a clean sanitary pad and two little safety pins wrapped up tight. She also had a brush and comb, a necklace of heavy beads, several photographs, some dried flowers and recipes for the making of home-made wines, Irish soda bread, and potted meat.

These two people were lovers. For most of the day, in their separate climates, they would sit by the hole in the wall exchanging conversation, peeping at glimpses of one another, able to see half a face or a hand in close-up or get a total view at a distance. They made up poetry for one another which only had meaning for themselves alone; sometimes they would hold hands through the rock, although they could only do this for very short periods of time because of the awkward height of the hole and the pain caused by being half bent and by the cold sharp rock rubbing on their arms. They would exchange bits of food – blackberries and raw rabbit meat, ripe grapes and mushrooms – and they would pass bunches of grasses or flowers from around the base of the wall to each other with passionate love messages whispered from the heart and from their deepest feelings. Although they had not properly seen one another or touched each other properly, they felt for one another in the tenderest way, and were swept by full passions that could never be consummated because of the wall. At times like these – especially was it hard when the moon was full – they would sit close to the hole and weep and moan for each other, longing for something the other could give were it not for the cruel wall that parted their starving bodies. Many long tortured hours they passed in this way wishing the wall would melt. But it never melted, it stayed there hard and enduring, as if it had always been there and would always be so. They had no ideas on the subject of how to remedy this terrible situation for it had been like this so long they could hardly remember when it was, the day they had found themselves, each at a side of the wall. Their love had begun on that very day, even before the sound of their singing voices, and with the rapturous discovery of the hole and the first blissful touches of the hands, and with the dreadful realisation that they could never come closer together than this. All through the years they had yearned but never thought it could be any different. They knew as if with an inborn knowledge that the wall was too deeply set to be tunnelled under, too long to be walked around, if indeed it had an end anywhere, and much too hideously guarded at its crest.

One day the man began to think that he could not stand it any longer. His body and emotions had taken all they could; he was racked with desire and his head was full of pain with inner weeping. He suggested to the woman that they should part. He explained that the idea had come to him that there might be other lands where a person might live, over the horizon, away to the north and south, things they had neither of them dreamed of, other loves perhaps, other climates and better food. He felt just then that anything would be better than to sit here forever just yearning for something that could never be had. At first, when the woman listened to this idea, she was so deeply shocked inside herself that she became as stone, she neither spoke nor moved for a day and a night, but lay with her head on the stone of the wall in a cold agony such as she had never before experienced. And then she began to weep, silently at first, then with little moans, then louder and from lower in her being, until she screamed in great pain, and cut her forehead on the blue rock and the blood ran into her dark hair, although she felt only the emotions caused by the idea. But the man persisted. He spoke to her soothingly and gently and he explained with a heavy heart that it would cause him an equal pain to be parted forever from her, but that it seemed the only course open to them unless they were to die here without ever having known any other thing than craving.

After twenty-eight days the woman had absorbed this idea into herself; she had turned it over, and tried to visualise the world beyond, without the man, perhaps with strangers, other women, more food, another dress, but she could feel none of it and gave up as the pictures refused to take shape. But she knew also that it would be thus, she had accepted the idea, and so she finally bent her head down to the hole and agreed with him that they should part. They decided to begin their separate journeys the very next day.

They spent the rest of the day gathering food; the woman tore off her petticoat and wrapped it around heaps of dried grapes, mushrooms and meat that the man had given her, and he took off his shirt and did the same. They spent a sleepless and silent night of unspoken doubts leaning against the hole, and at dawn they clasped hands through the hole, said quiet goodbyes and turned around to walk, he with his bundle, she with a bundle and a handbag.

They each walked for several hours, with such a weight of dread and despair in their hearts as they had never known; their feet dragged, their backs bent, tears ran gently down their faces, and they each tried to recall the feel of the other's hand through the wall, but already the impression was fading, and it was very difficult to feel anything. So, grieving, they walked slowly towards the perimeter of the north and south sides of the valley, and there in the distance they each heard strange sounds, smelt strange smells, and felt strange changes in the atmosphere. They were miles apart by now and it was not yet noon, and the way had been uphill.

At exactly the same moment in time, the man in the north and the woman in the south met strangers of the opposite sex, and these two asked them the same questions. They inquired who they were, where they lived, and where they were going. Sadly they both told the same tale, and the woman who now faced the man in the north asked him to touch her long fair hair and she made kissing mouths at him. He was immediately impassioned by this brazenness and, full of unspent vigour from the many dry years, he held her in his arms and began to make love to her, clumsily and fiercely, his own dark woman already forgotten. At the other side of the valley, she was just then succumbing to the advances of a dark man, a person more handsome than she could have visualised, raven and brown like herself, strong and passionate, and she was so filled with admiration and physical hunger that entering the embrace was easy. And then the two couples parted, after long kisses and greedy sighing. As they stood up they chanced to look back across the valley, and in the distance saw one another, infinite specks, but each speck duplicated, and because each had just then been unfaithful with a stranger, they each knew that the other had, too.

They were immediately filled with remorse at what they had done, and longed for each other again as much as before, and because they could now see each other even though it was at such a distance, they wished to be close again. Having tasted full physical contact with others they now knew that no bliss in the world could match what they would feel for one another, could it be achieved. They had the idea that they would run to each other

across the sinking plain, and somehow against all reason overcome the obstacle of the wall, which, from this distance, looked
very small indeed. So they set off running without even saying
goodye to their lovers-that-were-not-lovers, running and breathing heavily from the unaccustomed effort.

When they were about one mile apart they could see each other
clearly in the sharp white air which lit this part of the valley
giving an illusion of clarity and nearness. They paused, then, and
staring in wonder each at the other, a pure brave kind of love ligh-
ted them up from within, and it was as if they could see the pool
that was the hidden soul. They began to run again, and as the
ground levelled off, the sight of them was almost lost behind the
top of the wall; but this made them run the last few hundred
yards even harder. At last they came up to the wall, and ran up
and down at its base in joyous haste, seeking the hole. Soon they
stood opposite, and the woman shouted to the man that she was
going to climb the wall and the man shouted to the woman that
he was going to climb the wall, but they were so out of breath
with running that their words were all muddled up and lost, and
together they dropped the bundles and the bag at the base of the
wall and began to climb. It was easy to find hand- and toe-holds in
the rock and the old vines and in minutes they were near the top
where the cruel spikes stood waiting. If they looked upwards they
could see the tops shining bright. They wanted each other.
Together they made one last desperate push towards the top and
saw themselves close together at the narrow summit; as the
spikes pushed into their bodies and as the blood ran down they
stared in horror, not at the pain of Death but at what was really in
the heart and soul of the other. In terror they clung to one
another, closer and closer, hoping that it was not true, as they
embraced breast to breast across the spikes, their cheeks pressed
close with blood and tears; it was then that they noticed all the
other lovers impaled on the spikes.

Some were long-dead skeletons, dry and dusty, grinning skull to skull; some were mummified by the keen wind, eyes sunk in perpetual bewilderment and some were rotten and new, astonishingly quite new.

They turned again to see themselves, wondering dumbly at what they had seen stretching out infinitely along the wall, all the clasping lovers, no kiss or hand-hold there with either bliss or agony.

And very quietly they kissed as they clung and died there, impaled across the cold spiky barrier, feeling and thought growing more feeble every second.

In the north and in the south a fair-haired woman and a dark-haired man set off slowly to walk towards the wall, love stirring in the innermost recesses of their being.

Dormant Soul

'It is like being in Purgatory,' Lucy said to her doctor, visited reluctantly, eventually, because the thing was getting so very much worse. She could not work. Widowed, a freelance graphic designer, she could remain at home and was not therefore seen holding her head, heard moaning, seen shuddering uncontrollably. Lonely nights left her in peace to lie awake clutching blankets tightly so as not to go into the bathroom and swallow all the codeine, those tablets that even in triple dosage did not reach into the crawling pain inside her skull. As if her brain had developed sensory nerves and was being experienced as a mass of creeping stuff – by some other brain.

'Migraine!' the doctor had said, and all his treatments had failed. It transpired that Lucy was so non-allergic to substances suspected of causing migraine that this in itself was noteworthy. He admitted after six months that she was not suffering from migraine, *per se*.

Unable to get warm, even wrapped in her woollen garments and hugging, cheek cushioned, the coke-stove in her kitchen, hot coffee constantly sipped, hot-water bottle stuffed down the back of her slacks, she had tentatively suggested to him that as it was the height of an English but nevertheless hot summer, there might just possibly be something wrong with her circulation. He had snorted, impatient with hypochondriacs and incurability in all the manifestations of it which had been brought to his notice, checked her blood pressure and dismissed her.

'Take more exercise if you like, no harm there. Swallow vitamin B if you think it will do you any good, but in our affluent society *nobody* suffers from vitamin starvation!'

Ruddy cheeks twitching, clear eyes glaring. Healthy man. She had not gone back to him for several months after that, but wrestled alone with the desire to be dead. The razor blades with which she whisked off her body hair once a week became minor gods; she prayed they would come alive and slice through her veins. They did not. Her hands, held by some other force than the desire for oblivion, could not accomplish the act of slashing. She was so frightened of her deepest depressions that she began to refer inwardly to the lump of matter that would sit twenty-four hours contemplating space, so miserable that it could not accomplish the simplest tasks, as 'her' rather than 'I', and threw away the threatening and alluring razors. Hairy, she deplored her own odour which seemed peculiarly strong, permeating everything, rising above all the stronger germicidal bath soaps that she had tried, till it became a familiar part of the slowly progressing decay that was overtaking her little house that had once been almost too clean, shaming neighbours and friends who had looked in vain for dust to comfort their consciences. They no longer called, discouraged perhaps by her own inability to communicate anything except misery. And this was not widowhood that was causing her anguish; some other force within her drew her down into bogs of fear. And she did not know what it was.

Psychiatrists were out of the question; she had tried one who had dosed her with stultifying pills of varying hues which made no difference to the nameless sorrow, and which made her head much worse. Psychoanalysts were too expensive, and she had as little faith in them as other women might have had in priests, even given religion as a 'belief'. On her thirty-fifth birthday she entered her kitchen to make a cup of coffee and saw written on the wall: *Sole Indoor Meant*.

There was no doubt at all that she had written it herself, although she could not recall having done so. She would have liked to have wept bitterly about her state of mind and gone for a walk on the moors, blown out the nonsense, but she was much too exhausted and knew that this nonsense, whatever it was, had a consistency too thick to be blown away. She went to tell her doctor that she thought she was going mad.

'It's all right to go a bit mad, you know,' he said heartily, 'just so long as you know about it. It's when you go a bit mad and *don't* know about it is the time to worry. Join a club.' He had meant to be consoling. So she was not mad then, no need to worry that she wrote messages to herself almost nightly. Cryptic punning things such as: *Ikonoclassed. Mystichasm. Dog is Red.*

They were written in the nearest material to hand, sometimes butter on the tiles round the sink, tomato soup on the tablecloth, stove soot on her clean wall. Lucy read and stared and tried to recall when she had written those mad things. It must have been done during her sleep? One morning she found her blue poster-paint open and splashed on the carpet in her little sitting-room, but worse, her own handprints, identifiable by the simian line on the left and a small knife scar on the right, were plastered bright over her walls. Blue handprints. To ward off the evil eye. She might have laughed or cried, could not, and could not wash off the paint either. She was not superstitious, never touched wood. Why did she do these things?

'Why does she do those things?' asked Lucy aloud and alone.

'Menopause?' another doctor suggested, embarrassed when she explained that she was only thirty-five. She had aged terribly these last eighteen months, she realised. At thirty she had been often mistaken for a teenager. The doctor mumbled about it not being impossible but she thought he probably put most women's troubles down to their age, whatever the trouble or age.

One morning the message on her dressing-table mirror was clear and explicit: *Drink Wine Tonight.* It was written in gold-flecked green eyeshadow that she had not bothered to use for about a year. She was amused, if amusement can be expressed by thumping the head with clenched fists, reaching down inside for laughter that will not manifest. Well then, if she was telling herself that to be sodden with alcohol might relieve things a little, she would listen, and so she hauled on a raincoat and slopped down to the wine-store where she bought three bottles of cheap dry white wine. What would her husband have thought, seeing her now? Neither of them had drunk much. Which is doubtless why he crashed the car after that party. Six whiskies, two lagers, one gin. Flames twenty feet high and her lying on the grass verge, thrown clear and watching him die. Stunned. Unharmed.

Soon got over it though, as he would have wished. He hated sentiment, would have liked her married again. And who would marry this slut that she saw reflected in the shop window, shuffling through a thundery evening?

At half-past seven she was at home, drinking her wine and it tasted very good, chilled, cutting through the miasma of her mouth until by half-past eight the second bottle was opened. She felt almost hungry then and thought about the grocer's box, which had lain three days unopened in the kitchen. She never went shopping herself if she could help it but telephoned orders which were put inside the kitchen door, and she paid by cheque by mail. Avoid contact with people. Boring.

She was thinking, then, about Portuguese sardines and potato chips when she first became aware of Armaziel, who was making rustling noises the other side of the kitchen door. He stood back smiling and shining brightly when she entered, only a little apprehensive of expected rat or mouse, holding a large book which she intended to throw. It was a Bible, and Armaziel smiled the more to see it, for he was of that race that has been mistaken for angels, even in the days when Jacob dreamt. The widow Lucy was too drunk by now to throw herself before him or to hide her eyes from the super-detergent whiteness of his garment, so she stood nevertheless awestruck that anyone, even a bloody angel, should have been able to enter her so thoroughly locked house.

'What are you doing with my potato chips? Who are you anyway, you long-haired, shimmering weirdo?' Wine was good for her level of communication, she reflected, reaching out for the box of chips that the angel held.

'I was just going to bring them in to you, together with a little cream cheese, but it seems the cream cheese is "off". You should have put it in the fridge.'

'I should, you are right. My domestic standards are not what once they were. Do I assume that your familiarity with the nature of such earthly things as cream cheese rules out entirely the first impression I receive, which is that you are an angel, from Heaven?' Lucy recognised her own familiar style of drinking speech. Sort of pompous, careful, witty in an old-fashioned, boring sort of way. Drunk as anything. An imitation of windy old academics – such as her husband – who were very boring under the influence. They made obscure references and the humour got more dry as they got more wet. And she didn't believe in Heaven either, so what if it said 'yes'? And then there was the question of guardian angels. All in the mind. And what wasn't, when the philosophy was really running free?

'I am from another planet,' said the angel. So *that* was it. She would now be supplied with details she did not know she knew, so that it would be all real, undeniable. Maybe it (he?) would take her for a ride in a UFO like Adamski and those lunatics. Oh Jesus Christ, was this madness? It was not unpleasant. It was good to have company. The shining being was nice.

'There are no such beings as angels that I know of,' said Lucy's new friend, and she shook her head slowly.

'Tell me more,' she requested, drinking on.

'We have often been called that because of our dress materials which have for centuries been far ahead of yours. And our hair and wings of course.' Yeah, and the *wonderful* complexion.

'Of course, the wings.' Down to his heels they were. White and beautiful like an enormous swan.

'Our way of visiting people on such planets as Earth who are in distress, you see. Mainly we only visit people in certain mental and emotional conditions. And for a very good reason which I have to explain to you.' Lucy opened the potato chip box and held it out. He took a few and munched. Apparitions *ate*? Lucy began cramming and crunching. Potato chips were maddening. One could never quite eat enough at once, until suddenly you realised you were so full of them that you were ill.

'You have been ill for some time,' stated the shining one.

'I have, how did you know?'

'I have been observing you of course. I spend a lot of time on Earth, I'm what is called a guardian. I fight the demons of Sirius Eight wherever they try to grow.'

'You're sure you don't mean Sirius Nine?' asked Lucy, giggling, knowing she was drunk and having hallucinations and that she had once read a science-fiction story set on Sirius Nine. Or was it Eight? It was the first time in over a year that she had felt anything like happy; it was nice, this game with the unconscious mind. And yet, another part of Lucy had already become convinced of the reality of the person before her. It was her intellect telling her that the whole thing was imagination. Intellect could not always be trusted. Enough potato chips, where was the wine?

'Have some wine?'

'No thanks. Alcohol does terrible things to my flying ability, I fear. More dangerous than just having wobbly knees, if you happen to be up in the air.'

'I can imagine. How'd you get here?'

'Space-craft to pilot station, then I flew. It's resting just on the edge of your oxygenated belt, rather high. We hide behind a force-field, as I think you would call it.'

'I see. And you breathe Earth air?' Aliens schmaliens, where was his helmet?

'Yes, I breathe Earth air but have to take pills to balance up my blood. On my planet the air is much richer and purer.'

'Naturally. You wouldn't smog it up like we do. You're advanced.' Then she felt sorry for having been rude. 'Excuse me for being facetious, it's all rather unusual, I get like that in a crisis.'

'I know. Don't worry. Sometimes I get things thrown at me; people scream. I always try to get my new patients drunk before I arrive, it lessens the shock. They think they are having DTs, which is bad enough, but not as startling as the truth.'

'You amaze me, really. What is your name?'

'Armaziel.' Well, she had surely never heard that before. How inventive the unconscious mind. Collective? She would like to check some books. Like the Bible, Jung, Hebrew books. So interesting this, slightly swaying, better sit down.

'Lovely name. Boy or girl?'

'Sex is universal and irrelevant on our planet. We dispensed with differentiation about four thousand years ago.' Judas Priest! This was a real widow's imagination at work! She had always been a feminist and had not ignored a certain small urge of gladness under the grief at her husband's death. Bereavement was also freedom. What would have made everything perfect would have been the inability to be sexually frustrated, like this shining adrogyne who nibbled chips daintily but not effeminately. Sex was a perpetual nag at her body, drowned only by the greater pains of head and heart.

'Why did you come to me?'

'To help you out of your despair, but first to explain its nature to you. It is not what you think, but something more serious and rather astonishing. I shall have to explain or we can't effect a cure.'

A cure! To be well and normal again!

'Tell on then. I'll make coffee.' She put the kettle to boil but Armaziel refused coffee. He washed a glass and drank cold water. Lucy watched where he put it down so that she could check later. He began to explain to Lucy why she was so ill, and how to get cured.

It was the demons on Sirius Eight, of course, although

Armaziel only called them demons because they looked rather like black vultures four feet tall, and they had a habit of possessing human bodies, leaving their own bodies back home. It took them months to accomplish it, but they had the equivalent of patience due to a different time scale and total lack of emotional involvement with anything they did and the end result was a Sirian bird-demon perfectly disguised as a human being. An insane human being. They were trying to take over Earth in this way. Had been trying for hundreds and thousands of years. For just as long, Armaziel's race had been trying to stop them. Because if the Sirians were allowed to spread through the universe, Lucy was given to understand, terrible things would happen. Destruction and evil followed them wherever they got a hold. They were doing quite well on Earth, but Armaziel's crew were also doing quite well. The unobtrusive battle went on day and night. But psychiatry was helping the demons unwittingly by drugging patients. Once drugged, no help could be given, as it made the patient passive. She reflected upon how the number of mental patients was increasing, there had never been so many mad and unhappy people. Statistics of one in six women, for example. Around midnight when the wine was wearing off somewhat, Lucy began to know that it was all true. Armaziel was sitting on her wheelback chair with his lovely wings half opened. She interrupted him, just as he was giving her the main part of the recipe for exorcism of the bird-demon now possessing her, to reach out and touch him. He grasped her hand with his, and it felt cool and real and solid, and it encompassed hers. It was the first hand she had held for a long time, and she would have liked to weep, but the bird-demons had a grip on her emotions. They atrophied emotions so that their victims left their bodies gradually and without fuss. No noise in this kind of madness, just gradually being eaten up inside, an erosion of the spirit and the will. Yes, Armaziel was real and true and she could feel his goodness. It was not therefore nearly as chilling as it might have been for her to realise that the hand she grasped was the outer of two which grew, beautifully formed, from the same wrist, the second one placed facing the other, very flexible.

Armaziel pointed out that a person of human or more than human intelligence who has wings also needs two pairs of hands. For carrying things mid-air, for entering space-craft, for fighting off enemies. One pair would have been inadequate.

'We often say we need two pairs of hands,' said Lucy, wondering how she could have dreamed this thing up. But she had not, it was real. Doubt and certainty came and went, but mostly she felt certain of his reality. And it was the most reassuring thing, not frightening. She had someone on her side, someone who knew what was wrong with her, could help in a real way. Someone who cared. Even if it wasn't real? But it had to be, and she had to try his cure. Otherwise she was lost, bird-demon or unnamable earthly illness, it was all the same.

So she sat on into the night making careful mental notes of everything she had to do to repossess her own body again, eject the demon and lead a normal, healthy existence once more. It was not too complex at all, just rather silly in some aspects, and embarrassing. To get seven people to pray for you twice in one day for two separate half-hours. How? Ring up strangers, she had no friends left. There was no harm in trying, but what a fool she would feel. A matter of life and death, she would say. And it was, too.

It might well be the real cure, even if it was all an hallucination. It was a theme that recurred throughout history, angels appearing to people in distress, with a plan of action, instructions against evil forces. Shining swords and all that. She got up and made notes on the kitchen wall underneath the injunction to drink wine. The process of healing was going to be a mixture of prayer, magic and shamanism.

Armaziel told her that the reason some shamans had such success with their strange cure was because the recipes had been

THE POWER OF TIME

taken up aeons ago, not forgotten by more primitive people. Sometimes the prayer was enough in a newly established case, accounting for the success of some church exorcisms. But if there was one other thing besides the concentrated good thoughts of seven human beings that a bird-demon could not stand, it was tincture of benzoin. It was poison to them, like prussic acid is to humans. Shamans use lots of it. Either the demon left quickly, or he was gassed.

'Now I must go,' said Armaziel, 'and thank you for your hospitality.' He opened the door and went out closing it behind him. Lucy tried the door, it was locked. The key was hidden in a drawer. She checked. Armaziel called back to her.

'Fear not, it is one of our minor talents, opening locked doors.'

The following day, Lucy ran up pounds on her phone bill trying to get people picked at random from the book to pray for her for two half-hour sessions in one day. Four-thirty to five and ten to half-past. No special words or anything, just a concentrating of good thoughts and hopes, and perhaps even love towards herself. She began her calls with the words: 'Excuse me for bothering you, a complete stranger, but would you consent to pray for someone if they were in trouble and asked you to?' Some of them put the phone down on her after the word 'stranger'; some put the phone down after 'trouble' and some put the phone down after 'pray'; some went a little further, just so that they could be very rude to Lucy after she had explained what she wanted. It was astonishing how widespread was her cynical atheism; what was worse was the number of people who would not even think of helping in any way at all, and said so.

'You're in trouble, you get out.'

'Your own fault I daresay.'

'Immoral people always ask others for help, squealing...'

'Religious pest!'

'Go see a doctor.'

'You must be joking.' And so on. Lucy began to wonder about

people. Would people spare a thought for anyone else in trouble? Would such people who could not spare a thought for a soul in torment spare bread for a starving body? Armaziel and his fellows would be having a hard time of it here on Earth; most of the inhabitants were halfway ready for the other lot from Sirius whatsit already. But by the middle of the afternoon she had seven people human enough to go along with her. One was a Roman Catholic lady of eighty-three.

'Yes my dear, I'll pray for anybody. How many Hail Marys do you think would be enough?'

One was a Hindu shopkeeper. 'Yes Madam, I Shashi Mukerjee will pray. Perhaps you would care to call at our hygienic establishment in the near future. We stock everything for best eating. Two half-hours guaranteed, I pray every day many times anyway, it is good for the soul. Good day to you.'

One was an atheist. 'Okay. Anything for a laugh. I'll send you my love.'

One was a Christian Scientist. 'Yes of course, but if you call round soon I can introduce you to our little group. None of us is ever ill, one need never be ill. Right thoughts and right deeds, you know.' Lucy said that she was not sure that she could promise to call round, but that she might. Feeling guilty, thinking that one good turn deserved another.

One was a young-sounding person who asked Lucy to pray for her also. Lucy said that she would, but did not say that she had no faith. The girl had cancer.

One was a middle-aged businessman who said that he had not prayed for anyone, even himself, since he was a boy. 'If you think it would help. I'm not sure how, mind you.'

And one was a truck driver who said he would think of her on his run to Edinburgh. He was not religious, he said, but she sounded so unhappy. He wanted to know what was the matter with her, but she did not explain. She said that she could not tell him.

'Well, I once got a girl into trouble myself I'm afraid.' Guilt would help him to pray then, she thought, and began her other preparations, all according to Armaziel's instructions. She ignored carefully all her feelings that what she was doing was the action of a madwoman. It no longer mattered one way or the other; she just felt convinced that she had to go through with all this. If she did not, then the pains in her head and her depressions would get worse. She would die. If it did not work, well . . . but it might. Stranger things . . .

But not much stranger things, and certainly never to her, she thought, lighting white-block type firelighters in a baking-pan on the sitting-room floor. She shivered and shuddered, and it occurred to her that it was no wonder she was always cold. Birds had feathers and she had none. And maybe their planet was hot, too.

She drank the last of her potion. It was hot milk with an egg beaten into it and a lot of powdered nutmeg, sweetened with honey and heavily laced with brandy. This was to give her quick energy and stamina for what was to come, Armaziel had said, and the nutmeg was to open the edges of her mind, slightly. It warmed her a little.

She wondered what her doctor would think if she told him that this one mug of posset had done more for her than all his horrible sweeties. She felt more relaxed and warmer. Pills schmills! A minimal easing of the creeping in the skull. Nice. She settled further into her easy chair, inhaling the benzoin that the firelighters were soaked in, clutching three bay-leaves in her left hand, inhaling also the several sticks of incense she had lit and placed all around the room. Rose and heliotrope odours of argabatti, heady and fragrant. They hated it, Armaziel had said. She leaned forward and took some more bay-leaves from the packet, and threw them in the little fire where they flared and crackled, adding their own smoke to the room. Then she took the benzoin bottle and sprinkled it around her chair, ignoring the indelible brown marks it made on the carpet, soaked a tissue in the stuff and held it to her nose. It was clean and cutting and when she had taken several deep breaths of it she added the paper to the fire. Then she sat back, eyes closed, and waited. She checked mentally to know if there was anything she had forgotten, it had seemed too simple. No, it was all done.

She found herself yawning. Deeper and deeper yawns. Up they came from the depths of her lungs; she could not reach deep enough for the yawns; the air intake was enormous. Quite involuntarily, gulping to the peak of a yawn, holding jaws back and back like a sleepy cat, snarl teeth, like at the peak of an orgasm, pow! Air sucking into a vacuum cleaner, deep inside. Rest. Then another yawn. She was so preoccupied with yawning that she had no consciousness left to think that maybe there was not enough air in her room, that perhaps benzoin had this effect. It did not matter how or which way things worked; the yawns were feeding something within her, filling up spaces in her being that would soon have been filled with something else.

Then the tears. No emotion, no feeling; sobbing, racking moaning. Just tears. Tears in pearls, single and shining, tears in little rivers, moving like molten glass down the sallow cheeks, forcing through the closed eyes, hot and thick. Tears in salt ribbons, pouring, dripping, soaking the front of her sweater, tears that could have been caught in tearglass one two three. Tears for a gigantic crocodile.

Lucy's head was moving. How did this begin? Moving like this, in rhythm to some silent tabla, a wild, fast, intentional rattle and knock, the timing perfect. Gene Krupa never did better, nor Pandit Chatur Lal. I have heard gong players, thought Lucy distantly, touching metal with little sticks and the disc makes music itself, the rhythm helps to straighten the head, she had heard, but not like this! Rattle go the teeth, loose boom the brains like cod roe boiling in a pan. And the pendulum, it has been out of true all this time. It should go back and forth, regularly, evenly, and as the head swings side to side so fast, it makes the pendulum go right, like *so*. To a silent music, a source of something very important. More important than the heart and the blood. Something central.

There has never been such pleasure as shaking the head. I needed this and did not know. Why does not everyone do it? Why is it not generally known that head-shaking is about the best thing one can do? What a discovery. Shake shake. And in the jungles of Bengal the Head Dancers, Tamil, Telegu, swirling and shaking the hair like black corn-silk in a row, hour after hour. Flash of white eye among the perfectly manoeuvred hair, necks like rubber, they move round to touch the chest and then the back. Practice for years and years, initiated as children, some die of brainstorms, and here am I, Lucy, doing it without effort. My neck has no bones, it moves unbidden by me, I do nothing, something moves me this way.

My arms are beating on the sides of my chair and making signals in the air, out, in. Like Swedish drill or Balinese dancers. My fingers making symbols in the air and I do not understand. Whence comes the control, and I can never perform those party tricks where people separate their fingers. 'Can you do this?' they say, waggling the ears. Clever bastards, no, I can not do anything. But can you do this? Watch me, Lucy, sending messages with my hands. To music. You cannot hear the music? Well, I can.

My legs are battling with the floorboards, wild beating, such rapidity, on and on, still pouring with tears. Something is rising up within me, something good, and the head, the top of my head. Oh what happens now. Something is leaving. Something squeezed, struggled, writhed, pushed, scrabbled, slithered, scratched, fluttered. Out of the top of my head. And is gone. Rising within me, from my middle somewhere, something good. Up, through, into my head, filling my empty space. What is it? A substance. Warm sweet good. Unfamiliar. Remember. What?

Happiness.

Lucy slept deeply, in a protective haze of smoke that was poisonous gas to a bird-demon from Sirius Eight – or Nine – who surely now flew screaming and clawing and grinding and cursing like any old-time villain or thwarted evil genius, away to his leader, back to his own body, away, uttering imprecations. Foiled!

At just before ten Lucy awoke, feeling something stirring. It was hunger. She made herself a warm malted milk and took herself off to bed, smiling and sleepy and lay with the light on, relaxed, contemplating the sweetness of normalcy. To be warm as others are warm, to be alive and not want death.

The room filled up with still more light, and Armaziel stood there and told her that all would now be well; the seven helpers had prayed well, each in their separate ways, and were beginning again. She need do nothing more, just sleep. She would close now so that the bird-demon thing could not re-enter.

'Goodbye Armaziel.' She wished him luck in his never-ending battle, she thanked him, she lay and felt gratitude. He had gone, the light was dimmer. She put out her bedside lamp, closed her eyes.

'So much I never asked him. Where exactly is this planet, how long does he live, what about UFOs, are they his or the other lot's? Why choose Earth, who is winning...?'

Sleep without dreams for ten long hours.

The happy days were making happy weeks; Lucy's liberation from the bird-demon of Sirius thing was perfect and complete. No slimy trace had he left; he was gone.

She could look in her mirror and see that she looked young again, that her complexion was healthy. She could put what she liked in her bathroom cabinet; drugs, razors, they were merely useful, not threatening. She never thought of death. Life was good. Just to be alive and work and go out and come in and sleep and wake and eat. These things were good, because they were normal and without unusual pain. To get up from a chair without having first plucked up strength to make the effort; Lucy still took a delight in this. To wear a thin frock without hugging herself against the inner chill, this was wonderful. She did not often think of all the other sick souls who were possessed by the dreadful aliens, but when she did, the thoughts were difficult, and she soon found herself identified with her own happy present. For after all, how could she help? She had prayed in return for the dying girl who had prayed on Lucy's liberation day, feeling embarrassed, stupid, without faith. But as to how to repay for her health, that was another question. Because now she half doubted the reality of Armaziel. He had been, she thought, a figment. A figure come up out of the unconscious, in the nick of time as she hovered on the edges of a bad psychosis. Therefore there were no other people possessed by bird-demons from Sirius anything. They were sick in their own separate ways. Lucy could not help. And yet, sometimes at night, she would know that for a while it was all true, and that if she could find a way of warning the world about what was happening, she might help Armaziel in his fight against evil. It was her duty. But how to find the sick ones in the first place? How to tell them without being thought mad herself? It was impossible.

She thought all around the ways that she could make known the danger to Earth. Tell psychiatrists. In for treatment straight away. Write to some Church Prelate? Either no reply or she would receive a visit from a priest who would offer 'instruction'. The Prime Minister? He probably got lots of letters telling him that the world was being taken over by aliens. Maybe even had a special secretary to deal with that class of letter. The Secretary General of the United Nations? Much too busy to be bothered about Earth being taken over. There was really nothing she could do, she always told herself, and soon she stopped thinking about it. Her spare time, when she was not fulfilling commissions for layouts, she spent in painting out her home; covering up the blue handprints, the messages on the walls. Soon, everything in Lucy's life was normal. She thought perhaps she might make some gestures towards social life again. Supposing she fell in love and married? It was not impossible, but something about that idea made her shudder in much the same way that the bird-demon had; she was working *away* from having her soul eaten out alive!

One day in the late spring she wrote on the last wall in the house to be painted: 'Armaziel I need your advice.' She received no reply and so covered it with eggshell emulsion paint and went out to buy plants for her window-box. She got two trailing geraniums, six blue lobellia, six assorted petunias and some nasturtium seed. Excited with the prospect of a summer display of colour at her window she walked back through the park instead of taking the shorter route by the high street. It was a beautiful day.

There were children playing in summer frocks and cotton shorts, a dog racing up and down with a stick, mothers pushing prams. Birds sang and the air was soft; thousands of tulips dazzled Lucy's eyes and a mimosa scattered little yellow fluff balls around the seat where she sat to rest. All the seats were full of the old people of the neighbourhood: ladies with shopping bags and poodles, ladies with bags of crusts for the birds, old men with newspapers and pipes, old men with sticks and straw hats. Lucy recalled childhood Sunday afternoons; all that was missing was the band playing in the wrought-iron pavilion.

She sat back thinking that park benches were dreadfully uncomfortable, but that on a day like this it did not matter. An old woman already sitting on the bench began conversation. Lucy's heart sank. She had wanted to be quiet. Don't be mean, she told herself. The old thing is probably lonely.

'Yes, a beautiful day,' she said, and looked around, discouraging further talk.

'Been buying plants, dear?'

'Yes. For my window-box.'

'Nice, a window-box. I wish I was young like you, what wouldn't I do?' Lucy was embarrassed.

'What would you do?' The old woman thought a moment, and Lucy looked away across the lawns to where two swans glided on a small serpentine pond.

'I'd come in here and talk to old me, I suppose,' said the old woman, suddenly cackling loudly at her own joke. She rocked back and forth and Lucy laughed a little to be polite and peered into her parcel at her petunias. She should get home and plant them before they withered.

Lucy watched furtively as the woman opened her bag and took out handfuls of crumbs or corn and scattered it on the path. Instantly birds crowded round, unafraid. One of them perched on the outstretched wrist and was content to be lifted right up to the sharp, enquiring face. Lucy was amazed at how tame the birds were and put out her hand too, but they immediately flapped away, gathering close to the other end of the bench. Huffed slightly, Lucy gazed away again, and shivered. One could never really trust these spring days; should have brought a cardigan after all. She found herself looking again at the old woman feeding the birds and noticed how extremely poorly dressed she was, black tatters drooping, holes and shreds flapping. Pitiful. Thin and worn and dirty like a starved old crow. The breeze brought a wave of odour that made Lucy gulp and think she must move. How horrible, and how familiar. She gathered up her parcel of plants and tried to get up but could not. She recalled where she had smelled that particular smell, and it was herself when ill. This old bag of rags, possessed by a bird-demon. Then why so cheerful? One of them, now happy in evil. Lucy's head swam, crawled, ached. Lucy's voice would not say: 'You are one of them aren't you?'

The scarecrow figure with the hard little eyes looked directly at her, holding out a claw hand with a bird on it, and Lucy heard as it from miles away: 'Nobody notices old women, it's like a disguise. I've been coming here for years to feed my little cousins.'

Lucy struggled to her feet, fighting inside to keep out the *thing*.

Suddenly screamed out loud and came as a whisper: 'You're one of them!'

'Yes dear, been with them for twenty years or more. We save all the souls we can get.' She displayed to Lucy a face that clearly had a beak rather than a nose. Save souls? Is that how they thought, these evil parasites? Like some dreadful Sirian Salvation Army, *converting* people? Then getting the converts to convert others, possess them?

The sun went out.

The policeman picked up the black handbag from the bench and looked inside. No means of identification, just a lot of birdseed and a very small transistor radio. Expensive gadget for that old woman to have. He took it back to the station and made his report to the desk sergeant.

'Where'd the old bird go after the nutter attacked her?'

'Dunno. Disappeared in the crowd soon as I parted them. Gawd that girl was fierce, pelted her with petunias, kicked her, punched her, took me all me time to get her off. She was absolutely barmy, said she had discovered a bird-demon from another planet, and didn't we know Earth was being taken over? Going on awful, shouting and screaming. They took her up to St Luke's in a straight-jacket.'

'There seems to be a bit of an epidemic. Last week a similar case. Said we should tell the Prime Minister before it was too late. This bloke attacked a fella in a coffee bar.'

The desk sergeant wrote out a ticket for the 'Lost Property', and tested the three buttons of the transistor radio without result. Flat battery. He wondered if it was stolen property, and that was why the attacked woman had run off like that. He put it away in the drawer, and noted that there was another one like it. Very small and neat. It did not work either. Tell the Prime Minister indeed. They always thought big, these people, but acted small. Attacking a poor old lady. But they should be pitied really.

As soon as Lucy got an opportunity, she wrote over her hospital bed in hospital porridge: 'Armaziel where are you now?' and the nurse washed it off, angry at the mess, and gave Lucy an extra pill. It took two of them to hold her down so that she would swallow it, but the threat of a straight-jacket did the trick.

'Don't drug me nurse, pray for me!' screamed Lucy.

How cold it was in here, and Armaziel would never come again.

Elouise and the Doctors of the Planet Pergamon

Elouise sat in the waiting-room of the Out Patients of Central Theatre, dressed in a short white gown. She had been waiting for a long time and wished that someone would come to fetch her; she had read all the advertisements on the wall and found none of personal interest, all of them being for drugs with unusual side effects.

A nurse entered the room. He wore a scarlet mask that covered all his face except one eye, and Elouise knew that this signified infectious carcinaoma of the skin. She did not shrink with fear or disgust; she had played with children years ago who had that disease and it seemed she had resistance to it.

'The doctors will see you now,' said the nurse, so Elouise rose to follow. He led her down the corridor past mysterious doors and flights of stairs until they came to thick drawn curtains where she stood alone for a moment. 'Escape' occurred to her automatically. She decided that escape was not only impossible considering how important she was this day, but it was almost undesirable; curiosity made her stand her ground ready for the next experience, whatever it might be. She heard her name announced and felt herself led on to the stage of Central Theatre and then locked by force-field into the examination throne. Before her the theatre was filled with people. They were the Council of Doctors, and they numbered about a hundred; all experts.

She took out from her little handbag her mirror, observed her glistening pale hair and shining dark eyes and golden silky skin. Then she turned the little mirror on to the audience and was satisfied that many gave out squeaks of pain at the flash of light. Unusual if none among them had suffered some form of iritis.

The male nurse turned to Elouise and above the babble of voices he asked her if she had anything to say before examination began.

'I want you to release my mother from the prison hospital. She acted from the highest principles and the best motives, considering the fact that she is deemed schizophrenic.' Elouise felt very dutiful saying these words and also rather foolish. Mother was too mad to know where she was and, since recent events, had slipped completely out of the reach of other minds. The only response she got to her hollow request was a ripple of amusement for in any case her Mother had committed an unpardonable crime in allowing her only child to remain healthy until the age of twenty. It was almost unheard-of; supremely anti-social.

There was a shouted conversation about Elouise's radiography reports, blood tests, metabolic rates. Everyone was reassured that the pathologists were completing a list of test results containing information concerning the patient's haemoglobin, erythrocyte sedimentation, haemocritic reading, CSF, sputum, urine, faeces, gall-bladder contents. Someone screamed hysterically that the patient had a fantastic renal function and someone else remarked loudly that he had never ever come across such a perfect specimen of marrow. Someone maintained that he still thought that the result of his test would reveal occult blood in the stool, but his colleagues were dubious. Silence was called for and then the formal examinations were announced. Elouise hoped that they would not be as unpleasant as some of the tests already performed on her, and then remembered the last coherent thing her mother had said to her before being taken away.

'Don't let them get you down. Never fear a thing.' And Elouise simply sat and waited, quite relaxed. She took a good look around the theatre; great windows opened on to the surrounding forecourt, and inside row on row of doctors flopped down on padded seats. Behind her the backdrop, immediately before her the step that separated the rostrum from the auditorium, and in the ceiling very bright lights. No television equipment; this conclave was *in camera* although surely all Pergamon knew of her notorious self by now? She looked again through the windows across the flat land outside the forecourt. There were no other buildings to be seen but there were distant groups of people like herds of cattle browsing.

Matron bustled in from the wings. Immediate and profound silence ensued and Matron spoke. An efficient voice; a long-faced voice; a voice that was *we* and not *I*.

'Who will examine the patient first?' In the auditorium a man stood up, hand raised.

'Please Matron, I will.'

'Very well then, proceed. And then take your turns in orderly fashion.' Matron left the stage, and Elouise looked at her first doctor. Like a poppy unfolding, up rose the thin hairy body with green pallor at the neck and a corolla of bright red hair he waved towards her through the field of his friends, hypnotic and delicate. What wasting disease or chronic glandular disorder caused his appearance Elouise did not know and neither cared, he held no interest for her and inspired no fear.

'I got your lumbar puncture report,' he simpered as he approached. She cringed at the memory; manometer, gallipot and syringe. Unpleasant. But that was past, what now?

'Cross your knees.' Elouise crossed her knees and he opened a large briefcase which was fitted out with a tray of instruments. He took a soft hammer and hit her gently just below her patella. Elouise's foot came up and kicked the doctor under the chin which caused a ripple of laughter and some perfunctory applause in the audience. The doctor slowly moved his head away but showed no other reaction to the blow. He turned his attention to the contents of his case, checking and counting. He had a camel-hair paintbrush number six, three test-tubes containing mystery substances, three small plastic envelopes, a sharp pin and a tuning-fork. The tuning-fork he twanged loudly and looked up into Elouise's face and coyly asked her if she thought it in tune.

'Sounded all right to me,' she said.

'Good, good,' he murmured professionally and without warning stabbed her in the calf with his sharp pin. Elouise yelped and the doctor laughed and so did his colleagues.

'One all,' someone shouted. He opened a test-tube and wet his finger and dipped it in the powder therein.

'Taste that.' She tasted.

'It's salt.'

'And this?'

'Sugar.'

'Correct absolutely.' He put the third tube back in his case. He then opened one of the sealed envelopes and offered it to her beautiful nose.

'It smells of flowers,' she breathed.

'And this?'

'Corruption.'

'Too right it does,' he whiffed and hastily put it away. The doctor stretched out his thin pale hand and delicately lifted the hem of her short white gown. He took his camel-hair brush number six and touched her buttock with it where it flattened out on the chair.

'What does that feel like?'

'You might say the delicate touch of the wing of a newly-born moth at dusk or you might say you were tickling my arse.'

'Precisely.' She looked at him closely; it seemed that his eyes were made of plastic and that they continued into his head in a solid mass rather than that they were globes in sockets as other eyes. And yet he saw.

'Close your eyes,' he requested. 'Stretch out your arms sideways.'

Elouise did as she was asked but tensed herself against an expected tickle beneath the arm.

'Bring your index fingers together rapidly.' Elouise did. The doctor stood up, putting away his toys. He turned towards the audience.

'She has nerves of steel and all her senses in working order!' And he surprised nobody with this information. Matron bustled on to the stage.

'Kindly leave the stage,' she boomed at him. He floated away, defeated and disappointed.

'Next doctor please.' In the hush that fell in the spectators a wheezing could be heard, and the click of a gold pill-box and the next examining doctor took a dose of digitalis to stave off another heart attack. Purple-faced he fiddled with his stethoscope, his clubbed fingers having difficulty in grasping the rubber tube. He came to listen at her gently moving chest, tapped her sternum and ambled off, shaking his head. He drew no applause and little comment. Matron called the next doctor. Elouise looked out of the windows as she waited for the nurse to check a trolley of instruments. She noticed the small crowd of people drawing nearer.

'Swabs, vulsellum forceps, uterine sound, Cusco's vaginal speculum, bi-valve and duckbill specula, obstetric cream.' Elouise winced with distaste for all the metal looked cold and unfriendly. Surely her cervical smears had revealed all that was necessary about her reproductive organs? But of course, this occasion was a kind of ritual, a public showing of her amazing health. She relaxed and watched the doctor specialising in gynaecology approach. A thickset bull-necked fellow, he shuffled down the pink plastic steps and heaved himself up the step on to the stage. He scratched his arms constantly, setting his teeth together, flexing his chin against the sensations of extreme irritation and the pain of tearing skin. White flakes of epidermis and then dermis, blood-spotted, fell, floated and conspicuously hovered in the bright light. And he muttered that at least his asthma had abated, the while psoriasis ate him up. He creamed his forearms from a little tube and looked around for his instruments and his patient. Elouise looked at his inflamed arms and reminded herself that infection was not the cause of such sores. The doctor worked the lever at the side of the chair until it became a couch with Elouise reclining. He took a clean folded sheet from the bottom shelf of the trolley and cast it across her, then folded it back to cover all but that portion of her body from the navel down.

'Knees up, let them fall apart.' Under the sheet, Elouise examined her fingernails, gave a small sigh of impatience and boredom and cringed slightly as the cold metal speculum slid into her vagina. Painlessly she lay, ideas forming in her mind, stimulated by the cutting-off of visual impressions of any consequence. This was no way to live life, under a sterile sheet, with a lifeless instrument poking about inside one! There must be better ways of existing!

The doctor pressed a heavy hand down flat on Elouise's belly and peered up his speculum with a curiosity more normally reserved for medical students taking their first look at a cervix. Nothing unusual met his eye excepting the moist and living glowing health of that smooth muscle. He turned a tiny wheel that opened her womb. Waiting walls, the perfect place to begin life was all he saw. He left that place, too late for him, no business of his, there was nothing to cure. He packed his things and left it to muscly Matron to uncover Elouise, hoist the chair to an upright position.

She saw through the windows that the crowd of people outside was now at the great doors, and at that moment someone banged to be let in. A murmur of annoyed disturbance came from the doctors who already knew the diagnosis of their patient and were anxious to get all the formal examinations over with quickly, so that they could go and play golf. Once it had been decided what was to be done with the illegally healthy girl, life could go on as usual. And now there was a disturbance at the door. Someone went to open it, someone else shouted that the examinations were *in camera*, and someone else decided: 'Oh, what the hell!'

The doctors groaned aloud at the sight that met their eyes as the doors swung open. The Congenitals again! And marching on the Theatre, of all things. Oh dear!

Gibbering and murmuring, there they stood, the Congenitals delegation, the annual bid for attention and help. Swaying and twitching, wheeling and crutching, there they helplessly stood, demanding. Slobbering and jerking, moaning and hiccuping, leering and dragging, they had come once more for a subject to sacrifice to Good Luck, their only hope in life. They had heard of Elouise, and wanted her. Only the sacrifice of this perfect body could do anything for them, they had become convinced.

Elouise listened to the arguments going on at the door and began to realise what fate might be in store. She returned to her new idea, making efforts all the time not to become involved with fear. She did not know exactly what they could do to her, even if they got her; therefore she decided not to dwell on the subject. But there were drops of sweat between her eyebrows, and they shone like glass beads in the bright light. Poppy-head, the nerve specialist, noticed them and marvelled. He had thought her steadier than that, although sweating was far from abnormal under the circumstances.

At the door the Congenitals were led by a man with a head almost as big as his own thorax, the skin on his face having the appearance of severe scalding. A woman came to stand by him, her method of locomotion consisting of sideways leaps accompanied by upthrown arms and a glottal cry. Next to her came a blind man dragging a child on a wheeled trolley. The child howled constantly from ulcers caused by its own unceasing streams of urine and faeces, and a quivering patch of spinal cord that grew outside its body. A youth with a cleft palate and harelip carried an infant girl whose spine continued, joined to her flesh, down to the backs of her knees, and that ended in a naked pink tail that bent out like a hook. Behind them a woman lay twitching and foaming in the throes of a severe epileptic fit and close by knelt an emaciated youth with a cyanotic complexion and vacant eyes who clutched a hairless dwarf of uncertain age and sex. Deaf-mutes, blind, partially paralysed, deformed and mentally deficient of every kind abounded. A man looking like a lemon on toothpicks so thin his limbs, so huge his trunk, stood there and stared at Elouise, his dull eyes longing sadly for things he did not understand.

An officious doctor began to ask questions of the delegation, but Matron approached, pushed him behind her and began a formal interview.

'Why have you come?' she asked in a disapproving manner.

'We want you to give us the benefit of medical advances, comfort and money to live, not having had an answer to last year's question.' The words were spoken with little inflection as if learned by heart without understanding or hope.

'What *was* last year's question?' asked Matron impatiently.

'Why did you let us live?'

'Oh that! We told you before. It is our duty to preserve life.'

'But our lives are useless seas of pain and endurance. We are neither use nor ornament.'

'Well, everyone is sick on Pergamon, it's the law. Don't be so self-pitying.'

'But we can't earn our living, we are a neglected group.'

Cries of 'Sacrifice' began to rise from the Congenitals, although many of them had no wit to know what it was they demanded. Rights, rights!

Elouise was evolving a plan out of her ideas. The more she saw of the Congenitals, the less she wished to be given to them, whether they would kill her, make her Queen, or both. Elouise was lonely, she had always been lonely, even her mother had been too sick to communicate with properly. Elouise wanted to go and live in a place where there were other perfectly healthy beings.

She thought of the distant past of Pergamon's history, the time when everyone had perfect health through annual doses of Ananias McCallister's Elixir. Ananias McCallister, the Devil himself. His elixir had been the turning point in Pergamon's way of life, for the planet had become so full of long-living, healthy people that they had stood almost shoulder to shoulder, feeding themselves artificial protein that caused foul flatus that nevertheless their healthy bowels dealt with efficiently so that the outer atmosphere had eventually become a dense mass of floating sewer-gas, exploding mightily as meteors ran white-hot through it; the planet was even yet covered with massive circular marks like faery rings where fire had come booming down out of the sky; inconsequential dragon-coughs turning people to potash and nitrogen.

The new culture arisen out of those few remaining was disease oriented: health led to death, obviously.

Elouise's mother had told stories of other planets where people managed to live healthy lives and provide real food for themselves and keep the air clean and pure. Neither did they quarrel or take advantage of each other. Elouise sighed and closed her eyes.

'I am a throwback to better times than these,' she thought.

The Congenitals had been asked to wait outside until the examinations were officially over and a decision reached. The doctors began to confer, shuffling reports in triplicate, glancing idly, knowing that each prognosis stated 'Perfect Health'. Nurses brought in refreshments. Cocktail snacks and whisky in cut-glass tumblers were passed round, the atmosphere relaxed somewhat and epic tales of gold began. But one doctor insisted that he had not had his turn: he demanded the right to examine the patient personally, so Matron eventually allowed him the stage.

'I shall need a lighting technician,' said the doctor, an Ear,

Nose and Throat specialist. Elouise was not pleased at this inter-
ruption to her meditations. To accomplish her plan she needed to
be left alone. But there would be no use in grumbling, she had
best co-operate.

The doctor dragged behind him a wheeled trolley like a golf-
bag, and this he proceeded to fiddle with, trying to undo the
buckles as best he could, but he was hampered by a spinal stiff-
ness. Elouise thought he probably wore surgical corsets to sup-
port a slipped disc or some crumbling bone disease, for every time
he tried to bend he winced, drawing in air through rotten teeth.

'Nurse!' he blared out and the nurse drifted on to the stage,
dressed as if for an operation, masked and gowned and sexless.
Between them the doctor and nurse set out all the instruments
incongruously on the floor, and the audience chatted and drank.
Elouise watched one doctor who was so twisted with arthritis
that he had to lie on the floor every time he wished to refresh himself with whisky; to put liquid in his mouth while standing was
impossible, and although his colleagues would help him to move,
they would not feed him. One man rebuked him for drinking
alcohol but the arthritic doctor who was rapidly becoming inco-
herent, said that while it worsened his health, it was a good anal-
gesic and would shorten his life. Then, the lights were dimmed as
auxiliary nurses went round pulling close dark blinds across the
windows. The Theatre lights went very low too, and Elouise saw
the illuminated 'Exit' sign glowing at the back of the auditorium.
She had not noticed that before.

'Damn,' said the doctor on stage, unable to see anything at all.
The nurse came and helped him fix a headlamp battery, and then,
in the cone of brighter light that it shed, he looked closely at
Elouise.

'Open your mouth.' She opened her mouth only to find it
clamped open with a Doyen's gag.

'Say "ah".'

'Aaaaaaaagggggghhhhh!' Saliva dribbled down her chin and the nurse leapt forward to dab daintily with a bit of surgical gauze. The stuff was not very absorbent, and was scratchy to her skin. The doctor peered and poked around down Elouise's throat, and then, using a nasal speculum he performed a detailed anterior rhinoscopy.

'You've got a bogy up your nose,' he announced.

'Aaaaggghhh!' He began chanting a quiet liturgy which the nurse took down in shorthand on the areas of white starched linen and cotton available to him or her.

'No rhinitis, no sinusitis, no epistaxis, no polypi, no pharyngitis, no tonsilitis, no adenoidal hypertrophy.' He stopped for a moment, hand to forehead. Then he picked up Eve's tonsil snare in one hand and Gottstein's adenoid curette in the other and threw them on the floor, turned stiffly around, bowed one inch to the audience and left the stage. The nurse unscrewed the clamp from Elouise's mouth and handed her a bunch of gauze and scraped all the instruments into a heap and threw them into the wheeled bag. As the nurse left, he or she turned to sneer at the patient from under the mask.

'Such beautiful instruments would be disused museum pieces if we were all like you.' The whisper was bitter, the voice snagged up on negative emotion. Elouise rubbed her cheek where the clamp had bitten, blew her nose on the surgical gauze, and cleared her throat. She could now continue with her inner idea. Time was running short.

She relaxed every muscle, closed her eyes, mouth, ears. She began to say silently her newly invented formula.

'I want to be free. I want to go where there are others like me.' She repeated it slowly and rhythmically, this meaningful mantra, unperturbed by the sounds that came to her through her own wall of silence.

'Psychosomatic appeasement on a very high level,' and much laughter.

'Well, stranger things have happened.'

'Their luck might really change if they got her...' A cell in Elouise's head echoed with thoughts of what might happen if she was given. Torn limb from limb and eaten. Burnt alive. Put out for wild dogs. Left to starve on a guarded mountain. Made Queen. Put to breeding.

These thoughts disturbed her much and then she recalled her mother saying: 'Don't let them get you down. Never fear a thing.' But her mother had not known a situation such as this, it was not the same, this was desperate, urgent, terrible. Yes, the plan must go through, somehow.

She got on with her idea, acquainting herself intimately with everything happening in her body at that time. It was very noisy, what with thundering and rushing and squeaking and drumming, so that she hardly heard the fresh banging at the door and the sounds of impatience from the doctors. A delegation of Starving had arrived, begging for money and food. Elouise had seen the Starving before; two large eyes, sometimes minus lenses, great belly with umbilical hernia from inward pressure of gas, sticks of arms and legs, ulcerated skin, black patched and greyly flaking, suppurating slowly. There were many Starving and they lived in the dustbowls, scratching and whimpering day and night. The doctors and the normal sick gave charity quite often, but sometimes delegations came for more.

Elouise cut off her compassion, heard the doctors writing cheques and orders for food. If Ananias McCallister had been alive to see this scene...

In the forecourt the Congenitals and the Starving were mixing with each other, exchanging grief for grief, displaying their twisted and unfed children to one another, each father vying to be most deserving of sympathy for how little he could do to help his family. A wall was chosen for the banging of heads, and those that could not find a space used the floor. Those that could not bend down rent their hair, and wailing and whimpering and beating of the air and breasts began at first chaotically and then in rhythm. Feeling was running high. Even with charity cheques, what kind of a life was it? The question went up in the foetid air of the forecourt, rising and falling, passed about, reiterated. The doctors would have worried at the atmosphere out there had it been caused by any other group of people. But need they worry at enfeebled threats of people whose talents lay in basketwork and knitting, the making of felt pictures and the reading of Braille? Who among them could cast steel into sword, or spin a perfect gun-barrel? Which of them could lift a sword, or aim straight?

Secure, the doctors drank their whisky, argued lightly whether Elouise should be given to sacrifice or not, and aired their personal theories about what should happen to her otherwise.

Elouise heard nothing of what they said. She appeared to be asleep.

She was encapsulated, but capable of saying 'I'.

The rays of the sun lit up the scene in the forecourt, making it seem as if a Spring Festival were in full swing. A doctor predicted that no good would ensue from the happenings that day and a big man with red wattles said, 'She's not my type at all.'

Enclosed in the cavern of her own immaculate body, Elouise began to examine the walls. In a corridor of ridges there were waving plants, cilia reaching and retracting, snatching at the short white gown, trying to thrust her out. They banged at her knees.

'Back! Turn back! Foreign body!' they screeched at her, but she with her newfound will swept on, and the floor heaved but still she slid in the slime toward a division in the corridor. The left-hand fork would do fine, she decided. On and on. Into smaller passages she made her way and then stopped and fumbled in her handbag. Oh! Handbags! What a pest they were, one could never find anything. Paper and bottles and clips and mirrors and letters and make-up and manicure sets. She selected a nail file and a powder compact. She had never used the powder, perhaps it had been her mother's. Then, like many another freedom fighter before her she began her campaign by writing on the walls. With her nail file she scratched large the words: 'I want to be free. I want to go where there are others like me.'

Mucus bubbled up around her feet, blood ran down the walls, she opened the powder compact and scattered the contents about her in the current of air which blew first one way and then the other. The walls closed in on her, there was a rush of wind echoing, and a mighty explosion.

The doctors had finished the whisky, had come to a provisional decision about the patient. A doctor handed some papers to Matron who prepared to announce.

Suddenly Elouise coughed a great racking, whooping, echoing cough. A triumphal arch of sputum and blood leapt from between her parted lips followed by a cloud of what might be steam. She coughed again, clutching her throat and a dribble of blood marred her chin. Sweat poured from her pallid skin and she trembled as if in a fever.

There was a short and profound silence before an immense uproar broke out in the auditorium with clattering and screaming and the breaking of glass and the scraping of feet. A colostomy bag burst on to the pink plastic floor and was ground and spread by a gouty foot. The great doors opened and in swept a crowd of Starving and Congenitals. They saw the blood on the short white gown and became enraged, Starving and Congenital alike in accord, breaking and scrambling, beating and flailing with their skin and bone. Crutches made fine skull-breakers, glass eyes beneath feet broke legs and hips, calipers broke calcified teeth and a hearing aid choked effectively and doubtless sonorously one who would soon have died from cirrhosis of the liver.

Elouise became suddenly panic-stricken; weakened for the first time by physical ailment, her mentality had received a shock. And it would seem that her self-induced sickness had produced more than she had bargained for. How had she judged wrong? The urge to cough was frightful but with all her strength she screamed out for someone to release the force-field on her chair. Poppy-head, the nerve specialist, came wavering forward and threw the vital switch and she stood up to run but he stood grinning down at her, grotesquely pretty and obviously angered.

'You betrayed yourself!' he whinnied, lower teeth displayed in resentment.

'I don't know what you mean! I'm in mortal danger, can't you see?'

'But listen...' She did not listen, saw only his face come near in earnest discourse; brought up her foot with force to his groin which made it seem that he fell beneath a blade, harvested along-with the corn. She ran breathless and retching across the stage and found herself in a small store-room at the end of a corridor. Too late she saw that she should have made for the 'Exit' door. The shelves were stacked with rows of drugs and chemicals and cylinders and wads; she sorted blindly through them, shutting her ears to herself. Big action was what was called for, some sweeping, cleansing final act! Potassium cyanide capsules.

Oh, what a beautiful blue jar, what a fine decoration of skull and cross-bones executed in gold leaf. She clutched the heavy jar as if it were her baby and left the store-room and soon found the steps she hoped for; those that led up to the gantry in the flies. Up there she had a fine view of both stage and audience. The chaos and mess and smell were utterly disgusting.

She shook out the little glass bubbles so that they fell cracking on to the floor beneath, dropped the jar and ran as fast as her failing breath would allow, gown clutched over nose and mouth until she finally found her way outside into the pure fresh air, having banged the door shut, close, behind her. The last sounds she heard from that place were screams of mass-death and an ac-cusation against herself that she was in league with Ananias McCallister.

'Superstition, corruption, plotters,' she countered raspingly.

How different the evening from the morning. The day had started calm and golden; the evening descended triumphant and scarlet.

She passed the barren, gravelly land and came to open fields where she lay down to rest; all her body was in pain and distress, every sensation of malfunctioning totally new so that much harder to bear. She was listening to her own confused thoughts of how perhaps she had done her job too well, scored the message too deep, and wondering what to do next and where to go; thinking that to rescue her mother and hide away would be futile. Her mother would die soon anyway, and had she not bidden for freedom? Someone approached and flopped down on the grass beside her, startling her into terror and convulsions of coughing. It was Poppy-head, the nerve specialist.

'But you were in the...'

'No, I was not. I rose from your attack and left the place immediately. I thought you might do something horrible. I foresaw it.' She was too fatigued to move, lay back instead weeping and pleading, explaining herself pitifully.

He ignored what she was saying and spoke over her.

'You realise of course that you would have come to no harm if you had remained calm and waited?'

'No, no, they would have killed me.'

'Not at all. We had decided that you could act as a sort of living fetish for them, provided that they did you no harm. That way they would have been satisfied, you would have been accounted for. We decided that it was not your fault for being so damnably healthy, but your mother's.'

The dew was falling, making everything damp and chill.

'What shall I do now? I am so lonely, there is no place for me.'

'I suppose you feel like a special case,' said Poppy-head, rising from the ground, fingering his damp backside dubiously. Perhaps he would develop piles.

'But I am, I am, I'm different...' He turned away silently,

making it plain he thought that no excuse for what she had shown herself capable of; self-betrayal, mass murder.

'But they were so disgusting,' she murmured, knowing that whatever she said had become irrelevant.

She slept that night on the cold ground, disturbed by coughing and vomiting and dreams that she could not recall when she opened her eyes on the dawn. Her body was racked with sensations that she guessed to be pneumonia. She pressed her hot forehead into the cool herbs and then passed time watching a poppy unfold in the rising sun. She did not pick it.

'I only wanted to be free. I never wanted to hurt anyone.' Her words were blown away on the airs of Pergamon.

The Snake
who had Read Chomsky

They spent almost all their non-official working time, and their spare time, in that part of the lab which had been requisitioned for them. Although it was not large, it sufficed: to unravel nucleic acid chains does not require a dance-hall plus arcades. They were very satisfied with the robot assistance that Selly had allowed them, plus computer time, sub-electron microscope, chemical analyser, and all the animals they needed.

'Yes, certainly Marvene and Janos, if you wish to research into some aspects of the genetic part of animal behaviour then I shall be pleased to encourage you, just so long as your work here for me does not suffer of course.' Their work had not suffered, they saw to that. Their private work was not exactly what they stated, but it was near enough to deceive an observer who would be scrupulous and not snoop extensively. There was a little more to it than the behaviour of the cat but even to themselves they maintained a neutral attitude to their information, knowing only what they hoped.

There were mice being used, and a boa constrictor called Lupus the Loop who had a sole right to mice as food, and who possibly resented the fact that Marvene used a large proportion of them for her work instead of feeding them to him.

'Getting the information to link itself to all the cell types is the final key,' said Janos, taking a look at some mice who were hibernating in a lowered temperature even though they were a non-hibernating variety. 'These mice are hibernating but they will never shed their skin.' Janos very much wanted to have a coup with this research. He stood to be what he wanted for the rest of his life if all went well. Marvene glanced at him with concealed contempt.

'The skin-shedding isn't important at this stage, surely? If we stick to the line we are on we shall have the final tests ready in weeks,' she told him evenly and not without effort. Working in such close confines with one person for so long was not good for personal regard, but worse, it almost inclined one to show that bad feeling. She was taking extra pains with her good manners. She too wanted to be rewarded by the world for this work and she had no intention of allowing Janos to take the whole accolade, as she rightly suspected he would like to do. They had not discussed this aspect of the project, it would have been quite rude to do so, but instead maintained an implicit agreement that like all scientists they would share honours. It was certain that they had both been equally dedicated and both worked hard and with concentration. Not a moment was wasted in idle chatter. They had sufficient incentive not to waste their opportunity for they could also be revenged upon Selly, whom they hated. That greasy, plump, celibate person was not to be allowed to share any reflected glory from their work. He had irritated and disgusted them for so long with his unaesthetic presence, and they meant to be revenged upon him. It was worth the risk of discovery, once they had decided, the plan was irresistible. When they thought of this they would laugh together, but when they thought of their separate plans, they laughed apart, and silently.

Selly rarely visited them in their area, he went home at night to who knew what, alone in his bachelor apartment. Sour as old socks, Selly, white as suet but softer, secretive and full of bile. But very clever, and this they respected. It was one of the reasons they were at this lab, Selly's notorious cleverness. They had hoped to learn from him and in many ways they had. He was already near the top of the social list, even though he socialised so little. He was known for being something of a recluse, and for his genius and originality in demonstrating his ideas.

Selly had wished to demonstrate that light-obedient hormones were involved in flight patterns in birds, and he had caused a skylark to dive into the depths of illuminated water, singing. The audience had considered this very amusing. What had made it unpleasant was the way Selly laughed at the sight of the little creature trying to warble until it was drowned in watery light.

He had done some useful things also, in the business of providing food for the world's surplus people. He had produced a runner bean which was fifty per cent first-class animal protein. These could be fed on petroleum by-products, having the ability to make the chemical changes within their own metabolism, and also the useful ability to cleanse the soil by exuding a solvent which was biodegradable. It was true, Selly was no slouch in his work. As for Marvene and Janos's part in Selly's work, they were assisting him in breeding a two-kilo mouse which would at first be used in factory soupmeat and, after sufficient publicity, as a roast. So far the creatures had died before slaughtering could take place, so there was still work to do on strengthening the heart muscles of these little giants. These animals were fed on processed petroleum by-products. There was a vast store of fossil fuels since the melting of the polar ice caps had made it available. The lab in which they worked was part of a redundant atomic power station, ideal because of its isolation coupled with easy access by underground train to the living complexes. They took five minutes only to return to the other world. In one of the larger central areas of the building they had constructed a reproduction of a typical deserted domestic settlement of the lower classes. The actual work of course had been done by a work-gang from the lower classes. If such settlements could be shown to be suitable for breeding mice then some of them could be used, for there were many such ghost towns since the suicide epidemics. There was no question of experimenting with a real one, they were all too far away from civilisation. Their main problem had been getting the right light and darkness periods, because even though there was so little difference between them since the canopy came over the ancient skies, the animals all had residual circadian rhythms. All the upper-class human beings had artificial moonlight and sunlight in regulated phases because it had been shown to have an important psychological effect on brain chemistry, but the lower classes, for whom such things did not matter, lived in a dim limbo, monotonous and dreary.

As a companion work on food they were breeding a potato containing every known nutritional element in correct proportion for maintaining human life. This was proving harder than anticipated, because some vitamins destroyed others when existing in the same plant. But they would succeed, with Selly's guidance. It was going to make the lower-class menu very dull but that did not matter. Selly could have existed on such fodder for he was a very poor aesthete in the matter of food as in other things. This disgusted them. Selly did not enjoy life, he enjoyed ideas about life. He once confided in a rare moment of intimacy: 'There is a life of the mind which I have hardly touched upon yet.' They could have expanded on that comment but chose not. There was a sure way to get on with Selly and that was to flatter him. He accepted all compliments unquestioningly. In some ways, Selly was downright immature, a state not at all to be admired. She did not think him fit to live in the wonderful architectural fantasy of their upper-class settlement, he was an eyesore. They all had very small apartments, but it was one of the best specialist settlements in existence. The upper classes needed the stimulus of interesting surroundings, and interest had been taken well towards the limits both visually and kinetically. Their settlement was famous for its dissolving architecture; at any moment a balcony might disappear and drop people to their deaths. This did not happen so often that it was monotonous, but often enough to make living there exciting. In historical times, those people living on fault lines must have been exhilarated in much the same way, Marvene reflected. How ghastly it must be to live in the utilitarian warrens of the lower classes! Would society never find a humane way of ridding itself of all those surplus people left over since human labour had become almost redundant? Marvene hoped so profoundly, they were an anchor to a civilisation which needed to sail ahead.

If Selly were successful even with the potatoes, he would become a very high-ranking upper-class person. They thought him to be a totally unsuitable candidate for this because of his vulgarity. But whatever they thought, it was necessary to apply the art of flattery. He was always susceptible.

'Selly, I feel constrained to voice my admiration for your working method today. You are so stylish in your approach to what must feel like mundane tasks to one so advanced as yourself. I wish very much to cultivate your self-control.' Marvene smiled sweetly at him through her diamante-effect contact lenses. The twinkling was a stunning effect, and hid real feeling. Selly was not susceptible to female charm but in his genetic make-up somewhere there must surely have been a response to beauty, for once, just once, he had reached out to touch Marvene's hair, which had been trained to move constantly in shining coils, always changing its shape like a mass of slowly dancing snakes. Strictly speaking she was reaching above her present level of society with such styles, but sometimes beauty was forgiven social errors. Because she made such a beautiful model she had managed to get it done free but she had been obliged to have all the actichips inserted in her skull with only local anaesthetic...

'Thank you Marvene. I'm glad you appreciate the difference between mere routine work well done, and a truly aesthetic approach to the mundane. I may be able to give you some instruction on that.'

'Selly, I would be so grateful if you could. If I could only emulate you...'

'Marvene, it is all inner work. One has to control the entire self in order to control properly things like grace and care.' He didn't really have grace, she thought, he was just lethargic.

'If you talk to yourself Marvene, daily, and draw all your energies in towards your working self every morning, you will be able to bring more presence to your work.' This wholly patronising speech was typical and it made her angry. She already did this rather commonplace exercise every morning. She had presence, and style, and knew it, and she practised attitudes ready for the day when she meant continually to grace the highest levels of society. When Marvene had completed her research she would not only have put horrible Selly down, but have a weapon which could forever quell invaders, preventing war, and could possibly be used to keep the lower classes permanently occupied, if not eliminated. She would be remembered.

They already had the means of fixing Selly, and of testing out their work at the same time, but for mass use they needed a fool-proof method of dissemination which would disperse itself in a population per body-weight and type equally everywhere. If they could only have a few humans to experiment upon the job would by now have been done, but there was still too much opposition to human experimentation to make it popular, and it was certainly illegal to use human beings without their recorded consent, and this applied even to the lower classes, a very atavistic area of the law. With this work they hoped to justify human experimentation and thus earn the gratitude of scientists everywhere whose work was held up because of suitable material.

Selly was an ideal subject, being so predictable and stable in his habits, and in having no close friends. Selly could not be bothered with friends. He occasionally arranged some social life for himself of course, buying a dinner party for himself in some exotic building, but these occasions were only meant to keep his name in circulation, and to impress the influential. It was always necessary to keep in favour in order to get financial patronage. He was ideal, because any noticeable effects must be observed only by themselves until such time as they wished it otherwise.

'You know, Marvene,' said Janos, showing his small and boringly ordinary teeth in a slow smile of what in a stronger personality would have been consummate awfulness, 'I have to admire Selly for his independence of other people, especially women.'

'And what's so good about that?' she demanded icily, fire flashing off her eyeballs. 'I don't see where the style is in being by yourself. There's nobody to appreciate a lone person. One needs other opinions.'

Janos chose to overlook her anger, regarding it as one might a bit of flatus. 'If you're good enough and know it then nobody is going to think better of you than yourself,' he replied. He had that relentless argumentative tone in his voice which she had once found very attractive, believing it to be self-assurance. It was certain that nobody was going to think better of Marvene and Janos than themselves. Marvene still required that the whole of society admire her, as soon as possible. So did Janos of course, he was indulging in conceit with his words. He did not know it but he had managed without her good opinion for years.

'I have to disagree. An isolated opinion is not valid especially when the subject can not see the self from outside, which is a rare achievement. How can you ever really know what impression you are making?'

'I have practised projecting myself, metaphorically speaking, and using my imagination to know what impression I am making. Doesn't everyone do that, Marvene?'

'Of course, but it is a matter of degree and skill. It will still be a heavily subjective result.' He did not like that idea, clearly.

'If you persist in making destructive statements against myself I shall be obliged to be rude to you.' This formal warning was rather extreme so she knew she had gone too far. He didn't have good style, and tended to think that all negative statements reflected upon himself. He must be guilty about something, she thought.

'I apologise. I had not meant the statement to be destructive, merely in opposition.' He gave her a conciliatory nod, the kind meant to conceal the atmosphere, but his gestures always had a patronising tone which ruined the effect. She must find stylish ways of dealing with him, and was indeed working upon that.

Another problem was the question of reversibility in the chromosome interference. Perhaps the answer lay where she thought it did, in electronic control, but that posed problems for the masses. Not difficult for one subject, and things would go a stage at a time. She was determined not to rush. After a while, Janos seemed to have recovered from their little contretemps for he suddenly suggested that they buy a dinner party for themselves for the following night, and he suggested that with luck it might be possible to get somewhere in a fashionable building, perhaps the Cairns or the Herberg suite? Here was proof that he required the admiration of a crowd, but she let it pass and instead complimented him on his wonderful idea. They set about compiling a guest list, an unusual thing for them to do during working hours. They already had a few well-thought-of people on their social list, and several who might demean themselves for an evening. All their acquaintances were bio-engineers, it was rare to meet anyone outside one's own discipline, there was not enough time. This was a price which all talented people had to pay, but the rewards were greater than the penalties of course. They had been awarded knowledge implants as well as memory reinforcement grafts in their youth which enhanced their natural brilliance and capacity for application. Everyone preferred a hard life to the appalling possibility of being in the lower classes who had little in their lives except prescribed entertainment. They had very little spare time so she should feel privileged that he proposed using some of his time with her, but as it was not done to give a party without a member of the opposite sex as co-host, she did not make too much of the situation. She liked playing hostess and knew herself excellent at the task. When the overworked upper classes relaxed they tried always to make the occasion rare without always being monotonously outrageous. So what theme had he thought of?

'Animals. Fancy dress.' She smiled with glittering delight, her hair seeming to express a rise in her spirits. But it would be impossible for everyone to obtain costume in time for the following night. He looked annoyed and downcast, he did not want to postpone the occasion.

'Why not have animals but not costume – ask everyone to mime?' After a few tense moments his face showed reluctant pleasure. Fun, but not too spectacular. They must never be accused of self-aggrandizement. They got out all the invitations and replies of acceptance and ordered the Herberg suite to be done out to have the appearance of a twentieth-century zoological gardens at a time when animals had not been so rare. The food would be in feeding trays and the drink in gravity feeders.

They were especially pleased to have Selly's acceptance. To have Selly behaving like an animal in public at their expense would afford them some glee. What animal would he mime? They were sure they could guess. In order to have plenty of energy for the party they retired early and did not return later for more work.

The lab was at rest, and Lupus the Loop lay coiled on his simulated branch in the simulated moonlight, smiling to himself, for had he not been eavesdropping on them every night for months?

The party was a great success. Within the general benevolent atmosphere there were memorable moments. The sight of two well-known agriculturalists, who had made their name as the team to have caused real animal fur to grow on sheets of plastic, behaving like a couple of Nubian goats was worth remembering. It seemed that they could cheerfully mime mating for hours without being vulgar and very convincingly in spite of their very creative human appearance. They were both quite hairless and had gold eyeballs and teeth and nails but their acting was so convincing that few had to ask what they were.

Janos made a wonderful mouse. He nibbled his way through his food, twitching delightfully some imaginary whiskers. His very ordinary appearance seemed to fit the mouse image. He had never indulged in even so much as a tattoo to decorate his person, just like the lower classes who were obliged by law to wear uniform and were prohibited from any form of distinguishing mark. Janos, the little grey mouse, nibbling away at fame with determination. And Selly, the great scientist, being what she had hoped he would be: a cat. He rubbed round people's legs in a feline manner, getting titbits dropped for him, and being stroked and fondled although someone made the joke of treating him like a lab cat, miming the drilling of holes into the skull. He went so far as to jump on to someone's lap and attempt to curl up, his great bulk hanging down on all sides, making the catness of cat seem very droll indeed. Fat, satisfied, smug, comfort-loving, lethargic Selly. It suited him. He could make a purring noise and wash his face with the back of his wrist, where his watch lay embedded in his wristbone. This instrument gave not only astronomical information, longitude and latitude, time and date but the state of his brainwaves, blood sugar and nor-adrenalin. Few people still had these things embedded for they had proved to be painful to many people in later years. Marvene stroked Selly cat and told him what a lovely pussy he was.

'This is a lovely party Marvene. I shall remember this for a long time,' purred the monster feline.

'And I also,' said the man beneath Selly in a breathy manner. 'This is a wonderful idea, I shall tell everyone about this.' Marvene glowed with pleasure then, thinking that it had been worth the trouble if they were to be favourably talked about. Even the most brilliant upper-class person did not get funds if they were not in circulation.

Marvene felt that she should do a little more about acting a snake. She began to hynotise a female frog who had hopped over to her and sat crouched at her feet blowing a pouch and staring vacantly. Marvene slowly wound herself around the creature who put its hands over its eyes, as frogs in danger will, a clever touch. Marvene's extreme yoga lessons had kept her supple enough to coil backwards around another human being and to mime squeezing the life out of the frog, the proportion of the creatures not detracting from their dual performance. Everyone seemed suitably amused.

A rhinoceros, more usually an invertebrate engineer, came over to congratulate her.

'You have a gift as an actress as well as a scientist,' he grunted, swinging his invisible horn about on a great head, peering at little eyes full of stupid malevolence which was really a gaze of intellectual penetration. She liked the rhino-man, she was dazzled by his achievements and creations. His most famous work was the culturing of a hybrid toxicaria which could be absorbed in spore form through human skin, and when mature grow to twenty feet long with the ability to bore through bone, disposing rather definitely of any enemy unlucky enough to pick up its invisible spores. He had also of course developed an immunity for the aggressor. And this was not all he had done to improve the world. He had written whole series of papers on parasites of the universe, and presented one of the most controversial theories of the millennium. He was an authority on evolution, and had shown, conclusively for many, that Homo sapiens far from being the highest product of a chain of events was intended to be the lowest in another chain of events, but when the Sol system had been cut off in a crucial period in its development in order to quarantine it, that destiny had not been fulfilled. The Aldebaran Apple People had not wanted parasites, and indeed, not everyone on Earth relished the idea that humanity's true end was as a kind of maggot, burrowing through giant fruit.

The party was made complete with a tragic ending. A serious

accident or fatality always lent interest to the story of a party. For some, the main game of an evening was to walk home, the buildings being more active at night. There was a far higher risk of a step collapsing beneath the foot or a balcony disappearing leaving a person teetering on the edge of death with no choice but to jump; there was no rescue system, that would have taken the element of chance right out of the game. A few people did not care for this entertainment but they became impossible to socialise with, cowardice being so disgusting, and they were often relegated to live in the safe lower-class architecture. So a courageous woman who had mimed a dove all evening plummetted to her death on the deep glass floor below, showing that her miming did not extend to real flight. Exhilarated, Marvene and Janos walked home in amicable silence. Next day, everything was back to normal and both Selly's work and their own proceeded steadily.

They had made excellent progress, and Marvene knew that it was her insight which had made possible the step in personally controlling the subject. Selly needed a few more 'doses' to give them conclusive proof. But it was to be admitted that they had taken this line from original ideas of Selly's. He had connections with espionage, and had thought that if a human being could be made temporarily to behave in all respects including instinctive behaviour as an alien, there would be no chance of discovery when spying in other star systems. This of course applied only to those aliens whose outward physiology closely resembled the human. There were several important 'human' cultures having totally different metabolism to Homo sapiens and who behaved differently in many respects. For example, the Wilkins Planet race, who were of shining intelligence and naturally extremely advanced (more than humanity in some things) but who loped around at high speed on all fours and who had a mating season once every four of their years. He had been held up by lack of subjects, because although he had applied for volunteers, he did not trust the authorities to keep secret his research if he explained exactly why he required people, and this was requisite. But Marvene and Janos were ahead of Selly. Everything had depended upon what Selly had not quite seen, which was B/B serotonin pathways through the sub-electronic RNA polymerase. They had the potion which had made Bottom the Weaver behave like an ass, though they had never heard of him. Selly was to become the cat which he had so obligingly played at the party. She had given him a gift of sweets containing more necessary doses, and had the minute control constructed which she could activate whenever she cared to do so. She had come up with all these ideas while talking to Lupus the Loop. She often wandered in there to have a chat with him, it was an aid to projecting one's thoughts. This was her secret, the other two would have thought her slightly deranged but she trusted her instincts, when controlled with careful thought. Lupus the Loop seemed to tell her things which she needed to know.

'Tell me, Lupus, have you any idea how I can control the newly altered instincts of Selly so that he will not always behave under the new influence?' she had asked the great snake as he lay coiled and smugly full of food.

'It's perfectly simple,' the snake had seemed to say. 'You will construct a monitor which you will keep in your possession, transmitting impulses which will inhibit or release the metabolic pathways you have interfered with.' And it had been that simple in essence although difficult to effect. An extremely sophisticated form of radio control. Beautiful! She had hugged him in thanks, knowing of course that the idea had come from her own mind. Snakes do not have minds. But even plants sometimes spoke to Marvene, when she was alone with them. She had discovered as a child that you can talk to anything and get a reply, and learned later about the projection of the mind, and had then kept it all secret for such things were despised by intelligent persons.

Janos was straightening his papers which were all handwritten, which was very unusual. He kept them in an insulated box for safety but there was only ever one copy. Marvene was observing the mice. They were reprogrammed as dogs, and as she watched, one little male cocked its leg up and put a marker on an upright post. Another one was burying a fragment of bone and two of the females were playing together in an un-mouselike manner. Most amusing!

She supposed that Janos's ideas had an ecological beauty about them for if he succeeded in ridding the world of excess people, and making animals able to do the few tasks left requiring human labour then they could be cannibalised, whereas human beings could not, at least aesthetically.

That evening when they arrived for their session, Selly was in their part of the lab. They detested his intrusion but could say nothing.

'I came to find out why your mice were so noisy,' he explained, grinning. He was obviously embarrassed. He offered them a conciliatory smoke which they accepted, even though they were his last, but he said he had a new package. They smoked together in silence, then Selly said he was going, and did so. Janos immediately checked his papers but nothing seemed to have been touched. Was Selly snooping? There was no evidence. Marvene decided that she felt tired and left early, and soon after that Janos wandered into the snake house. The great constrictor was coiled rather torpidly except for his eyes which seemed to follow every movement. Janos did not like taking samples from this beast, he was secretly afraid of it but would have died rather than admit as much. He sprayed the skin thoroughly with a penetrating local anaesthetic and took a syringeful of spinal fluid from behind the head. His hands shook as he did so and he imagined that the snake knew he was frightened.

'There you are, Lupus the Loop, that didn't bother you did it?' he cooed insincerely. The snake ignored this transparent mollification. It was a very large specimen which had been reared in Nature, having all the instincts and qualities of the wild creature, which lab specimens did not show so strongly after a few generations. Someday Janos would like to visit Nature, that large zoological gardens which had once been called Australia. The snake moved, sliding like oil along the branch towards him. He watched spellbound, noticing how it could move without disturbing its surroundings. What intensity. What grace. Collecting himself he suddenly ran, closing the door securely. How primitive those creatures were, how far removed from himself. Shuddering he thrust the samples away and then suddenly noticed that Selly was standing watching him, and he almost collapsed with fright. Selly was holding a mouse, stroking it although he was no animal-lover. The unmoving moonlight illuminated the plump face making a mirror image of artificial Selene herself, smiling full at the trembling Janos who was in no social position to lose his temper and managed not to do so.

'I forgot something, I returned for a moment,' said Selly. 'I'm sorry if I startled you.'

'That's quite all right, I respect your attention to detail, you know that.' Selly replaced the mouse in the vivarium where it had been trying to build a bridge from the little island upon which it had been placed, to a happy land at the edge of the world where nuts and other choice scraps tempted. Together they watched the mouse in its occupation without comment. Selly nodded in benevolent approval, absentmindedly scratching his ear and shaking his head. Janos was very offended at this utterly disgusting behaviour until he realised with a thrill that Selly was behaving like a cat. Of course, the nasty man sometimes scratched himself anyway. He looked for the control which Marvene had been constructing and it had gone. Had she finished it, had she gone ahead without him? How long had she been secretly experimenting with Selly without his knowledge? Janos looked at Selly looking at the mouse. The fellow was drooling.

Shaking with fury he took his leave and went to find Marvene. She was there, outside the lab, and had been observing both of them through the glass door. She told him that she was looking for him, that she had a surprise for him. Confused, he told her that he thought he knew what it was.

'But watch this,' she said, waving the tiny box between a thumb and finger. She indicated Selly. They were fascinated to observe Selly slowly take off all his clothes and prowl round slowly, and then fat though he was, crouch down on his haunches and with much puffing and heaving somehow manage to get his leg up around the back of his neck where it stuck up pointing at the ceiling, his foot extended like that of a dancer. He slowly reached forward with tongue extended and made a bold attempt to wash his own genitals, pausing to nibble at something bothering him on his thigh. Janos thought: I shall remember this moment all my life. It is one of the great moments of science that we are privileged to witness.

They were all invited to another party, and this was very exciting, the host being the renowned Roald, who had made breakthroughs in bringing back seals to land and breeding them as household pets. Miniature seals were a favourite in many homes, lolling around on sofas and balancing things on their noses. To have reversed evolution in this way was a considerable feat and might lead to a further breed of useful seal. Selly wobbled with anticipation.

'It is to be a swimming party. What a sense of humour the man has!' Janos laughed aloud, a thing he seldom did, usually expressing amusement with breathy exhalations. He was delighted because he swam very well indeed and would be able to exhibit this talent. Marvene was less happy because she had never swum well and had no confidence in water. The pool contained dolphins and she disliked them, fearing that they might bite and imagining that they could read her mind. She knew that they did not bite but still the fear was there, secreted behind her immaculate eyes.

'I may go in aquatic costume,' Janos said, 'if costume is allowed.' Marvene dreaded that there would only be seafood which she could not bear.

'I hope they have seafood,' said Selly. 'If there's one thing I like it is a nice bit of fish.' But the main thing to be glad about was that they were privileged to be visiting Roald, for he had a very high position, and following so soon on their own party they could make a continued good impression. Each would have preferred to have a reputation alone, but together was better than nothing.

Work continued without further discussion, and Janos locked away all his notes when he was done, and hid the key.

The party was going well when they arrived and they were well received and introduced to important people. They were feeling confident of themselves and Marvene had resigned herself to not making much of a showing in the water and had draped herself at the edge of the pool, bravely throwing her supper to the dolphin, which did seem to be reading her mind because it always leapt a split second before she threw a morsel. Janos was posing nearby eating prawns and clams with evident enjoyment. He planned to dive into the pool when there were not many swimming, and execute a graceful water dance. If he had not been a scientist he could have been a great water athlete. Selly was chatting easily with Roald himself, and several important people stood near them waiting to have a word with the great man. Suddenly, Marvene saw her chance. If Selly misbehaved here he would be forever out of countenance. She activated his new behaviour.

Selly suddenly crouched on the floor on his haunches and got himself into a complicated position whereby he could lick the backs of his own thighs. The effect was immediate then – good! Had he done that at their animal mime party he would have received applause, but one *never* repeated a performance or did anything out of tune with the prescribed atmosphere. Roald stared unbelieving at this awful display, seeming at a loss, and other important people tried to ignore Selly, everyone suffering from acute embarrassment. Janos was horrified.

Why had she done this here? Did she not realise that it would bring bad attention to all three of them? What lack of tact! He decided to try to attract attention away from the scene, and ran up the steps to the diving-board, sparing a look of hatred for Marvene who was actually displaying her glee at Selly's display. He prepared to dive, calming himself for an especially elegant performance.

Selly, while engaged in his behaviour which gripped him at first without his realising that he was doing anything at all unusual, noticed his wrist monitor because of his tortured position bringing it right in front of his eyes. His brainwave readings and noradrenalin were abnormal. They would be normal for a cat though, and of course, all manner of other realisations came with this knowledge, and these made him snarl and begin a howling growl which made the blood run chill. He could take his revenge immediately without a show of power, without explanation. He would bring them both down, if he was to be ruined, then it would not happen in solitude. It must be Janos who had done this thing to him of course, he believed, for he had read Janos's notes fairly extensively in his spying. But his discoveries had enabled him to do something very similar to Janos. He had not believed that they would dare attempt this on him, but he had been waiting his chance to experiment with Janos.

His hands felt very clumsy because his thumb did not want to oppose itself and his claws wanted to retract in a most uncomfortable way, because he did not have claws. With a triumph of control considering that everyone was staring at him as if he had gone mad he activated a control directed at Janos.

Janos was poised for action. He looked down to judge the height and was overcome with waves of prickling terror at the sight of the water. Water! He had come the wrong way. He turned to retreat, wobbling wildly between diving skills which he knew he had, and a total unfamiliarity with water that belongs to mice. He clutched himself with his little front paws, balancing on his hind legs by an act of will, and people turned to see a man hesitating to dive because of lack of nerve. He was creating a totally unfavourable diversion, but his rodent instincts made him tremble and stay. There was derisive laughter from one or two impolite guests and Roald glared at them, then at Janos. This spurred him to action and he fell into the water with a disgraceful splash, squeaking with fear which he could not master. He floundered around trying to swim but a lab mouse had no inkling of such motion. He panicked. Marvene collected herself and without thinking slid into the water to rescue him. She swam well. Janos had activated her snake instincts thus ensuring her increased confidence in water, although it was certainly still not her favourite element. The audience were impressed with Marvene in spite of themselves, and she was obscurely aware that she had done something amazing and unaccustomed. While the disgraced Janos was being taken away to dress and the impossible Selly escorted to another room to hide himself, she enjoyed a certain amount of qualified glory. It was while she was experiencing a strange desire to slither away underneath a piece of furniture that she guessed what was happening to her. Her jaws drew open with reptilian fury. There was something so obviously wrong with her now that people left her alone. The three of them were in disgrace, it was demonstrated that they were no longer desirable. Marvene knew then that all the work would come to an end. It would be impossible to find another good place in upper-class society. She burned with hatred of her two colleagues. They had stolen the work and used it against her! The very thought filled her with the will to kill them both. She felt that she could strangle them slowly while telling them why she was so doing, and then swallow them whole to eliminate them from her ruined world.

It was discreetly suggested to her in a message from Roald that she leave the party with Selly and Janos. They were ruining his party. She acquiesced with graceful dignity and as she glided away she looked her host in the eye in such a way that he felt threatened. Everything was over now, what did it matter? Then the three of them were out in the night. None of them spoke, there was too much suppressed anger beneath the tough veneer of politeness for any to dare, at first. Janos's upper lip twitched dangerously and Selly's mouth was ajar in a silent snarl as he regarded Janos with malice. He had hunger in his face and Janos felt threatened, a paralysis seemed to have overcome him. Marvene slid away from them which broke the gaze and the two men followed. Selly loped along silently on the balls of his feet, going ahead and returning, quickly but without fuss, circling them and then trotting off like a shadow. Marvene glided quickly then, head held erect, fixing Janos with a gaze, and he trotted agitatedly, head down in his shoulders. Around them the fantasy of the city glowed, the illuminated towers and balconies and flights of stairs and terraces were beautiful, everywhere glass, every aspect designed to astonish and amuse. Marvene spoke first.

'Janos, I am going to kill you. I am going to punish you for spoiling my life. There is nothing you can do, you are going to die.' He kept his nervous eyes upon her and tripped over the bottom step of a winding flight which led to a broad esplanade, a favourite nightwalk because of its elevation over an abyss and the astounding view. The banisters of the stairway were hollow and filled with small alien lifeforms from other planets. Janos had always loved this walk, he always stopped to take a look at the lizard people or the gloriously beautiful butterfly people in their simulated environment. Now, he would have given a lot to be a prisoner in a bottle like these highly intelligent specimens; anything would have been better than to have only space between Marvene and himself. Suddenly she reached out to grab him and he jumped, he ran up the stairway at speed but saw Selly ahead, crouched on all fours. The grotesque image of fat Selly crouching to spring almost made him squeak with hysterical laughter, he was out of control. In a blind panic he whimpered and ran down again. Marvene reached him and almost had hold of him by the neck when Selly leapt with a screech. The stairway beneath them all disappeared instantly and all Marvene could hear was her own ghastly hissing shriek, and she clung to a balustrade, winding herself around it clinging, watching the little butterfly people escape as their prison dissolved. They would not live long. And Janos had lost the night game, he fell to his death among a cloud of exquisite wings. Selly had changed direction mid-leap and somersaulted out into space in a wonderful arc to land with ease upon his feet on an impossible balcony two flights below. He crouched there moaning with the physical shock, looking down to see Janos land on solid glass. And then he looked up at Marvene, her hair coiling wildly.

'We shall all die. I shall kill you myself. None of us has a life now.'

'And we have come such a long way together.'

'Not together.'

'I'll switch off the control if you will. Do we want to be like this?' It was self and not-self, this snake that she felt to be.

'No. You are a snake. It suits your nature. And it must have been Janos who did that to you.' Probably true, it didn't matter now. She ran then, bitter and wild, not home but making for the lab in the underground, down to it through the glittering arcades aware that Selly followed. Kill herself? Where was the courage for that, how do snakes kill themselves? She was drawn to her most familiar surroundings, and stood among the cages, uncertain. She reached in and picked up a mouse by its tail. It kicked as she dangled it over her open mouth. Selly got there, howling eerily with laughter and reached out a paw to get the mouse for himself. The little creature was dashed away and ran to trembling safety in a heap of mouse-bedding, heaps of paper shredded but still showing that it was covered with Janos's handwriting. Then she laughed too, for he had been careless; now there would be nothing left to show what the research had been. The two humans engaged in a clumsy struggle, Marvene lacked weight and Selly was too fat to get her arms around to squeeze and he was hitting her with the flat of his hand.

Behind him on the bench were the dissecting knives, and she reached out and grasped one. She pushed the instrument into the side of his throat and cut, and cut. He was thick and tough and she could hardly believe that he was dead when his weight went slack and slid to the floor in a great pool of his blood. She found the control in his belt pack, examining it with a detached curiosity to see if it was a good copy. She felt different now, the impulses in her had changed. She felt active and tense but more like herself. She felt disgusted that she had almost eaten a mouse. What a powerful discovery they had made. She turned over in her mind ways in which she could use this to make a new life for herself. It was a powerful control weapon. Perhaps she could still be famous if she completed the research alone? She had nobody holding her back now, crippling her sense of style. She turned from the mess and wandered into the snake house.

'Marvene, I have waited for you,' said Lupus the Loop, smiling with pleasure. The hallucination of his actually speaking to her was very strong. All the disturbances she had endured had upset her mental balance. 'Chomsky was right, Marvene. That ancient debate is at an end. Language is innate you know.' She stared at him, knowing perfectly well that the vocal cords of snakes were so . . .

'Selly very kindly gave me his powers of verbal communication when he gave me his own instincts. You didn't know he was trying that, did you?'

'You can not speak,' she said, obviously expecting it to interpret.

'Did you hear a voice my dear? I am transmitting to you telepathically, my usual method of communication with other snakes of course.' Marvene laughed thinly.

'What an imagination I have sometimes. Dear Lupus, come to me then, tell me more. Give me answers out of my own brain.' But she had not read Chomsky. He glided to her and swiftly wound himself around her, head down and gripping tightly.

'Marvene, I want us to mate. I have needed a female for some time but my cruel imprisonment here did not allow that. Snakes are more passionate than humans realise, and Selly too had his passions. Secretly, he much desired you my dear.' She screamed again and again, begging him to let her go. He was embracing her desperately, frustrated and in anguish. He gripped her tighter and her bones slowly snapped and the breath went out of her so that she could not scream any more. Finally, possessing her in the only way he could, he swallowed her whole, taking his time, covering her broken body over with his own beautiful elastic skin.

The little mouse who had escaped was busy. It was releasing its fellow prisoners, who were not only grateful to be released, but said so.

No Coward Soul

I am standing in the centre of a howling desert storm, metallic grains tearing as if to strip me to the bone. I can find little air to breathe and that is full of poisonous gases. My lungs burn, my senses turn in on themselves like struck snakes, whipping back at me for subjecting them to such awful terrors. But I am on a quest and shall persist in the face of everything. I am stronger than I have ever been, my powers of concentration and my determination will carry me through. I come here seeking powers that no human being has yet had, and I must not fail. Like a knight in ancient times I must run the gauntlet, I must be fearless.

If only my limbs would behave properly; they thrust themselves against my control, grotesquely so that I laugh. It must be the atmosphere in this dreadful land, this frightful country on the deserted planet of Amygdalanea.

Everything here is designed to trap the traveller. I am deceived by strange visions, tortured by horrible thirst and hungers, by sexual desires which I feel will drive me insane but which sweep away as suddenly as they took me, leaving me mercifully drained and as dry as an old dying woman. I go forward, dragging myself through the tempest, wary of the ground which has hidden quicksands, unseen steps, rocks which seem to move into my path as if with intent to trip me, hurt me. Everything here is hostile. Everything is against my plan, but I shall win.

Nadine prepares everything very carefully as she has trained herself to do. The room is entirely sterile. In the corner is an ozone-ioniser quietly aiding continual purification. This entire project is a work of art. The carefully placed automatic film cameras will record every stage, for she wishes to exhibit the process as well as the result. She has written notes of all her intentions. It is only a matter of checking and double-checking; taking everything a step at a time. She has taken the appropriate light-hypnotic drugs, her hair is very short and washed with alcohol, she has administered local anaesthetic. The mirrors are all in place so that she can see exactly what she is doing, magnifying glasses are to hand, and the carefully tailored arm rests are covered in sterilised cloths. She lowers herself into the specially constructed couch, placing her head on the moulded pad. She is an expert with fibreglass and resin and made the couch herself. All the instruments are sharp. The telephone is silenced, the door is locked.

'So now, Nadine, you can begin,' she says aloud.

She takes a scalpel and with great care makes an incision in the image in the mirror. It is the top of her own head. When the flaps are laid back all neatly clipped and the area cleared of blood, she takes a tiny circular saw, adapted from a dentist's drill, and cuts a large area out of her skull, lifting the object which resembles something found on a beach, and laying it in a steel dish. The look of it amuses her. The only discomfort so far was the noise of the saw which she hates; the whining sets her teeth on edge but that is over. As she takes the first fine probe from the stepped-down electrical rack she has to calm herself. It is very exciting.

This is the culmination of three years of secret work. Autosurgery is not unknown in the world of art, but this will be the most sophisticated project to date. She has spent a lot of time practising and researching, picking up knowledge from medical friends, reading, and performing similar operations on dogs and cats. She knows the process by heart. There are important differences between animal brains and her own but basically everything is the same, and she is perfectly familiar with human models. First of all, it is a matter of bypassing certain areas of this delightful grey matter, to reach a deeply seated spot.

There were figures approaching. This was to be the first confrontation.

'Say who you are!' a loud voice demanded. She prepared to present herself with dignity. A lot would depend upon what she said and how she did it, but someone else spoke in different accents.

'What the bloody hell are you doing here?' The voice was very cultured, very angry. And also someone else.

'You stupid twat comin' down 'ere at night, yer've bleedin' well asked for it!' Somebody leapt at her and gave her a clout on the arm with something heavy and she squealed, all dignity forgotten, anger surging in response.

'I am Nadine Quilling, an artist, and I am here seeking peace.' Her mouth filled with sand out of the gale. The attacker grabbed her clothing and the pain in her arm was excruciating. 'I'll bleedin' well do for yer—got any cash?'

'No. Nothing.' She was pushed backwards and fell over a sharp rock, managed to roll on to hands and knees. Fear got her by the skin, hairs rising like pins. Was this how it should be? Where was the rational discussion?

'Get to your feet woman, immediately, and explain yourself.' She did so, to face a man in tweeds with a bristly moustache. He carried a shotgun. His face was scarlet with fury. The storm dropped somewhat and she spat out sand.

'If you trespass on my land you will be shot as like as not. I don't tolerate poachers, I don't call the police, I act. You'd best be off or you might get a blast up the behind. What are you doing here?'

'I'm on a mission. I seek peace.'

'Bloody conshy I suppose. No patience with 'em.' The man did not seem to be aware of the others poaching on 'his' land. The youth with the weapon was doing a kind of war dance, laughing to himself. 'She seeks peace, tee hee, she seeks peace.'

He was painted in an extraordinary manner, his face a canvas, his skull almost shaved and dyed with some lettering which she could not decipher. The third person was more menacing; he had an unhealthy spotted complexion and mean eyes like a furtive rat. His clothes were poor, everything greasy and worn. He looked cold and underfed.

'No money. Them with no money pays somehow.' He moved his hand and brought to life a flick-knife which he gestured with in a sly, gentle manner. It made the blood run cold. The three were obviously not together, but they were all against her.

'Somebody like you shouldn't be out here at night, it's dangerous for those that don't belong.' Suddenly the painted youth went for her but she was faster than he was and grabbed the thing in his hand, a heavy cosh. All peace missions forgotten, she swung at him at the same time as aiming a kick at the shotgun which went off with a dreadful sound mingling with the screams of the man with the knife who got the full blast. The youth went down with a grunt and she turned to the tweedy squire but he was running away.

Things were not going at all well, but at least she was whole and safe.

Notes on my Autosurgery, by Nadine Quilling

I have always had a violent nature. All my life I have been the victim of a terrible temper. I once almost killed my little sister; it was only the timely intervention of an adult which saved me from putting the kitchen meat-knife, an instrument of surgical sharpness, through her throat because she had once more stolen my teddy-bear. School was fraught with fights. Teenage saw me, an intelligent girl who could pass exams easily, wandering the streets of the city with a knife and a gang of acolytes, looking for trouble. I am told that when I was a baby I screamed almost all my waking hours, bit my Mother's nipples and then the teats off feeding-bottles. I was always loved in spite of everything. I was a wanted child and my violence was not bred in a soup of Freudian deprivation or parental error. And they had wanted a girl.

I have always been abnormally strong, able to win fights with boys and later able to beat any man at Indian wrestling. All I had to do to win was to unleash in myself my ungovernable rage and direct it into my arm. The sheer fact of existence fills me with fury, it is as if I was born full of resentment and rage at being in this world. I should have been born somewhere else more suited to my talents, which in spite of the flowering of my intellectuality, resulting in being recognised as unusually clever, does not make me feel at home on Earth. My destiny is not fulfilled. I have never felt that.

So I am going to alter this state of affairs. Earth is where I am and will be, and I am fully tired of losing friends with my evil moods. Many things have already been tried of course; I have been to psychiatrists and neurosurgeons ever since I was little. My parents refused to allow me to have brain surgery because they feared the crude methods might turn me into a vegetable. They were correct, but the answer still lies in brain surgery. That is why I have devoted recent years to learning everything necessary about manipulation of the human brain. I am an artist, as is well known, but painting ceased to give me satisfaction as did fibreglass sculpture. I have worked in performance art, and this new project is very much a result of those years I spent doing quite extraordinary things in front of people in art galleries. Now, I intend to solve the central problem of my own life. Rather than trust myself to a brain surgeon, I myself will effect the radical change in temperament needed to make my life peaceful, without altering in any way my intelligence, perception of the world or motor functions. More than one piece of autosurgery has been successfully carried out, although some have unfortunately been obliged to call for medical help due to exhaustion.

This operation will be painless and I do not anticipate fatigue. There will be no problems with main arteries; success will lie with skill and delicacy.

Having located my own amygdala, which is the seat of the disturbance, I shall implant permanent pathways to that and to nearby areas so that I can self-administer appropriate chemicals to the exact brain area needed whenever I feel slightly irritated, which is often the prelude to a fit of rage. I shall never again be out of self-control.

I hope that this process will become recognised as a valid tool to people similarly afflicted, to violent souls of all kinds who wield terror over others, to anyone who destroys the peace of the world by unleashing the powers of darkness which reside deep within their natures, whether there by natural accident or unfortunate distortion. I intend to benefit people instead of being remembered as one who ruined her own and other's lives because she could not keep her temper.

Everything is prepared (see notes on procedure).

I have no fear.

She had several chemicals prepared in readiness. No one substance was a panacea. It would require experience to know which to introduce at any one time; there was the monthly cycle, occasional illness and medicines to be taken into account. Deep in the hypothalamus, many chemicals have many effects. Any interference must be as precise as possible, unlike the offerings of the chemotherapists she had encountered over the years. She had steroids, hormones, cannabinol, cannabichrome, adrenochrome, ergotamine, delta-1 form tetrahydrocannabinol, suprareserpine, norepinephrine, psilocin, and her own invention, her own serotonin invert. It had hitherto been thought that serotonin was not after all a useful psychotherapic tool, but she had not been convinced from her reading. She had extracted her own serotonin and distorted its indole structure to resemble that of lysergic acid derivatives. The scar on her belly showed where she had opened herself to take the necessary samples from the bowel lining, and with the help of a biochemist, a dear friend who had no idea what she was actually engaged in, had mimicked this precisely and could produce it in the lab next door, which had once been a kitchen.

The only advantage of possibly getting someone else to do what she required was that a qualified brain surgeon would not be as excited as she was during the actual operation. She could not be too tranquillised. Her advantage was that strength of character goes hand in hand, paradoxically, with a vile temper. Her rage could tear the world apart, and she was making it construct a new world.

Everything would be okay, said an optimist deep within that part of her which she now probed with a fine, erect, sterile wire.

It rained, it rained, and all the world was mud. The mud smelled of death and effluents, of petrol and shit and lead. She wore dark green wellington boots and a sou'wester hat, and in between, nothing. What could logic do in such a world, you would get wet eventually anyway. Trudging after her mother in the snow it had been like this, the boots sticking in the green slime and clay beneath the perfect whiteness. Not far to go now lovey, soon be at school, put your feet where I put mine or you may fall into a bog, this field is full of bogs under the snow. Out there though, in the countryside the snow was never blotched by specks of soot. Lifting high the infant legs, in the end the warmth of the schoolhouse full of enemies, now to be faced, her mother gone to work leaving her small and precious, intelligent, very bad-tempered girl in the hands of ignorant teachers and children who would laugh at the fur-lined hood her mother had sewed, and call her Eskimo Nell.

On and on now through the terrible humours of this planet where the weather was never good, was always dull and wet and cold and wretched, oh to be in England, now November's here!

Everything looks like a sea of diarrhoea, even earthworms could not thrive in this cold stuff, and they will survive almost anything. Planting daffodils, she had often marvelled at the lively worms turning in their graves, indignant at being disturbed to make way for a bulb which would also survive the ghastly winter and thrust forth beauty and laughter enough to delight a crowd of Wordsworths whose hearts would lift at the sight of those glorious sex-organs.

But now it was serious, and she was alone, no Mother to guide and cheer and it didn't look much like anything at all had been planted. But as in fairytales and horror stories, there was a light on the horizon. Was it a house, a palace, or a Will-o'-the-Wisp come to lure her to her death in the bubbling morass beneath the outer shell of the planet? There was only one way to find out. A wind whipped up, full of gall and ire, blowing the rain of sulphur from far hills fit to rot a frozen mammoth. But this was important work, her legs must carry her – towards the lights. It seemed to take an age, the knees weakening, the fingers long since dropped off with cold for all she knew, and hunger and thirst driving her mad to the point where she thought perhaps like Scarlett she might go with the wind and eat the very earth. Rhett and Ashley were nowhere to be seen when real trouble was brewing. Her senses were not deprived, therefore she need not have been looking inward so much, deep into the sea of associations, not always as free as some literary critics will have it, but the outer world was so bloody awful there was nothing for it but to be inward as well as go on, like Milligoon, to Christmas backwards, or the light. It would have been perfectly possible to forget what world she was out to change so awful was the world she was in, but deep in her mind it was there; the ideal, the idea, the id, the drive onwards to the light and salvation.

The light was in an office block in a car park with no cars, but the door opened as she approached it much as doors in hillsides open to those in fairytales or those with heavy shopping bags in department stores. A secretary in a nylon overall waited.

'Do you have an appointment?' That phrase, how many desperate supplicants has it put off forever, how many at the end of their tethers have simply stepped backwards and knotted the tether into a noose for their own necks?

'Yes,' she lied.

'Well if you will go into the waiting-room I'll ask the chief to see you in a moment.' On the waiting-room wall the posters. A skull smoking a cigarette, a reminder to have her cervix checked, a warning about toxicaria (but who eats dogshit anyway?), a holiday poster for spectacular trips across the Great Central Commisure, complete with arranged simulated brain damage so that presumably one would not be able to read any more boring posters. The magazines on the table: *Country Life, Vogue, Punch*. Instruction on how to go walking in the country dressed in a side-slit scarlet dress with high sequinned shoes, feathers in the hair, and punch somebody, possibly an unsuspecting Pig.

And then the cross of Jesus on a handout, advertising Western Meditation which would change the world, person by person, relaxation was the key to eliminating all warfare. Jesus, with his coterie of thugs around him, instructing them how to spread the message so that all future generations would be able to torture and main and kill in His name. The only one among them with any wit or foresight, Judas. And his girlfriend Mary of ill repute turned from a healthy woman into a foot fetishist. If he comes again, it will be different. She herself would personally attend to him. She Mary Amygdala would personally duff him up for all the pain and trouble and misery...

'The Chief will see you now,' said the secretary who had glided in on the thick-pile carpet. With no word she followed, dripping evil-smelling mud, and then stood there in front of the vast and dignified desk covered in the hide of an unfortunate animal. She faced a pair of gleaming spectacles which did not quite hide perverted intelligence shooting forth like sun-rays at her disreputable appearance.

'Have a seat.' She resisted easily the temptation to pick up the seat and bash him with it; sat on it, squelching bare bum, and the interview began. She gathered together her confidence.

'I understand that you are applying for a passport, and a licence for agriculture?'

'You understand correctly.' There would be no point in revealing negative emotion, it would get her nowhere, but the sight of that face was making adrenalin build up from underneath making a stagnant sewer in weak conduits. The fury of ages was in her, in front of her its cause. All in one package, a manifestation of what fucked up the world.

A white, clean, bespectacled, masculine, self-assured, unscrupulous, self-controlled, reasonable, rational, patronising, helpful, fatherly, brotherly, friendly, efficient, trained, qualified, educated, powerful, potent, virile, monied, God-fearing, authoritative, secure, polite and democratic male. He must be democratic or she would not be here at all.

'Well, let's begin at the beginning,' he said, relaxing visibly, the bristles on his face taking a slightly downward curve. She looked with her telescopic and microscopic eyes and saw his pores open and exude micrograms of sweat containing bacteria, ethyls and esters from whisky, urea and after-shave.

'No, that's too far back. Let's begin now.' The whiskers made an arc in space which would have delighted Einstein, but nothing else showed.

'Well, put it to me then in more detail. What do you require of this office?' he was being patient.

'I wish to have free access to the hypothalmic and Amygdalanean territories and, after soil-improvement, grow new crops, guaranteed disease-free.'

'You must be aware that it will cost you millions, and that there are strict laws governing what is grown here?'

'Yes. But I am prepared to pay a large price, and you would gain in other areas also.'

'Would we though? Our ecology is already very carefully balanced.'

'I noticed that, outside,' she said with sarcasm. And then as he reddened slightly, she told him what she planned to grow. Hybrids of cannabis sativa, peyote, various medicinal plants, and also in underground caverns, with sun-ray and infra-red, anticipating his pointing out that the weather here was too stormy and cold for such crops.

'I see.' With glasses like those he should have been able to see but he clearly did not, quite.

'And how soon would you wish to commence work?' It was funny how some things commenced and others began.

'I wish to commence immediately.'

'I see.' There was a nasty ashtray on the desk, carved by some sad hand driven to torture alabaster. She saw it slowly lift itself and slowly work its way through his cranium, shattering slow blood over the room, and this vision warmed her while she waited.

'Well, if you will just return to the waiting-room I shall run a few things through the computer and then we can discuss it further. We cannot promise anything.'

'Of course not,' she said, knowing that it would always be true. Out in the waiting-room she deliberately chose another chair to mark with an arse-print. There was a mirror, she got up and went to check her appearance. The top of her head was open, the scalp laid back like turf, clipped short and neat ready to lay down on a prepared surface. There were wires sticking out of the grey brain, a smudge of blood on her forehead. No pockets, no handkerchief, so she wiped off the blood with spittle as best she could. She sat on yet another chair but she was dried out now except for her own humours, damply steaming on even the grimmest day. She was summoned again.

'Well, I've checked a few facts and figures and there certainly seems no need to terminate the application at this point. It will go before the Board next Thursday and we will let you know of their decision by mail.'

'But that's no good, I need to know now, I've got everything ready, it is a matter of life and death.'

'My dear lady, it is not a matter of life and death. I'm afraid there is no other way. We have to be democratic about these things, we can't have just any old project going through without a vote and we cannot rush these things.' She thought of attempting to bribe him with promised cash, but he had another idea.

'Of course, if you would like to discuss it further here and now,' he said in a different tone of voice, looking at her breasts. He turned round to a drinks-tray behind him, then she picked up the alabaster monster and hit him with it hard. She stormed out past the open-mouthed secretary, determined to go ahead with the project anyway. So, it was illegal! Anarchy was the reply.

Outside it was still raining and there were no other buildings. It is at such moments that anger changes into despair. There had been a lot of anger so there was a lot of despair. Slumping along in her wellies she cried bitter, desperate tears. When they got into the schoolyard at playtime the other children ganged up on her, pulling her ringlets. Outnumbered she ran to the lavs to hide and found frightful things written behind the door. Outside in the yard, under the shelter, were cages of baby white mice. Everybody got to look at them except her. She wished it would be tea-time so that she could go home. Then the bell rang and she opened her eyes, aware of her sterilised room, the alarm set to go off every ten minutes as an aid in case of unconsciousness. Not infallible, but it had worked now.

It was wonderful the way nothing hurt at all. In a superstitious corner of her mind she had not quite believed that brain tissue does not itself feel.

She steadied herself and selected a cannula, very gently worked it down into the tissue until the point made contact where an electrode had been. The matter closed around it as if welcoming the foreign object. The cannula was obtained through a biologist, a size used for goats. She had told him that she was doing a lifesize sculpture of a brain operation on a goat, a perfectly possible thing for her to be engaged in. The top was adjustable so that she could have it exactly right, hardly protruding through her skull when replaced. She had not known how thick her skull would be, but judged correctly that it had been quite thick from the number of knocks it had taken during fights without cracking. Two more cannulae went in without trouble. It was now a matter of testing to see if they were correctly placed, although she already felt sure. But she did not want to be the victim of perpetual appetites or to feel continually hot, or cold or have her judgement and senses distorted in any way. A few millimetres and she might not be able to read, or to smell certain things – but she reminded herself to concentrate now and not digress upon morbid possibilities.

A human brain is not like an animal brain precisely, and doubtless human brains were individuals also, just like faces and hands. She only knew this one, and it was the first meeting.

Suddenly the weather cleared and she was in a burning desert. A beach, not a desert. There were few people about at this time of day, but no mad dogs. A sailor with his trousers rolled up and his peaked hat awry. The Greeks were friendly and good tempered, the men much too friendly but pleasant. Nearby a tethered goat munched on kitchen scraps, its golden eyes blank with greed. The sailor came and sat down beside her, jogging her paintbrush, ruining the sketch she was making.

'Hey steady on, look what you've done!' He looked but obviously could not tell there was anything amiss. He put his arm round her in a strong grip, hurting her bare arm, and put his other hand on her breast which was clad only in a tiny bikini top. This was so unexpected and unusual, all the Greeks she had met spent a lot of time chatting and being charming. He tried to kiss her.

'Get off you bastard what the hell do you think you're doing.' In any language the message was plain, from both of them. He had no smile, no charm, not a typical Greek but horribly handsome and knew it. She started to struggle but he persisted, murmuring the one word 'fuck'.

'Oh sod off you pig,' she said, and got her strength together, heaving him off as she stood up so that he rolled in the sand. Perhaps he was drunk, again unusual for a Greek. He was on his feet again and instantly at her but she got her ankle behind his to bring him down. He was very strong but now she was furious and crashed her fist into his teeth making him howl and bring his hands up. Her other fist went into his eye and her knee into his balls, bending him double as she sprang back. She grabbed her sketching box and hit him on the back of the head with it, flinging tubes of paint everywhere. He fell groaning, then silent. She spent a lot of time getting back the paints except one which the goat had eaten, packed everything and watched the sailor getting to his feet, bending over again to vomit. He gave her a venomous glare and shook his fist but she shook hers with more determination. He staggered off, and she went in search of some lunch. Thank heavens she had her strength, the world was not always safe for women.

She lay back sweating profusely on the sterile sheet. The sun, the effort. The doubt. What would have happened if she had not been able to zap him? It was not possible to think about it, saliva came into the mouth with revulsion. She remembered now, she had given the ruined sketch to the goat.

So, a little more work and the worst of this project would be finished. She took careful measurements, deciding to bore the holes now while she was still steady. A high-speed drill can rip through anything and needs great care. Little jokes about holes in the head flittered through her mind as she finished the job. Then, the electrodes again, the fine probe. Just testing.

She suddenly felt the blissful, orgasmic waves passing entirely through her, a wonderful feeling of pleasure, but had the presence of mind to switch off the current. It must be like that for deep-sea divers; the symptoms of euphoria were so pleasant that she might not wish to surface. Already she was tempted to switch on again. No wonder animals would starve to death rather than stop pressing the buttons. She pressed her own and was instantly flooded with a feeling of happiness, physical sensation so agreeable that it must surely be the way flesh was meant to feel? She switched off, trembling. She took a while to calm down, administered more local anaesthetic and a mild tranquilliser and set to work again. Another probe.

Vennors the Lizard Lord stood before her, snarling to show his terrible teeth, his immense and splendid ruffle standing up to impress and intimidate. His claws were terrible and his anger great. She had trespassed into the innermost secrets of the Keep, and she must die.

'So, you call yourself a seeker?' he hissed, his tongue slithering to manage her language. 'You come to spy on us from Earth! You will not be the last to have been disposed of here on Amygdala-nea, oh bride of Death. What say you?'

'Aw shaddup Vennors you oversized newt. I've telegraphed the contents of the scrolls to my colleagues, you might try anything but you can't spoil the project now. We now know that you've been stealing precious metals from the lands of Maruzzi and Magoun. We have you, Vennors, what are you going to do?' For answer he extended his claws and lashed out at her, but she was quick and lithe and dodged expertly, meanwhile drawing her sword. As she swung it around her head she felt its power flow through her arms like electricity. Her shoulders flexed, she took her stance, and as the creature darted forward she hacked off one front leg with a mighty sweep. A frightful roaring filled the cavern like thunder in the Hippocampal deeps but still he advanced, eyes red with rage, green blood spouting on to the precious tapestries which he had plundered from the weaver's of Heschel's Gyrus. She thrust with the sword deep into his rumbling breast, needing all her strength, the strength of conviction, through the armour plating and into the beating heart as evil and black as his plans. He who had tried to destroy her world was now dying.

'Earthwoman thou hast done for me,' he groaned, blood dripping out of his mouth. 'But tell me this. How will you now return to Earth? My minions have destroyed your ship. Did you think we were complete fools?' She sprang back, pulling out the sword which smoked with his acrid humours, and ran for the door, down the thousand steps of his tower and out into the perpetual twilight of Amygdalanea. The grey plain stretched before her, the only relief her wrecked ship. She thrust her sword into its scabbard and put up her hands in supplication.

'Oh, Board of Medical Directors, how will you help me now?'

The thing is, she thought lazily, cleaning her instruments with alcohol, I need the angst to get me out of scraps, but would I get into the scraps in the first place if it wasn't for the angst? There were always outside circumstances which would excite anyone to ire and wrath. But those who were mild and turned the other cheek, did they get raped, beat up, slaughtered? Well of course they did.

She placed a drop of cannabinol down the central cannula. Instant trip, thoughts going on several levels, delight and distortion and mystery and humour. Great fun. And not a bit of aggro anywhere. When it was over she lay dreamily smiling, thinking, well, it works just fine. Amazing. But she was lazy, she just wanted to lie there, existing, taking pleasure in being around. She took a look in the mirror at the exposed brain and found it hilarious. She laughed and giggled, feeling the lovely humour rise up from her diaphragm in waves, the funniest brain she had ever seen. A person could live like this, just laughing at their own brain. There was a loud knocking on the door of her apartment. Instant alert. Who was it. Go away. Keeping quiet, wishing them away. Eventually it stopped, they had assumed she was out, had not heard her laughing, she hoped.

Last stage of the operation, placing the skull with its holes over the ducts, perfect fit. Then the scalp, stitches. Antiseptic. Shot of penicillin, adjustment of drip feed to include high ascorbic acid, take that out soon. Her brain cleared of the last molecules of cannabinol and she felt fine. If it wasn't for the oxygen cylinder she would have liked a smoke. The cannula ducts were obvious but she would wear a hat until her hair grew again. Resting she waited until she felt quite certain she would not feel ill upon getting up and slowly sat up. When the dizziness had gone she began putting things in order, had a whiff of oxygen and went to make a cup of ginseng tea. She washed her face. Everything was fine. She hoped that the films were good. About three days convalescence, probably, taking it easy. Quiet, and sleep. And then there would be the matter of obtaining horticultural sun-lamps, good manure and fresh seeds. And a clean water supply down there in the caves. Whole tracts of Amygdalanea were wasteland; she would make them blossom. The alarm bell rang so she went to disconnect it. There was the important matter of getting Vennors' minions on her side to assist with repairing her ship. She would be their leader now Vennors was dead. The phone rang as soon as she plugged it in.

'Hello Nadine, your phone's been out of order, I've been trying to get you for days.'

'Hello, who is that, this is Mary Amygdala speaking.'

'Nadine, quit joking, there's a party tonight in Elsie's studio, can you come?'

'You've got the wrong number, this is Mary Amygdala you

creeping Jesus.' She slammed the phone so hard that the plastic cracked and she picked it up and crashed it against the wall, knocking a pickled cat's brain off a shelf. She was about to start screaming when she remembered. No need. The cannulas. She dripped a small dose of her own special serotonin and was instantly in a different frame of mind. She must have been suffering from post-operative shock. She cleaned up the mess but felt slightly weak so went to sit by the window, pulling the cord on the blinds. The view outside was of a dismal November afternoon with rain and gusts of wind blowing garbage around. It was enough to depress the spirits, but she wasn't going to get upset; perhaps the weather would improve by the time she had finished her convalescence. The afternoon mail arrived and she noticed that there had been other mail. She opened the most ominous one, which was disguised as an electricity bill, but she could decipher the strange script. It was a declaration from the minions of Vennors of their sworn enmity and a refusal under any circumstances to help her.

She went to sit by the window once more. Tears ran down her face. Not tears of anger, but the tears of the timid and ineffectual. Only rarely as a child had she ever felt like this. Perhaps she would never be able to return to Earth. Perhaps they would stop her crop-growing scheme. If she went out perhaps she would be attacked by louts? There must be ways of dealing with situations without force but they were alien to her. Surely though, she had taken the right course? One thing was certain, nothing in her world would ever be the same again.

Black Sabbatical

Jeremy went down to the magician's house again. He knew it would be a pointless visit, but there was nothing else he could do. There would be the ritual pipe of hash, the same request from himself to do something about finding his wife, and the regretful refusal. But they would not part before a larger sum had been offered and regretfully declined. The old man would say that he could do many magics, but not the magic of finding a lost woman, dead or alive. And surely she was dead? Surely.

Jeremy saw his small friend El Frieda on the way. Or was her name Elfreda, he would never know. She could speak English and French almost fluently, but she could not master the writing and spelling – any more than Jeremy could master Arabic, which in return she tried to teach. He had spent hours with her on mutual lessons, without much success. She was eight, born in Marrakesh, visited Casablanca once, and lived most of her life here, about ten k's from Ain Leuh. She sold prickly pear at the side of the road, or rather, sat hour after burning hour and sold perhaps two dirham's worth in a week. Sometimes she begged in Marrakesh when they visited the house of her uncle, and at this she was very skilled. Jeremy and Jean had first met her there in the square, peddling henna which had spilled out on to Jean's white pants-suit, causing some upset. They had met again in Ain Leuh the day of Jean's disappearance. They sat together on the dusty step to talk. Jeremy hoped that someday El Frieda would bring him news of Jean. He knew that it was a stupid hope, but he hoped it. He had two hopes. One was El Frieda and her possible news of a ginger-haired white woman in the house of some minor shiek, or the magician who would conjure up her whereabouts with his bones and drugs and filaments into the other world. Jeremy knew that he was out of his mind, but inside his mind it was too painful to exist. Inside his mind he had murdered his wife; outside of it she had got lost in the desert through her own bad temper.

'What have you to tell me today, El Frieda?'

'Nothing, Jeremy sir. I made no sale. Fifteen kilo of prickly pear I have to throw in the ditch, it is rotten and last night only couscous without meat. My father he said no meat for her she is lazy. But it is not that, he does not want me to be strong. You see, the magician has spoken to my father about me, he has me marked from birth, he says. I am the strongest of the family.'

This news was not of an unusual nature, for El Frieda's father was a great friend of the magician, and the old men traded insults as readily as cloth or slippers. This marking of the girl child as the strongest would be little more than an attempt to damage the ego of the opponent. Bargaining took many forms in Morocco, not least of which was veiled insults. He laughed.

'Fear none of them, El Frieda. You will get meat tonight.' He gave her a fifty franc piece, and she hid it under her robe, somewhere in a little purse tied to her belt. Then, when the coin was safe, she thanked him, kissing his hand and looking up at him slyly. He hated her to do things like that, it was servile. And the look in her eyes was something that upset him more than anything he could think of. It reminded him of Jean after they had had one of the torrential and frequent quarrels. For a little while she would become like a doe or a spaniel. She had often quoted from *A Midsummer Night's Dream*, smiling and pawing his arm. He wondered sometimes if Jean had been slightly psychotic. Always raving about independence and yet unable to be alone without falling apart, the screaming, the bickering, the attempts at total domination – that they had both made. He admitted for a moment that he had loathed her and that they were very ready for a divorce. She had given him three children and brought them up very badly. They would never be what he called 'normal' not only because of the manner of their mother's death, but because of her shabby treatment of them. She had not infrequently shouted to them, aged four, seven and nine, that she wished they had never been born. They were accidents, did they realise. . . ?

He turned right away from that picture of her. He did not want to remember. It was unnecessary. All that was necessary was that he find her, dead or alive, and get her back to England for a proper burial. He covered his eyes with shame at the slip. If she was *dead*, a proper burial!

And then begin work again. At the end of his sabbatical year. He also had a great deal of work to do on the book that he was supposed to be writing that year the college had granted him. A book on Moroccan tiles, both the tiles of the mosques and of the market squares, the common work on wells and fountains, house floors. It was to be lavishly illustrated, and it would make him quite a lot of money. But he would have to go back to work as a teacher of ceramics eventually. In seven months time.

'I must go to the magician's house.' El Frieda had gone, she had left the step silently, almost certainly to visit the market where fly-blown meat was sold. She was so much older in her ways than any of his own children – for eight years old she was truly astonishing. But so were all Moroccan children. Self-sufficient, independent, sly in trade and bargaining and the ways of Europeans. So he went on down the deserted street to his friend's house. The magician. He had been introduced to the old man by one other that he had met and confided in on the day of Jean's disappearance. The fellow had been sitting in a tiny café in Kasba Tadla, the nearest source of any police so the locals had told him. Weeping with sudden rage and humiliation, he had told the old fellow everything, all about their terrible quarrel in the desert that night they had camped with the children, having missed the way at Ain Leuh and taken the Sahara road by mistake. How they had accused each other in louder and louder voices in the silent night, the children quiet or whimpering by turns, Jean trying to cook rice and meat on the last whiff of camping Gaz, the worry about not having enough petrol to get back to the main road the next morning, the bickering about whose fault it all was, and his plea that a night in a desert was surely an adventure, could she not just relax and enjoy it? He had said that just to enrage her, knowing that she had always had a dream of a romantic night spent under canvas or under stars, in the desert, but that to have to cook and quarrel during it, and then not to make love, which they had not done for months, would be hurtful to her dream...

The old man had surely not understood half of what he had told in English and broken French, but he had eventually written down an address with the help of some other tourists, and gone away, leaving Jeremy with only that to hold on to. The police were trying, but what could they do with such a case? For the fact was that in the sandy waste, not a hundred yards from the metalled road, Jean had suddenly screamed, thrown down the pot of stew into the sand, bawled that she was finally and forever leaving him, and run off into the black night bellowing like something wounded. Which she undoubtedly was. They both were. He had followed her just a few steps and then gone back to the tent and the children who were frightened of being left alone. And in the back of his mind was the thought that if he got lost in the night, they would have no one to look after them. There were black vipers in that desert somewhere, perhaps not so near to the road, but quite possibly. And scorpions. Jean was in danger. They were all in danger. He could remember everything about that night. She had not returned. He had waited. He had stoked up the fire. He had sung songs to the children. He had shouted to her, for over an hour he had shouted. He had tried to sleep, got up, waiting for dawn. He had finally drifted off to sleep sitting up and jerked awake with the sun in his face, the howling of one of the children loud in him. No Jean. He had driven up and down the road in desperation. He had not known what to do. There was sandy waste everywhere, no habitation. He could not imagine what had happened to her. Stolen by a passing truckful of Arabs? There had been no trucks. Out in the desert, collapsed with scorpion bite? The land was flat, she was not in sight. Gone over the horizon on foot? If so, into some of the most hostile and hallucinatory country in the world. Perhaps she was living with Berbers? But it did not seem likely. She would demand to be taken back to a town, and they would not dare refuse. There were no wild animals large enough to eat her, as far as he knew. So he had driven back to Kasba Tadla, told the police, told the man in the café, arranged for the children to be flown back to the grandmother in Wales, saying hardly anything to them, for what could be said, except that he would return home when he had found their mother. He did not feel he could cope with the situation with them still with him. He could not look them in the face. He felt they looked at him accusingly, sometimes.

But he would find her. After about a week he had got himself together sufficiently to visit the address he had been given, which had turned out to be the village magician, not a local man, but one from the Sousse. He had many tattoos on his face and hands and ankles, and had no hair except a tuft on the top of his head, rather in the manner of some Red Indian tribes. He had not spoken at the first interview, and Jeremy had not discovered what his trade was until the following night in another café, where the local Arabs had told him with much respect and some scoffing that the old fellow was certainly the only hope of finding a disappeared wife. He would demand a large fee.

'There are not many men with wives worth what he demands. I have heard of disappearing women, but never have I heard of one that was found by that old dog. He wants too high a price, and there are many women.' This witticism had brought a great deal of laughter up out of the half-stoned group, sitting there sucking up inferior hash mixed with terrible tobacco. But something about the magician had fascinated Jeremy, and he had returned the next day. They had gotten on to the subject after about the fifth visit. There had been grins and nods and shakes and extra hash and mint tea but neither price nor task mentioned clearly. It was not going to be rapid, and Jeremy was anxious that something be done quickly. Eventually he pleaded for speed, and the old man had said simply: 'It is not likely that she lives. But I can bring her back to life if she is discovered, dead.' And the rest of that interview had been silent. Jeremy had sat on, finishing his mint tea, and had returned to his small hotel without comment. He had been vastly amused by all that, having had no idea that such nonsense still went on in the modern world. Especially in that part of the world, in a Morocco which was in many ways enlightened. But the old man was from the Sousse, far south where Africa began to be more African, strange, nameless regions of desert, oasis, secret villages and moving caravans that went to Timbuktu. Wild men who had an annual kind of Durbar at Tantan, where nothing else happened all the remainder of the year, it seemed to exist so that they could come from all over the Sahara and show off their prowess at horsemanship and shooting. And superstition was abundant amongst such people.

The old man was living here only as a visitor, he had been there almost a year, but the locals told Jeremy that he would go away again after the spring of the following year, he travelled around like that to avoid the police keeping too close a watch on him, for his practices were illegal. He healed people, found lost things, put curses on those who cheated and occasionally did things for crops and sick animals. Especially was he good with tomatoes which seemed prone to tobacco virus at times. He could cure that with certain incantations. He was not a very usual figure, and his magic was not local magic, therefore the more powerful. Opinion was divided in the cafés about its effectuality. Jeremy was full of scorn about the whole thing, but there was nothing else that he could do; it was a kind of sociological survey that he was doing. He might even perhaps put a bit about the old fellow's rented house in his book, for it had some magnificent tiles. Jeremy had already taken several photographs. The Moroccans were always so hospitable and generous; he was merely being friendly with one of the local characters; he was not really consulting a magician. The heat was intense. It was towards the end of August, and there was a strange heavy humidity in the air along with the dust, and everyone, even the Arabs, seemed to be suffering from a kind of hay-fever. There was a lot of dysentery about amongst all those tourists that passed through; he could see in every party a white mask beneath the requisite tan, and several visits to the lavatory were quite usual. He himself had seemed to recover rather rapidly from what must have been hepatitis and now felt strong and alive and very well indeed, even in the heat and dirt. His hotel was primitive, with a filthy outside toilet arrangement, but he did not complain. He had to stay here, it was the only possible place to be, where the police could find him. When they found her. Which of course they would not. She had disappeared. It was as if she had wandered off the earth into another dimension that horrid night. Just like Jean to die in such a manner. Inconvenient, dramatic, hurtful, troublesome. Why the devil could she not have caught typhoid and popped off quietly in a hospital, where they all knew where she was and could mourn her and forget? They would have been recovering now. As it was, they could not speak of her in the past tense. Alas. And his moods fluctuated like that, from hard bitterness, to sugary regret and sentiment, even to the glorious passion they had experienced together so many years ago when they had first met. He caught himself saying things out loud like:

'Jean, when I rescue you from this hell, we'll love together just like the old days, we'll recapture everything we've ever lost.' And then he would hate himself so much for the schmaltz and the Hollywoodish hollowness of himself that he would make himself do something that he detested, walking along the main road and back three miles each way, but a pastime he had discovered exhausted him thoroughly enough to put him to sleep the instant he got back and lay down. He went to the police station every other day. One day they advised him to return to England; they would let him know if anything turned up. They were extremely sorry, but they could do nothing more about the unfortunate case. They were embarrassed. There really was nothing more to be done. But he told them that he was writing a book and that it would take him several more months, so he would not be leaving. Wearily they looked at his passport, visas, permissions, bank-book, and waved him away. He was doing no harm, he could of course stay. But to find his wife, that was not possible, except per-haps by a miracle.

The old magician specialised in miracles. At a price. Today Jeremy seated himself down on the blue and white plush cushions and after a while of pleasantries they began talking about the price. Jeremy had not mentioned the business of bringing Jean back to life if she were found. He did not want to go into that. He just did wonder, though, if this man had a gift for psychometry. If he gave him Jean's handbag, for instance, could he perhaps send where she might be found? It was not too ridiculous; several tales were told locally of his successfully finding objects at a distance by this method, and water divining was authentic enough, and there were people like Peter Hurkos whom he had seen in a film. Tongue in cheek of course. But it was possible. Perhaps. And so he rationalised his presence in the magician's house.

The old man seemed not quite ordinary in many ways. For instance, he never told how he opened the door without getting up. Jeremy had watched for a thread but there was none, and yet, when the magician waved his hand the door would open or close at his bidding. It could seem rather eerie in that cool, dark room after coming in from the baking heat and noise and light of the street. Very impressive. After a long while spent discussing the origins of the tiles on the floor the old man suddenly spoke in a slightly different voice.

'My bargain with you is unusual. I need for every large magic one wind-dried corpse. They are quite common on the edges of the Sahara, certain people bring them to me, but there are never enough. I need special things from them for my magic. You understand? But in your case you are wanting to find just such an object, for your wife is surely that by now? Well, bring her to me and I will give her life. At one other price, something I cherish even more than money.'

Jeremy pretended at first that he had heard nothing. Then, desire for logical order prevailed.

'My dear fellow, I do not know where to look, or I would not ask for your help.' How stupid and mad these old Arabs could be. It would all turn out to be a riddle full of wisdom in a minute, they could often not distinguish what was hurtful and real from...

'But I will give you a talisman first that will lead you to her. It will be simple. You will walk out one night from the place where she left you, and before dawn, you will find her. I have never failed in such. I shall take from you for that two hundred dirham. And then bring her back to me and we can speak again of things. I shall be happy to see you.' The English was incredibly good, hardly any mucked-up syntax, a very good accent.

'Where did you learn your English?'

'As the son of the wealthiest and most powerful magician in the whole of the Sousse, I was sent to Gordonstoun Public School, in Scotland. For a period of five years. I have also a degree in biology at Sussex University, but my career was predetermined. I have a calling, and my father taught me more than any other person or persons. And this is more lucrative. I charge high fees for great things. Everyone comes to me either in the first instance or the last resort.'

'And you expect me to believe that you have actual magical powers? How did they go down at Gordonstoun?'

'I had not been initiated at that time. My father taught me his craft after puberty and before I returned to Sussex. Naturally, discretion forbade me to mention my powers in the common-room, although one was tempted to curse occasionally. I was once insulted, but the consequences of my revenge would have been out of proportion in England. Here, things are different. And I have no abiding interest in modern Western biology, it is too thin, dealing only with appearances, not with realities, it is just not satisfying for a lifetime.'

Jeremy was already making this information into a story to tell the staff when he returned to his job. 'There was this old magician fellow, topknot, hash pipe, robes, the lot, then he tells me he was educated – of all places! And what's more – a degree. . . !' The old man had stopped speaking. Jeremy took his leave as soon as he politely could without discussing further anything about Jean. Possibly the story about his education was not true; the whole thing was becoming more unsavoury. Perhaps he was not only a charlatan in magic but in ordinary things too. Many people had found it advantageous to say that they had a degree, when they had been nowhere near a university. But Jeremy could not quite decide what the advantage would be in the old man's deceiving him like that. It was quite senseless. A figment caused by the hash, perhaps.

He made his routine call to the police station, knowing that if they had any information they would have come to his hotel. Then he went and posted the letter to his mother and the children. They were all, or possibly just one of the boys, to come over for a two-week vacation. He doubted the wisdom of their coming to the scene of their mother's disappearance, but his mother wanted to come, and there would be the problem of what to do with the youngsters during her absence. Maybe it would be better if just the eldest boy came, he was very sensible and capable of travelling alone under the care of the air hostess. There was also the expense to be thought of. During a sabbatical year, there was no pay. He had saved up for this trip for many years. Jean had grumbled often about the penny-pinching for what she sarcastically sneered at as his 'fabulous trip to the orient', although she had always wanted to go abroad even more than he did. To him it was work. The book on tiles. He went home and sorted out some slides and prints, and went over his notes for the introductory chapter once again. He could think of no improvements.

The following afternoon found him in the house of the magician again. As usual the door opened as if by itself, and Jeremy as usual gave it a hidden ritual sneer. Nylon thread magic! He sat and smoked, and one of the servants brought mint tea, and the magician said that unfortunately that day, he had no time to stay and talk. He was very sorry but he had visitors. They were old friends of his from Essouiria on the coast. So Jeremy took the hint and got up, noticing as he did so that the outstretched hand of the magician was not held for him to shake, but held a small package. He automatically put out his hand but stopped short of taking the package until the other nodded his head, with some impatience. It was a small bundle of something wrapped in yellow silk of the kind he recognised as being 'shantung', his mother had extolled the virtues of such material when he was little, and he remembered petticoats and knickers hanging on a bedroom chair. They had been very soft and thin and papery, and they had needed a lot of careful ironing. He fingered the package. Perhaps this was not shantung, but a similar Moroccan silk. He began to undo the knotted silk thread that was wound around it.

'No, no!' shouted the old man, very angry. Then Jeremy admitted that he was holding the talisman, the thing that his rational mind told him he would have no dealings with. He made as if to return it.

'Your one chance, friend. And the price before you leave, if possible.' There was a terrible hardness about him now, very cold with small glass eyes. Well, Jeremy had the money on him. Against all wisdom he carried cash, and it was for this purpose. He had had the same cash in a manila envelope ever since they had first started discussions about the price of services rendered, many weeks ago. In a dreamy way he took the envelope out and counted out several five pound notes. They were more valuable to Moroccans than dirhams or francs; it was illegal but that seemed beside the point.

He left the house without further exchange and found himself lying down on his bed, sweating, feeling sick. He must be cracking up to do a thing like that. Wasting all that money on a packet of rubbish! He must chuck up this sabbatical year and go home, get another job, set up house somewhere, provide some security for the children, leave all this nonsense behind. If only he had come alone in the first place, none of this would have happened. He had enough material to stick a book together, he could do it just as well in England. He had a touch of fever which he hoped was not dysentery. He slept although it was only four in the afternoon. It was dawn the next day when he awoke, and he had dreamed of a blue lake in the Sahara, which even in the heat of the mid-day sun was icy cold, too cold to bathe in, but heaven to drink. But the more you drank the more thirsty you were.

He got out of bed and made mint tea, terribly impatient during the infusion but not daring to drink water from the jug. Then he dressed and packed a small bag with a change of clothes, went out and bought food supplies from the little general store, loaded everything into the Rover and set off. In his pocket, buttoned securely right against his chest, was the bundle wrapped in yellow silk. He was there before sunset and slept in the back of the Rover, wrapped in a handwoven blanket that he had paid twenty dirham for and had been offered the same type of thing at half that price the following day. Everything changed from day to day and place to place in Morocco, there were no constants. He found the place where they camped, for there in the sand was a can, a deplorable object he thought, kicking it. He knew it came from their supplies, it was an unusual brand made in small quantities in England, brought as a treat and opened that night by Jean in an attempt to soothe him. Oyster soup with Guinness. So he stood there for a while determining in his mind which direction she walked away that night. He mentally placed the Rover and the tent and the moon, and decided that she walked away from the road in a slanting direction towards – but there was nothing to go towards.

He set his compass, checked his flask of water, and set off. It was slow progress, the sand was fine, almost dust, and his way was impeded by scrubby growths that might in spring become flowering bushes but were now like primitive grave-markers on an ancient battlefield. He walked on leaning forwards and slurring his feet because this was easier, and sometimes looked around to see if there was anything appearing on the horizon. It would seem that this plain extended infinitely. Then he saw a distant cloud of dust rising up, a minor whirlwind, and stood gazing at this for a while; there was nothing else to be seen. He sometimes thought that through the dust he could see distant mountains, but it was uncertain, amorphous. He went on and the sun began to go down. He did not think that perhaps he had better retrace his steps, try again another time, that he had been foolish to come without a sleeping-bag. He did not think of anything. He did not even remember that he was looking for anything any more. The business of putting one foot before another became everything. He was exhausted, drenched in sweat, and longed for a breeze. There was nothing. Near him the air was still, there were no more plants, just red stones and occasional lumps of glittering quartz. He continued. He had pains in his back and his head, and his insides churned. Perhaps he would have dysentery again, that was a nuisance. No tablets seemed to help that condition. There was not much light left. He stopped and looked around. It was almost certain that there were mountains in the distance now. The dust had settled and they were clearly visible. The red evening light struck them; they looked unreal, like volcanoes suddenly broken up through the ancient crusts of dust and sand. Like Japanese paintings, thought Jeremy. And he lay down in the sand, shifting around to move small stones. He looked up at the stars appearing; he felt cooler, he slept.

He lay on the couch in the magician's house. They had given him mint tea, and, alone in the upper room in the cool shadows, he thought about getting up for a while. He had got up yesterday for a short time, it had been quite successful. But he still felt very weak, and events were not always clear. He was still not certain if his mother and son had been to visit yet, or just the boy, or whether their visit was yet to come or if they had decided not to come at all. These ideas were uppermost in his mind all the time he was awake, and worried him very much. Stick to things which had really happened. The old magician leant over the bed, saying that he had done very well, he had been clever. Grinning knowingly. But before that, coming to the house with El Frieda at evening. And the child crying loudly into the silence as the old servant woman led her away. He could make no sense of that. And Jean's dust-proof watch, still ticking. He put out his hand to the small octagonal table and picked it up. An expensive watch that her father had given her for coming-of-age, years ago. It was wound annually, dustproof, waterproof and shockproof. It kept perfect time, according to his own watch. Which might not be correct. But Jean wore that watch all the time, sometimes even in bed, which angered him unreasonably. He put it down again and very slowly and carefully got out of bed, staggering slightly and upsetting the small brass tray that had held the mint tea. In about thirty seconds there was the old woman in the room clucking away and halahar-habing away at him. She seemed very concerned.

'I am much better, tell downstairs. I am coming down. Much better.' Shouting at her, using his hands. As if she were deaf and stupid rather than foreign to him. He managed to get himself into some clothes and went down. There was no one in the magician's main room. He went on into the kitchen, and there was only the old woman washing drinking glasses in filthy water. Something was cooking on the earth stove, and it smelled very good. The scents of cummin and lamb and rosemary drifted in from the courtyard, and he thought perhaps his appetite was returning. It was a good sign to enjoy the smell of food, for a long time it seemed that he had no interest, for dysentery had that effect.

'Where is the old man?' She pointed with the wooden spoon that she stirred the stew with, and Jeremy went across the little courtyard and tapped upon the door.

'I am pleased to see you so well,' said a voice behind him, and there stood the old man. The door he had knocked on remained closed.

'I am much better. Thank you. You have been very kind. But it is time I started to get my affairs in order. I have things at the hotel, and there is the Rover somewhere, and there is the visit of my family, and my book to write. You have been very kind, so very . . .' The magician was holding up both his hands.

'Everything is in order. We have long since got your things from the hotel; everything is paid for you, and the Rover is in the street at the back of my house, and is guarded constantly by boys. You have nothing to worry, all your things are very safe. About your family, there is some mail for you which we got from the post office.' The old woman handed him three packets. There were thin letters from two of his colleagues and one from his mother. She had made arrangements with Aunt Jessie to have the children for three weeks at the very most and would be arriving on the 14th, Marrakesh Airport. It would help if he could fetch her, or perhaps if not then he could let her know and she could make her own arrangements. Imperious as ever, disguised as sweetness and a willingness to oblige. Nothing puts me out, Jeremy, but it would help if you could just do this, or that . . . he felt like tearing it up for a moment but folded it carefully, then got it out of the envelope again, and looked at the date.

The 10th.

'What date is it?' he demanded. It was the sixteenth. His mother was already here. Alone, angry, there would be scenes, explanations.

'Do not worry, I had her met with a car at the airport and she is staying in an excellent hotel, and has a guide of the souks who is reliable. She had already spent rather more than she intended. Her purchases include three sets of Safi drums for the children.' The man was not looking at him, but was watching a scorpion in the dust at his feet. Jeremy jumped backwards and staggered. The old magician pointed at the insect, and it remained perfectly still.

'You must have opened my letters!'

'Such indiscretions are neither mine nor necessary. I can read the contents of letters just by holding them.' He moved his hand and the scorpion dashed forwards but scuttered around his naked foot as if frightened.

Jeremy did not know what to say. And then: 'What did you tell her about me?'

'I told her that I was your doctor and that you must not be disturbed for a day or two. We got on rather well; she is a pleasant lady with delicate manners. She will visit here this evening for dinner. You had better be bathed and dressed properly by then, it would seem that she is the kind of person to be shocked by your appearance.' Jeremy looked down at himself, and the shabbiness of it was not good. Dusty, and his toenails needed cutting. Odd, that, he was rather meticulous about such things. And then the hand exploring his own face. Long stubble, unprecedented in his life; his hair on his collar; his fingernails, long and filthy.

'What has been happening? I do not remember everything.' And as he said it, he did remember something, the date of his journey into the desert. He had been away, somewhere, for almost a month.

'You were ill for a long time after your return. But everything is

all right now. And my part of the bargain is completed. You will
see her soon.'

'What time is she coming?'

'She is here now, but you are not quite ready for her. Go bathe.'

'I thought you said tonight...'

'Your mother tonight. When you are ready, you will meet your
wife again.' He did not speak, for the words would not come, and
he wanted very much to fell the old man, see him bleed in the
dust, have done with all the horror of this charlatanry, the holding out of the awful ideas, the possible miraculous truths. He realised he had almost believed everything the man had said since
they had met; something had made him believe, partly, against
his will and reason. He hated. He hated. He almost fell down into
the dust.

He was sitting in the main downstairs room, clean, and smelling
of some sweet-scented soap that he would never have chosen for
himself. He was shaved and brushed, cross-legged on the blue-
and-white plush cushions, and in front of him there was the glass
of mint tea in its silver holder, on a small brass tray bearing the
symbol of the Hand of Fatima. The door opened.

Jean paused a moment before entering, and then rushed
towards him, smiling. She knelt in front of him and reached out
her hands, and he stretched to touch her. Her reddish hair was
just as it had ever been, not white with the sun and in strands scattered on the sand. Her skin was its own milky fairness, the
freckles the only dark marks, no dry blisters and black burns. Her
eyes were their own pale grey, smiling out at him, not the gloating
pebbles smaller than their leather sockets. Her teeth showed only
a little, her very good teeth; they did not grin horribly from black,
dry, shrunken lips.

'Jeremy.' She spoke, not as before, sitting beside him in the
Rover all those miles, only stupidly sitting, shrivelled and bent
and black and uncommunicative, turned in on herself as if

forever, hugging her stomach as if she had a pain, although she had been beyond pain.

'Jean.'

'Call me El Frieda,' she said softly. 'The days of our dissonance are over. I live again through her.'

There would be no explanations, the old man never explained anything. Jean seemed to shed light in the dim room; she softly rose and led him up and out by the hand. They went out into the late afternoon sun, and the shops were opening, and people were slaking the dust at their steps with buckets of dubious liquids. They passed El Frieda's house and it was all shut and mourning flowers were dry at the step. Children in the street began to follow and gather, shouting. The English phrases that he heard he did not like. The Madman. They were all laughing. Then at the end of the street he saw the large black car stop, and his mother get out alone and stand there. Then when the car had gone, she saw him and started towards him, arms outstretched. She came nearer and nearer, and as always when they met and Jean was there, she ignored her until she had embraced her son. He hated her for that, Jean had hated it too. He looked at her to see what reaction there was. He looked at her and looked at her, he could not take his gaze away towards his mother, who was talking rapidly.

'Well I must say you are looking well my darling, to say that you have had such awful adventures and been so very ill. The doctor told me all about it, he is *such* a nice man. I was to meet you at his house, but I see you are out and about already, taking a walk. Who is this little girl? How is your book going? I half expected to see you sitting up in bed. I have brought you one or two delicacies, I do hope the heat has not...'

She went on and on; he just went on staring at the thing at his side. It grinned and grinned. It looked terribly happy.

Living Wild

Cruelty has a Human Heart,
And Jealousy a Human Face;
Terror the Human Form Divine,
And Secrecy the Human Dress.

The Human Dress is forged Iron,
The Human Form a fiery Forge,
The Human Face a Furnace seal'd,
The Human Heart its hungry Gorge.

William Blake, *c* 1794

I awoke in the night, a very unusual occurrence. I never got to sleep quickly, but when I finally did it was always as if I had been transmuted into stone. I once slept through five and a quarter hours of electric alarm clock.

I opened my eyes, and I had the impression that I had heard a kind of roaring, some sudden happening of sound that was not a jet plane and not a thunderclap but which could have been a great wind. Some vortex out of the sky, coming and going like the impulse to make love when the body is exhausted. Hot, rapid, hollow. It was cold in the bedroom, which was unusual too because the whole house was heated by small-bore steam pipes that my Stuart had fixed himself years before, in an attempt to dry out the ancient fabric of our house. I could see the full moon low over my laburnum tree, glowing red hot through the miasma rising off the nearby town, diesel exhaust and smoke and steam and particles of gypsum dust, all sucked up in the inhalations of the moon, making cancer in her ancient body. Someday she would issue an endless flood of polluted blood from some secret orifice, rain it down into our puny tides.

But why could I see the moon? I always slept with the thick velvet curtains carefully closed. The window was open. I never left the window open; I had always been frightened that an owl might fly in and tear out my hair. A white owl, hooting and infested with fleas. Or bats, possibly worse. There were no curtains at the windows, that was it. Still torpid, I could not bring myself to get up and discover the curtains on the floor. I supposed there to have been a storm which had blown open the window and dislodged the rails from the plaster, which was crumbling in many places. Annoyed and shivering, I put out my hand for my cigarettes and lighter. I would fumigate myself a bit first, before coming to a decision about getting up. In a moment I might want to visit the bathroom and then perhaps make a malted milk, I thought. I have always hated getting out of bed. I got the cigarette packet and put the firmer, tipped end in my mouth. I scrabbled around for the lighter on the bedside table, which was higher than my head, it being really the cupboard end of a Victorian sideboard. I touched a plastic ashtray, a paperbacked book of Blake's *Songs of Experience*, and then something small and cold, with a tail.

I shuddered under the blankets for a long time before the taste of chewed tobacco brought me to my senses enough to realise that what I had touched was not a dead mouse dropped by an invading owl, but the bowels of my lighter, the wick and cotton. I had no recollection of having had the thing to pieces, as I sometimes do when it needs a new flint or wick. It always took me hours to get the bit of wire through the tiny hole; I was so useless with my hands that I sometimes thought I must be slightly spastic. I would sit up in bed with bits of spring and flints, fiddling and poking far into the night. Yes, I thought, I had given up in despair. I surfaced from my steaming cave and fumbled for the switch on the cord of the lamp. It fell to pieces in my hand, bits of plastic rattling on the pediment of the cupboard and then swallowed silently by my sheepskin rug. I cursed and lay back for a moment, controlling my temper. I could tell it was not going to be an easy night, because with me, if one thing goes wrong, then many do. I would have a man in to fasten those bits of switch together. Then it occurred to me that the wire could be live so I edged away towards the opposite side of the bed – Stuart's side – and got my feet trapped in the tucked-in blankets. In a few weeks, when Stuart came back to discuss a reconciliation, would he sleep there again? I thought of that with both longing and apprehension and struggled with the covers impatiently, drawing in my breath. I yelped with pain. It seemed I had lost the filling out of my front tooth; I must have swallowed the bit of silver amalgam when I brushed my teeth the night before. I got out of bed and found my robe and slapped around on the wall for the main light switch, and when I found it nothing happened. I felt around then for a sweater and jeans, it seemed as if I might not get back to sleep for some time. I could not fasten the zip of my jeans; the little metal runner that locked the nylon teeth had come off. Almost in tears I just fastened the button and abandoned the idea of shoes. There seemed to be a lot of things on the floor, none of them shoes. The curtains were in a heap, and when I lifted them up by the nylon rail, they slid off the ends and the flexible rail sprang up and knocked something off my dressing-table with a crash. Cursing, I threw it down and tried to shut the window but could not, for the old metal catch had come off. It was a very stiff window because of being rarely opened and I heaved at it to try and jam it when the whole pane swung outwards and fell out of my hands down to the greenhouse below. The awful sound stopped, and I stood with my hands gripping my shoulders, all huddled up, ready to start wailing. I was horrified. Naturally. It took me a few minutes to decide what to do, to collect myself at all. Then I thought I would go and fix myself a drink and a snack. Calm down a bit. I could not find a doorhandle. I panicked then, I think. I recall running at the door with my shoulder once or twice, oblivious of pain, and there was a dreadful noise of rending wood, and somehow I forced my body round the side of the door where it had broken away from the flimsy frame. There was dry rot in the house, but still, I must have used a lot of force. I ran downstairs weeping, holding my shoulder with one hand and my mouth with the other, and was almost projected into empty space by a board that came up under the carpet, which was loose. I tried all the lights in the hall, but there was nothing happening; and I picked up the phone but it was dead. Reeling and frightened, I ran into the kitchen and put my foot into about four inches of water. I started to wail and incongruously and childishly had only one thought at that moment: honey. I wanted several spoonfuls of Tasmanian honey, and then a hot drink and a snack.

I sloshed around in the wet and dark looking for the gas cooker, but it wasn't there; and where the stove should have been, there was just some rubble under water. There was a smell of gas. I could believe none of it, and yet it was true. Somebody had swiped all the kitchen equipment.

Ridiculous. Alarming. I ran outside on to the lawn which was a sea of mud from the rain which was pouring heavily. The moon had gone behind rain clouds or the ends of the Earth. I hugged myself under the old laburnum, still aware of my desire for honey, but my passion for the stuff was not greater than my fear of going back into that house. If there was still a kitchen cupboard and honey in it, it could stay there. Everything was wrong in that house, and besides I had other thoughts forming, rising up in me like news of a death when one always thinks first: no – it can't be!

I was adding up details like a computer that contains the inevitable answer to a problem but cannot deliver it until all the necessary circuits have been connected. Lighter-case, electric wires, dental filling, curtain screws, window-latch, nails in floorboards, carpet hooks, zip fastener, cooker, stove, doorhandles. It was a list like an ironmonger's nightmare, and there was one other thing on it that he could not supply. My wedding ring.

My hands were naked, empty. There had been a strange wind out of the sky. There had been a disaster. It was not an enemy hydrogen bomb, it was not germ warfare, or anything like that. It was not enemies from this planet at all. I felt convinced of it. I began to know it. I could almost picture the great ships zooming down, pausing, giving out some frightful magnetic flash. I could hear again the sucking sound of air rushing into empty spaces where all the metal objects had been. And see the ships accelerate away with their strange bullion. They needed metal, we had it. So they took it. Some strange race of thieves had come in the night and lifted all the metal from the planet Earth. Every nerve was alive in me with intuitive knowledge. I was certain, and I said aloud: 'All the metal has gone!' I did not call out or scream or call for help. Who could help and who would hear and what could they have done? And did I want Them to return? They must be terribly powerful and probably unscrupulous and frightful. If They could do that, what else might They not do? I sort of jumped around in the mud and bit my knuckles and wept, but this was only for a while. I wanted to get my pragmatic side working. I saw myself as ludicrous and one among millions of panic-stricken people. Vast numbers would die in crashes and shipwrecks; buildings would crumple, bridges would suddenly not be, all machinery would disappear and scatter conveyor belts and bottles and boxes everywhere; lifts would plummet, surgeon's knives would disappear mid-operation; the sheer magnitude of this happening made me reel mentally, and I realised with horror that it would mean starvation, especially here in England. No transport meant little food. There would be riots, massacres, fighting for food. There would also be disease because of no sewers and there would be fires from escaping gas. My first knowledge, most important, was that I must, somehow, survive. I began to walk away from the house. There was only one other house nearby and that was Henderson's. As I passed it I stole some of the hard pears that overhung the road and stuffed them down my sweater.

Henderson was a widower, and he was probably dead; he worked on the night-shift at the gypsum mine, and I thought he would surely be trapped forever down there, the metal cage gone up like his shout for help.

Our house is on the edge of a 'green' belt in the Pennines. The wildest moorland and valleys, accessible only on foot, are within ten miles of roaring mills and evil mines. I had set off from the house with some vague idea of making for the town, but I began to realise what an illogical step that would be. I began to wonder why I had not gone back indoors for shelter but I knew really that my instincts had served me well enough, for if there were to be rioting crowds and mass panic, I should aim for some safe solitude other than a house. People would mauraud everywhere in search of supplies; I could be killed for my few groceries and my blankets. I hurried on, changing directions, taking a road that led to the meadows. It was still raining heavily and I slapped along in my bare feet and met no one and nothing. There was of course no traffic at all. Peace and silence – if I could find somewhere secure.

As I began to climb the hill away from the town, I passed the small mental hospital that had once been a manse. I could hear voices at the other side of the high wall, but the place was inaccessible from the main road; they had taken out the great gates and walled it up, doubtless to prevent patients from running out into the traffic and to create privacy. I found toe-holds in the huge stones and hauled myself up to look precariously over the top. There was broken glass set in concrete, but it was worn smooth with the sulphurous airs and driving rains that sweep the hills and valleys. A man in a white coat sat on the front steps, head in hands, weeping. Two pale women in nightdresses, dishevelled hair blowing, bent over him, comforting, persuading.

'There, there, Doctor Markowicz, come inside ... we'll look after you ...' So that was Dr Markowicz! I could not help smiling at the spectacle of the psychiatrist so soon broken under shock, and his two madwomen apparently trying to be sensible in a crisis. I had been given a note to take to his outpatient's sessions by my GP some months before, but I had not kept the appointment. I had not liked the idea of discussing my private life with strangers; my trouble was not serious, only worry and overtiredness when Stuart and I decided to separate temporarily. In this world, the only person who can really help is oneself, so I told that self. My Yorkshire independence bordered on stubbornness, I daresay, and still does. It pays in the end. So, independent, I slipped back on to the pavement, my hard pears sticking into me, and slopped on faster. I had to get across a meadow, and then I was in open country which belongs to nobody. It was all National Park. But in that meadow stood a bull that I had many times admired from a safe distance. He was a magnificent shaggy beast of a Highland, a famous sire and a fierce character. Did I dare walk past him without the protection of barbed wire? If he charged, could I run fast enough to get over the stile at the other end of the path? I had to risk it. I decided I would rather face the bull than a rabble of humanity. It was possible that he would not even notice me, of course, because although the dawn had broken, the moon was gone and it was a gloomy morning with all the rain. Could bulls detect by smell?

I gathered all my courage into one inhalation and began to walk quickly. I was more than halfway across when I saw him turn his head and stare at me. He put his head down and pawed the ground, and I stared back at him, not breathing for sheer fright. I got over the stile and almost collapsed with trembling at the other side. The bull turned and walked a few steps. I had won the battle, not with the bull, but with my own timidity. I have always been so easily terrified, it was a triumph. As I thought of the stately home nearby, I felt once more less brave. They had a pride of lions in a paddock to entertain the visitors. Was I to face them too? Bitterly I reflected that antique furniture was surely enough to attract visitors on a Sunday? Lions! Appalling! And there were no guns to shoot them with; I could only hope that they would forage for their food amongst the hordes in the town. Would the Duke be the first to go? In my distress I was becoming facetious, as I always did, and which had so irritated Stuart. At inappropriate moments I could be counted upon to make some inane comment, and it had irritated him.

I was longing for a cigarette. This was one certain way of giving up smoking – no cigarette factories, no money or machines, no cigs.

But it was not going to be wonderful, it was going to be hard – and for me of all persons. It had been a standing joke in our family, my ineptitude. I had caused my brothers endless amusement as a child; it had filled their idle time, making fun of their stupid sister. But I did know my way across the hills for they had allowed me to follow them on their way to summer camps, although I had always been sent home before teatime.

'Reet, thee gan' 'ooam, our Emma Jane. We gunna camp up at Mermaid's Pool and tha's only a lass.' So, walking in the wet and dangerous morning, the first day of the Earth without metal (and I wondered if only the smelted metal had been stolen, or vast supplies of ores also), I determined to visit Mermaid's Pool, and Madwoman's Stones, and Kinder Downfall, and the many stone circles. I would see them all, they would be my home. I would complete all the journeys that my brothers had made, and I would do it alone.

If my child Leonora had lived, she would not have been the kind of girl to be sent back home. She would have been as good at camping as she was at sewing and cooking and almost everything else she tried. She was almost a prodigy; she just *did* things. Once she was shown how, a skill soon became hers. At seven she had been taught some elementary stitching by Mrs Henderson, who died shortly before Leonora herself died. She had made herself a petticoat in a week and taken it proudly to school to show teacher, and the woman had accused her of lying, of having had help from me. If she had had help from me, the thing would have been ruined! How I hated that schoolteacher for humiliating my little girl. I had been humiliated many times at school but always for being stupid. School lessons were no problem to Leonora. Monday arithmetic did not blacken her Sundays with dread, tracing maps did not bother her. I recall my geography lessons, the tracing paper like ice, slithering, floating, black graphite marking me up to my elbows, the blurred edges of Africa, holes in the paper from my concentration and little wrinkled tatters from erasing. Torture! Shame! And Leonora learned to play the violin. Doubtless, the friends we then had thought her less of a musical genius than we did, but to hear her play – it baffled me. How could any person, let alone a seven-year-old girl, manage to move her fingers like that, one at a time and meaningfully? I had never been able to entertain anyone with anything except my daftness. I remember one party where I was a great success, really made everyone laugh. I could not think of a fruit beginning with 'A'.

That first night I slept in a gully on the edge of the moors. I had seen no human beings all day; I had just kept on walking and had eaten a stolen pear when I was very hungry.

I was so exhausted that I did not mind the cold and the wet, all I cared about was that I was safe from the hordes of panic-stricken people. I was alive and alone. I kept thinking I heard things in the sky but saw nothing. There would be no more planes, I knew. I was just worried in case the thieves came again for something else. Nothing happened.

I was several hundred feet too high above sea-level for any real warmth in the camp I finally made. I spent hours trying to make a woven shelter out of bracken but I could not make it watertight and windproof. When I found my tiny cave I was exultant. It was really no more than a hole under a huge rock, entered by a natural fissure that could be blocked with stones at night; but it was dry, and when I swept it out and made a bed of dry bracken, it seemed the most adequate home I had ever had. It was a long time before I succeeded in making a fire, but after the first few attempts I did not give up but decided to try every day for as long as my patience would last – longer than that I swore – and I did try every day, rubbing sticks in dry bracken and fibres until it happened for me. I kept telling myself that I was no more stupid than anyone else. I had hands and brain and will; I would have them co-ordinate. Being alone, I had no derisory audience except myself, and I told myself to shut up. I knew the fire would start because I had a clear picture of it outside my cave. One day the smoke went up thin and miraculous and fire came. I never let it go out but fed it with sticks and peat. That fire represented everything I had longed to do on those holidays of my brothers. They, poor souls, had always taken matches. If they had been there to see me, they would have sworn that I was not the sister they had known. I spent many hours sitting by my fire, dreaming about those days and those camps that had been forbidden me, until in the end it did not matter any more. Nothing hurt in the dreams. I wondered how my brothers, the two remaining alive since Charles had his accident, were faring in this emergency. I supposed the disaster to be world-wide – after all, why pick on tiny England – and therefore Harry in Brisbane and Joe in Nigeria would be in some kind of predicament also. Dead? I would never know, unless people invented something without metal that would go so far. I visualised winged horses – it seemed like cosmic inefficiency not to have evolved winged horses.

I thought a lot about Stuart. We were to have met that winter to discuss a reconciliation, to see how we had fared without each other. I felt horribly convinced that he had fallen in love with someone else. I had last heard of him in London. What a place to be in a crisis! Was he dead? But I had no time for mourning the unknown. I was still full of the vacuum he had left in me, and his possible death meant only that his absence would continue, which it might in any case. Leonora's death. I thought about that at nights by my glowing fire. If she had died suddenly instead of a bit at a time, it might have been better. But we should not have had that seven months of constant communication when I never left her alone. In the end we became telepathic for one another. Leonora became more and more like me, until at last she surpassed me in ineptitude. The mattress at the foot of the stairs, because she fell so often. The bed in the lounge, because she forgot how to walk. Her sticks of arms and legs, like the withered roots of some useless vegetable. The violin in the loft because she wept at the sounds it made for her. If they had taken away that tiny bean of stuff from within her brain, they would have taken her life with it.

'Nurse her at home, we can do no more than you.' Spoon-fed, bottle-fed, voice twisting, cracking, losing sense, babbling and whispering and then ceasing. I tried to recall if I had been to her funeral or not. I could only recall tea in plain white china, white ribbon bows, and thousands of flowers. And seedcake.

But I did not spend all my time dreaming. There was the business of getting food. There had been plenty of blackberries and bilberries, and although my gut writhed at first, they filled me sufficiently. Then I found a crop of mushrooms. Cautious at first, not certain which were deathcaps, I finally became confident and astute at looking in the right places for them and even had a source of chanterelles, which I stored dry. There were a few bird's eggs although it was the wrong time of year for there to be many, and it was because of these that I learned to climb. I tried to make a bow and arrow, but I could not make a string strong enough to last more than a few feeble twangs. I cursed myself for an idiot for not looking by the roadside for an old auto tyre on the way up, but how was I to think so far ahead? I suppose I must have been planning on a temporary escape at first, I was to see only one sheep, and that was away before I could get to it. I had always thought that sheep stayed outdoors all the year round. I was full of lust for its flesh and skin the moment I saw it; living wild makes essentials spring to mind before any humanitarian consideration.

There were plenty of rabbits and rodents and grouse, but these too eluded me. I had luck in finding two hazel-bushes incongruously growing in a patch of beechwood by the river. I stripped off every nut and stored them in my cave, rationing myself to a very few each day.

But quite apart from scratching about for food, there was the pleasure of the landscape and the delight in roaming the hills. In only a couple of months or thereabouts I had become hardier than I would ever have thought possible, and my tattered jeans and sweater kept me warm even when snow came. Barefoot, I was not at the mercy of slipping leather and sliding rubber, I felt secure on high ledges, gripping with my toes. I learned to run slowly to keep warm, and the lack of cigarettes, which had been a trial at first, had allowed my lungs to expand. I breathed pure air all the time and felt health rise in me as it had never done before. It was a mild winter compared to some those hills have, and the snow only stayed right on the top of the highest peaks. I went up to Madwoman's Stones in the snow and stood in the centre of the perfect circle and looked all around at the vast whiteness of the moor. From that vantage point only wild country could be seen, not one man-made scar was in sight, except the circle itself, and that was no scar, it was an object of wonder to me. I became keenly aware that I was living the same kind of life as the people who had built that circle of stones and the barrows grouped around under the heather. Or was I? Perhaps they had been very civilised people, and there had been much more to their building than these few stones. I sensed some ancient intelligence. The earth was full of it; one had only to stand and listen and smell. I thought of the people over in the valley. Were they reverting to crude savagery as I had feared, or were they perhaps making a new kind of civilisation such as there had been thousands of years ago, before metal had been smelted? I still had little confidence in human nature and no real curiosity to find out.

And then came the terrible time. Fear in the night. Padding of feet and growling and snuffling outside my doorway of stones. I woke in the night to the sounds, and I think I have never been so frightened. I could smell a strong animal odour, and I peered out between the boulders and saw the shaggy hair against the moon-lit sky. I heard the slap of great lips, and I was taken back about thirty years to when I was very tiny. At Whipsnade Zoo I had seen and heard my first lion. This one had come up from the valley searching for food. I thought it would be the end of everything. If I could not outrun and kill a sheep, I could do nothing to a lion. I sat on the floor of my cave and prayed to some nameless power that it would go away. After a while all was silent. The next morning I crept fearfully out and began tending my fire. There was a dreadful crashing of bracken on the hillside, and I looked up to see the creature leaping down towards me. I was inside the cave and had drawn in the stones to blockade it before it reached me. It growled and snuffled again, and I lay curled and trembling in terror. My free life was at an end. Many hours passed; two dawns came and I was appallingly thirsty and the stench of my own excrement was horrible. I decided to die.

It seemed then as if that had been my mission all along that trip. To die. I would go outside at dawn the next day and wait to be attacked. Maybe my reactions would make me run, but not far. He would leap on me and kill. I would rather give myself up to the beast than die in filth and fear. After I had made that de-cision, everything felt better. I began to doze comfortably and drifted into a series of dreams.

Then I rested in the milky quiet between sleeping and waking, waiting for the dawn when my death would happen.

And then a vision came to me. All the paranormal had become the normal, we humans were changed. An evolutionary step had suddenly taken place. It was the dream of the mystic and the ama-teur yogin and the magician and the alchemist and the mad scien-tist come true. Suddenly. Why? I was not sure but I felt that it was some kind of test. And yet, if it was a test, who was the examiner?

I had seen no vision of God, did not believe in personality beyond the human. The test perhaps of the Universe itself. If humanity proved useless in its new function, then might it not be sloughed or moulted like an out-of-season growth? Had we ever been anything else to the Universe, were we any use in the *pattern*?

Did I in fact have new powers? I had facility with my body that I had never had, it was certainly as if I had re-discovered myself, expanded, grown. What about the thieves from space then? Were they a figment? I then supposed so, but I had severe doubts about my supernormal abilities. And yet had I not communicated telepathically with Leonora all those years? Sometimes when the edges of the circle had encompassed other things . . . and I was to die. I had decided. I would speak to the lion with my heart. I would calm him, befriend him. If I failed then death would come, and my vision would be a mere hallucination, or else I was still too stupid to benefit from new powers, or I would probe my new power in one direction at least. The vision would be true and all would be well. I pushed away the stones and crawled outside. With my eyes closed I staggered upright and held out my arms. I reached inside and gathered together all the thing I know to be love. I thought of the lion and I let it flow towards him. He crouched at my feet, lolled his great head, and made a soft growling. All was as I had hoped.

It was a male so I called him Leo. My new powers did not include astonishing originality, nor did I succeed in finding any other thing within me except a sense of expansion in general. I could not move stones except with my hands. If I sent messages to any person, I received none in return. I could not transport myself except by walking. It was disappointing, and yet I had my friendly lion. He hunted rodents and rabbits for me and I gave him most of the kill raw and roasted bits for myself in the hot ashes. We went for long walks and scrambled around the hills, and all the time I was trying to think what to do about my vision. I had seen that humanity was unaware of what had happened.

Perhaps I had been chosen to tell them? But I let the weeks of winter slip by without acting on that possibility. I wanted no part of it. I was not ready to return to the world; the idea filled me with dread.

A day came that could be called a day of spring. It was clear and blue, and the little river ran bright and noisy over the pebbles, and the sun seemed to avoid the small white clouds that came and went rapidly. I had found a few wild violets and primroses, and this had made everything seem splendid and full of hope. I called Leo and we set off to go up to Mermaid's Pool. I had somehow not dared to go to this place alone, but now that Leo was with me, I had no misgivings. The paths are very steep but not impassable, even after the landslides that melting snow had caused. Perhaps if my brothers had not been so certain that I could not manage the climb, I too would have camped up there with them. We went straight up through a wood that threatened to slide away in its own leaf mould, scrambled from root to root and then out on to sheep-tracks that led to a rocky escarpment like sea-cliffs, from which there was a magnificent view of the Downfall, a narrow watercourse about three hundred feet high, catching the sun like a slit filled with gold. Leo seemed more in his element the higher we climbed, and he joyfully crashed about in the patches of bracken that grew taller than myself, and for him it must have seemed like Africa that day. Then came the stony place where nothing grew; the floor was grey grit that would someday become the white sand that lit up the river bed below, and the rocks piled up on each other with an eerie regularity that seemed like an ancient fortress more than a fortuitous scattering of compressed mud. Then we had to achieve the impossible. There was a scree at an angle of forty-five degrees, made of shale and sand, and it seemed that two steps forward made three sliding back. If one of us slipped, there was only a voice before flesh met rock far below. I had learned by then how to decide not to be frightened, and so we went up, and then suddenly, at the top, everything was changed. It was like no place on earth that I had ever been.

We were not at the top of the mountain but on the lip of a huge cup, like the drinking fountain for a Great Horse, and the lees of the draught were still shining there at the bottom of the amphitheatre of stones that had grown soft with moss and bog cotton. The very far edge of the pool met the sky where the water seeped silently away underneath the skin of the earth, and the few clouds swam in the water and slipped off into the blue without a tremor. It was a silent and enchanted place, without birds, and Leo padded without sound amongst the rocks, and I did not shout or sing, although I might have, so exalted that day had become. It was impossible not to hink of the gods of the place and to feel that a secret had been penetrated and to sense also the men from the Stone Age who must have hunted here and stood where I stood, looking out through space towards the farther hills. I looked at the waters and the stones, and I thought that they were now the densest matter available to mankind, the lowest order of substances. I thought I could sense, almost as a scent, finer substances in and around me. What if the stones were 'lost' also – what would become of humanity? We would become finer than air, have no bodies, and there would be no planet Earth, for it is rock to its heart, molten, as I have read. If we were unprepared for our 'loss' of metal – it would be the end. Dross in the Universe, denied existence by the very order of things.

I removed my rags and stepped into the waters and swam three times around the rim of the cup, caressed by weeds and making as little mark on the surface as possible. To splash and play would have been sacrilege. When I had got dry and dressed again, Leo and I explored the place further, and he found a dead sheep, mummified by the drying winds. It lay like a white scar in a brown hollow, sunken slits where eyes had once missed nothing beneath the black foot; no flies and corruption, just death come and gone when the time was right. I had made the decision. I would go and tell the world how it was with things. I would come down from the hills.

The next day we set off to go down into the town. I was full both of dreadful uncertainties and sound convictions. I felt I needed miracles to prove my message. Would a tame lion be sufficient? Should I not be able to change water into wine, heal the sick? Were there other people who had realised the new potentials? If so then all would be well; I could add my word to theirs.

When we had reached smoother paths I threw away my clothing. I felt that a prophet in raggy jeans was unsuitable for the message I had. I sat astride Leo who could bear my weight for I was as thin as sticks and he was a strong animal. Once we were over the hilltop and had passed a reservoir, we could see Glossop in the valley, and beyond it the fantastic panorama towards Manchester. On a clear day the view is perfect for about twenty miles. Even the smog cannot obscure the Pennines. It is the meeting of the ancient and wild with the modern and ordered – ordered only into chaos. Buildings smother the earth. I looked and saw smoke in the morning sun. Smoke rising in rose and pearl and amber until the dreadful beauty became unbearable. Smoke has risen on those hills for three hundred years, ceasing to belch ethereal Hell only on Sundays. Coal and coke burning in great metal boilers, metal rolling mills, metal looms, metal on the soles of the clogs and metal toecaps to prevent bloody accidents, metal shovel metal cog metal nail and hammerhead cage wrench wire lock can gate trap hopper chain.

I could hear myself screaming as if it were some other woman, and I was aware that my voice reached Manchester and travelled out from the planet at a tangent and carried straight on out through the masses of space until it reached the heart of things. I was no longer conscious of what I had screamed by then, and I received no reply. I roared in rage at the furnaces below me, I yelled and bellowed at the forges with an anger and fury like a tunnel of fire, melting all things to incandescent likeness. My anger was at the deception I had suffered. I had been brought to believe that humanity was evolved to something greater, and it was not. The metal was there as it had always been. Nothing had changed, any fool could see it. Only on Sunday had the mills rested, like the gods that they were, shaping existence. My humiliation was enormous, it was the greatest and stupidest and most foolish boob of my entire useless silly life. I had surpassed myself in idiocy. I felt I could never speak of it to any person, that I could not live with myself. I saw clearly that I was insane, deluded, the victim of my own twisted perceptions and mad logic. I was the arch-jumper-to-conclusions. My so-called thinking had produced a monstrous set of deductions, and a rare exile. I had no sense of humour to soften my mistakes.

We ran on and I cut myself on barbed wire – somehow I had succeeded in either avoiding the stuff or not noticing it. We were approaching the bogs. I read a notice concerning foot-and-mouth disease. The whole countryside was banned to people until further notice. Thank you, I said to the filthy bacteria, for accomplishing my certain solitude. I must have read about the outbreak and stored it away as a necessary element in my approaching psychosis. Madness is secret and cunning and efficient at proving watertight cases.

And my lion. A grotesque but lovable combination of Chow-chow and Great Dane with maybe some Irish Wolfhound. A large, dumb, shaggy sire come to comfort the mad lass. He could not bark nor could he roar. Perhaps he was strayed from home like myself, perhaps his owners were tired of feeding such a hulk and had let him run off. He could only course along beside me and raise wildfowl in stupid canine joy. I was so ashamed. I was so deeply ashamed of myself, a familiar feeling of mine all my life. There was no point to such a creature as me. Down in the town there were official sanctuaries for stray dogs and naked crazy women. Not the same sanctuary, we would have had to part.

We came to a place that I knew and had always dreaded, for

once my brothers had in play threatened to put me in it – a bottomless bog of slime marked by a prehistoric monster called the Penny Stone, although the euphemism could not cloak its meaning. It stood erect and potent over millennia, a perpetual reminder of the necessity of continuing life. I defied it.

I allowed myself to slide forward into the mire, sucked into what my distorting imagination thought of as a womb. I closed my eyes and deliberately relaxed against the cold, and loving hands of velvet mud caressed me, and I was lapped about by tiny secret streams that ran beneath the hair of the slough. I would join the others who had died there, for the place had the reputation of claiming those who dared to touch. I lifted my hand and marked black on my forehead where the stuff would reach, and I smiled happy in the knowledge that all would soon be over. I desired oblivion and it was obtainable. I felt to be airborne then and the dark was lit with softly coloured lamps and everything was smooth and there was a sighing in my ears.

I later became conscious of pouring rain and I spewed mud and bitter bile. The dog was not there. I had a wound in my shoulder where his teeth had held me, and my scalp was torn. I must have been half dragged out by him, and perhaps instinctively saved myself by levering myself on his body. I could not spend time weighing up the relative values of his life and mine, but I shall always remember. I had loved the odd beastie and he had loved me. Then I was empty and exhausted.

It was a night of reconciliations and realisations and acceptances. I wondered if I could ever again trust my perceptions, if I would ever be certain that I was not tricking myself into the fantastic through the misapprehension of the commonplace.

I had put my hands on a wringing wet tissue on my bedside table where I had left it after crying myself ill that night when the space thieves came, and I had thought it first a dead mouse and then a lighter. I had failed to find a curtain screw because something in me had decided that there were none. I had set the scene so deep in my mind so that when I awoke on the night of a bad storm when the power lines were down and the roads quiet because cut off by flood, everything would fit to make no less than an earth-shattering experience. A time had been reached when either enormous changes took place in me and my life, for the better, or I would degenerate into psychosis. I could see it in retrospect. The strange thing was that I had indeed woken to my mad self, but it had changed me for the better. Some people do not need quite so much as thieves from outer space and a vision in the wilderness plus suicide attempts to grow and change and become themselves. Or maybe they do but never get the chance!

I sat outside a shooting lodge all that night in the rain, getting the mud washed off me, and going back over events. The filling in my tooth had been out for weeks, but all memory of the avoided dental appointments had been wiped out conveniently by someone in me who had a more amusing idea. The window catch had been hanging by one screw for months, and a high wind could have wrenched it off. And I, in my crazed state, wrenched off the entire frame and also smashed the rotten door-frame. Not easy but not impossible. There was hardly a sound in the house. Old and decrepit but beautiful, it had had no attention after Stuart left. He had done a lot of work, but there had been still much to do, and I was useless and hated the intrusion of workmen.

Everything that night had made me think of vanished metal. I had left the broken light-switch in despair and a futile attempt to mend it. Who but a person deluded would try to switch it on? And I chose to find jeans with a broken zip. I had another pair with metal studs but those would have put a hole in the case. The telephone had been cut off because I had not enough money to pay the bill. What an act I put on for myself. Turning left into the utility room instead of right into the kitchen, thereby not finding any stove or cooker but a flooded floor. That room always floods in storms, the doorsill was missing and we never used it for anything but storing fuel. The unfortunate mental patient who

thought he was Dr Markowicz – or had I deliberately misheard –
comforted by two resident night nurses. Did they persuade him to
return to bed and sleep it off – what would they have done with
the more acute 'case' leaning over the wall? And I had braved a
bull securely fastened in by green plastic-covered fencing, difficult to see in twilight, impossible to see by someone who has
already decided that it is not there. For me, the metal had gone.

It was not a meaningless delusion. I had not become Napoleon
or Mary Queen of Scots, condemned myself to cosy incarceration
in a new and more congenial world where I was the biggest and
most important around. I had accomplished something better
than that with my psychotic inventions. I had moved lead and
iron out of my being, heated them, transmuted them and sur-
vived. My vision was of my self. By the time I was on my way
back home under cover of darkness I knew I had never been more
myself. There was the problem of how to insert myself into a sane
world unnoticed. I needed a hot bath and some clothes.

It was like housebreaking. I should hate to be a thief. I could
not endure the stress, I thought – and then remembered; I had
endured stress. I had proved myself.

Everything was different. New carpet, new paintwork, a new
lampshade in the hall by a telephone which looked as if it might
ring. The television was blaring away in the living-room. Stuart
and I had not had television, we had liked each other's company
until Leonora's death made islands of us. I risked going upstairs,
meaning to look for some clothes. The hinges of the bedroom door
were set into new inserts of wood, the craftsmanlike sort of job that
Stuart would do. Who had done all this work? Had he returned
and sold the house, or done it up waiting for me to return?

In our bedroom the light glowed softly from a pink shade that
was – had – been mine, and in the bed lay a strange woman,
asleep, her head a flowering of blue rollers. At the foot of the bed
in a crib lay a baby. I held my breath to look over the neat blanket
at the very young baby with little flames of dark hair sticking to

its forehead. I felt tempted to loosen the cover but dared not touch at all. If I had touched I would have clutched the infant up to me and kissed and burned with love. I was too late. The house belonged to someone else. Was this Stuart's new woman, or was she of a totally new couple? No idea of property crossed my mind at that time, it did not occur to me that the place was half mine no matter what. The woman opened her eyes, looked at me and then closed them and turned over. She dreamed then of a naked filthy wild woman with tears running down her face.

I crept out into the night, cringing at the teevee noise. I slunk down the road to the Henderson house, knowing him to be on nightshift, broke in, had a hot bath and borrowed some clothes from those still left. From then on my story has been one of slow but increasing success in making my own way in the world. Someday I intend to call again on our house, a long way now from where I live and work.

I intend to find out what is happening to Stuart, find out about the woman and the baby – I have even thought that perhaps she was a delusion, a large piece of wishful thinking on my part for where I would like my own life to be. But not yet. I'm not strong enough yet, I don't think. When I'm good and ready within myself I'll find out.

Meanwhile my life is better than it has ever been. I work with my hands, I cope with situations, I am independent. It's that independence that gives you the feeling of well-being. I know that now. And it gives you confidence in yourself.

Sometimes I think I'll take a vacation camping on Kinder Scout – in a more conventional style, of course, with a tent and a few items of necessary comfort. Or something more adventurous, somewhere abroad perhaps. But if I get a dog I can't take it with me because of quarantine. Problems, problems!

At least they are ordinary problems. Nothing so elaborate as thieves from space, or being attacked by lions. Not for a long time. In fact, to be truthful, life can be just a little bit dull.